MONSTROUS

Monstrous Book Three

SAWYER BLACK

DAVID W. WRIGHT

STERLING & STONE

To YOU, the reader.
Thank you for taking a chance on us.
Thank you for your support.
Thank you for the emails.
Thank you for the reviews.
Thank you for reading and joining us on this road.

MONSTROUS

Chapter One

THE FOG SWIRLED AWAY as if it didn't want to touch her. Spreading apart like curtains to her stage. She stepped through and was greeted by the applause of rain.

Someone told her not to venture into the mist, but she couldn't remember who. An older man with hard eyes, a cane, and long gray hair. He kept popping into her mind, his worry creasing the lines on his skin even deeper. She felt his strong hands on her shoulders. His long beard tickling her cheek.

She reached under her dripping hair and pulled the edges of her collar forward. Hissed in pain, throwing her head back and covering the heat beneath her jaw with a bare hand, wrinkled and pale from the cold and wet. Her hand came back red with blood.

Her face wrinkled in disgust and she wiped her hand on the front of a pant leg already smeared with crimson. It seemed to leave a glowing trail, sparkling with whatever light could reach it. She squeezed her eyes shut and shook her head.

She was looking for someone who'd been with her, but

she couldn't remember his name or what he looked like, or even what separated them.

She looked back into the fog. It was always so dark here.

Got to find the way home.

Home?

Where is home?

Her feet felt like wood inside her heavy boots, shuffling across the uneven cobbles. Buildings on either side loomed over her as if bending down to block out the meager view of a dark sky that had only the occasional flicker of a candle to light it.

Eyes pierced her from every direction, glittering in the dirty orange glow behind hazy glass panes. Through the crooked frames of empty windows.

Dread crawled into her throat, keeping pace with the sun as it rose above the horizon, and her breath burned in her lungs as she forced herself to walk faster.

But she had no idea where she was going. Or where she had *been*. The fog had seemingly permeated her mind. She remembered a blue light dropping from her blood-slick hand. Her cry of despair as it shattered on the rocks. The old man shook his head in disapproval, and she cringed from him in shame.

Chittering laughter from behind!

She raised her head in alarm and turned. Slimy movement and splashing footsteps. She squinted into the depths of the roiling mist and saw roving shapes darting in and out of the shadows.

Moans of pleasure and growls of anticipation.

She kept herself in the middle of the lane, keeping space around her to swing her balled-up fists, but preparation became panic when her hand fell on the empty sheath at her waist.

She forced herself to walk faster, her feet slapping echoes off the inky walls.

Her teeth chattered as a shiver racked her shoulders. Hot breath plumed in white jets, contrasted with the thick brown mist swirling about her knees and rising up to her waist. She knew if it closed in to surround her, if it rose to cover her face, she would die.

Scraping footsteps slapped in time with her advance, and she felt something graze her hair. The fever had finally weakened her, making her prey. An easier target with every drop of blood dripping from her throat. Heart pounding, temples throbbing, she threw herself into a shambling run.

A groaning cry rose from her throat, pulsing with her steps. She held her hands in front of her, swiping at the mist that curled around to slow her down.

Filthy steam rose from a sewer grate, washing her with a reeking rot that clung to her soaking clothes.

A wall of white, and she skidded to a stop before smashing face-first into the side of a rusting delivery truck.

Her groan rose into a frustrated wail. She struck the metal with a fist, and the empty cargo box boomed like a drum. Rasping laughter rose all around, and her eyes rolled up in terror as she spread her fingers, feeling the truck's length as she skirted its edge.

Its loading doors pressed into the greasy wall of the building to her right. Not enough room to squeeze past. She dropped to her knees, the sudden change in elevation making her head pound. She saw nothing but shadow beneath, save for a pair of glowing eyes winking in and out of the rolling fog.

She jumped to her feet and slammed her back against the building, scraping her nails across the plaster and brick. A gray hand reached out from under the truck, and she kicked at it, just short of making contact.

The laughter turned into wordless shouts. Hisses and growls. Eyes appearing like stars. Leering faces with their details obscured by mist. Baleful hate and slavering grins.

Her hand brushed over a stone molding that transitioned into a doorway. Flaking paint from a wooden door, and she pressed herself into the empty space while questing for the knob.

She couldn't remember how to pray.

A small overhang blocked the rain, and she could feel the tears streaming down her face.

Her hunters pressed closer, and their shapes bloomed from the mist.

Her hand found the knob, cold and oily under her touch. She closed her eyes, giving it a frantic twist, and the door fell open, sending her tumbling into the darkness.

Her teeth clacked together as her ass planted on the rotting floor, and pain jolted up her spine. She scampered back, her hands sinking into sticky filth, and the eyes in the mist widened in surprise.

Her toe hooked behind the rebounding door and she kicked it shut, flopping to her back with the effort.

The door slammed, shaking the wall and shuddering through the floor.

She dug her fingers into the grit, bugs and worms writhing under her hands.

Then she lunged forward, running her hands up and down the jamb until she found the lock. A heavy bolt that squealed in the hasp. She strained against it, a scream hissing through her gritted teeth, and the bolt drove home.

Her body sagged in relief, then flung away when the door rocked from the impact. Again, something slammed against the door. She screamed, covering her mouth with filthy hands and opening her eyes to their limits. She pressed her back into a dark corner and slid down to sit with her knees drawn to her chest, staring up at the silence above her.

"Help me," she whispered. "Please."

A window next to the door, black with grime, darkened further with crowded shapes.

The door creaked with every blow, pale light creeping around its edges. She covered her ears and waited for it to burst in with every dark beast from her imagination spilling through. The pounding stopped, and she slumped with a gasp as though a weight had been drawn from her shoulders.

A knock on the door, nice and polite.

Shave and a Haircut.

The ceiling creaked as something skittered across the floor above. Dust sifted down like powdered sugar on a pancake. Hurried whispers from behind the door, and the shadows cleared from the window.

Another knock, and from the floor upstairs, the response.

Two Bits.

The darkness deepened, growing as if a shroud had been tossed onto the street. A darkness so impenetrable that her eyes bloomed with color under the strain of trying to see. A sense of gathering behind the door. Whispers and scraping that drove fear even deeper into her gut.

Silence from upstairs. Nothing from outside. She leaned forward, straining to hear, and the seconds ticked, marked by her shuddering breath.

The door tore from the frame. The combined shriek of the creatures pierced through the shattering wood and into her ears. And then they were on her. Clawing and biting, fighting each other to reach her first.

She screamed, her ragged voice lost among the howls, and the darkness was absolute.

Her wrists and ankles held in stabbing grips. She drew a breath for another scream, and their rotten stink coated the inside of her mouth. In her mind, the old man looked away, covering his face with shaking hands.

Light exploded into her eyes. Into her *mind*. Beaming through the hanging mist, illuminating her attackers in a blinding flare. Sagging gray skin and hollow cheeks. Sores and blisters. Greasy hands and filthy faces. Rotting clothes from every era of history.

They released her, jumping back to face the light, their faces slack with terror. The glare stabbed out of the shadows as if from an opening door, and a colossal red demon stepped out with a beacon on his shoulders.

The blinding light receded, and the beacon became a beautiful child. She caught her breath as the creatures scrambled back, and the child rose from the demon's shoulders on pearl-white wings tipped with black. His eyes, one blue and the other gold, glittered with swirling light, and his hands ended at black claws curled around a shimmering sword longer than he was tall.

The demon spread his arms. His muscles bunched and rippled, veins roping from his wrist and bulging from his thick neck. Black claws sprang from his right hand, but his left wrist was capped with a dented coffee can. The demon grinned with gleaming fangs.

"Howdy, fuckers." The voice rumbled from his chest like a diesel truck powering up a hill.

The demon stepped forward with a roar, and the little angel bounded from his shoulders, the sword swelling with fiery light.

Her attackers charged across the room with voices joined in a screeching wail that sliced through the air like a tornado siren. Scarlet blood flew into her eyes. Into her mouth. She curled away, but their screams of pain and terror clawed at her sanity. The demon's roar, and the angel's cries of rage.

Bodies hitting the floor like wet sacks. Mewling cries severed by the whistling slash of claws.

Her hands and feet were numb. Cold and leaden. Her face burned, and her chest bubbled as she cried. A gentle hand under her legs, her shoulder leaning against a warm chest. Her body rose into the air as her mind spiraled into the darkness of her fever. She passed out with the salty taste of blood still on her lips.

HUSHED VOICES IN CONVERSATION. The rocking rhythm as the demon's strides made her sway in his arms.

Where are you taking me?

"She's very pretty, isn't she?" The small voice said — the angel.

"Yes, she is." The demon's rumble. "A little old for you, though, isn't she?"

"No, Henry. I meant for *you.*"

The demon laughed. It sounded like a shovel digging through sand.

"Doesn't matter. This one's not for *me*, no."

"Why not?"

Yes. Why not?

The silence yawned for so long that she didn't think he was going to answer. When he did, his voice was tight with pain. "Because I still love Samantha, buddy. And I'm starting to finally learn what that really means."

She felt the sorrow in his voice as her own, and she turned away, settling back into troubled sleep.

. . .

SHE WOKE to angel's face hanging above her. Her teeth chattered with every inhalation, and her pulse thundered behind her eyes. Heat rose from the neck wound. Cold radiated from her hands and feet. She didn't know why she was dying, only that she didn't want to. Tears welled in her eyes, and the angel blurred as he reached out to touch her forehead.

"I don't know if this is going to hurt or not," he said, his quiet voice sad and apologetic.

Pain shattered every forming thought, and her scream rose to fill the empty space in her brain. Her head was filled with fire. Burning into her neck and flowing into her lungs. The scream emptied her air, and she couldn't catch another breath.

Her diaphragm seized, cramping under her ribs. Her heels drummed on the soft padding beneath her. The angel removed his hand, and her air returned in a whooping breath that flooded her with healing relief. Lost memories followed, and Aela sat up, pushing herself away from the little angel's touch.

She massaged her neck where the Ravager had dug into her flesh with a dagger, and her hand came away clean. Smooth skin met her fingertips, and she looked up to ask the angel what he'd done, but he was already walking away.

She sat in an attic room. Yellow light flickered from an oil lantern in the corner. Bright and cheery, it danced behind its glass shield. Another lamp in the far corner banished the shadows, and Aela smiled. Evil rarely did business in the Forgotten by candlelight.

She sat on a plush couch with deep cushions and pillows. She was smearing it with her dirt, and she snatched her hand up, ready to apologize. She looked up into the demon's eyes, and *Sorry* died on her lips.

He sat in a leather recliner. His black T-shirt stretched across his chest, barely holding his bulk. A white peace symbol distorted by his muscle to look more like a peace oval. Brown cargo shorts with ties dangling from the knees, his feet wrapped in fuzzy penguin slippers. Cute little beady-eyed smiles over his toes.

Dark hair hung across his forehead, and he swiped it aside with the gnarled stump at the end of his left wrist before snapping a newspaper back up to keep reading. Old and yellow, cracking where he held it. *WALL STREET CRASH!* in faded letters across the top.

The angel looked like an ordinary boy. But *beautiful.* White T-shirt and shorts. Silvery blond hair lying perfectly on his head. Pure skin. His eyes still hovered in her mind. Blue and gold, quietly commanding.

He passed by a wooden desk and grabbed a book on his way to the leather chair. He jumped up to perch on the demon's shoulder, then opened the book and rested it against the demon's horns like a music stand. Chin in his hands, he stared at the book with a furrowed brow.

Aela remembered everything from her trip into the Forgotten thanks to the boy's healing hands. The *other* demon she'd been escorting to Solitude. The enchanted blade coming at her neck. Her narrow escape.

But her memories couldn't help to sort *this* madness. An angel sitting on a demon's shoulders, his eyes inside a *King James Bible.*

She cleared her throat, and they both looked up at her in the same motion. She was suddenly afraid to ask her question, but she cleared her throat again and shrugged.

"Am I dead?"

The demon looked at her in confusion, tipping his head like a dog listening for his master. "Aren't we all?"

Chapter Two

HENRY OPENED the old newspaper and folded it in on itself to read the inner pages. A pot roast recipe caught his eye. Adam's warm breath washed into his face. Henry smelled peanut butter and the old bible's musty pages.

"*I'm* not dead," Adam said.

The girl smoothed greasy black hair from her forehead and shrugged with a sigh. "I was *born* here, so I guess I'm not dead, either."

Henry raised his eyebrows and looked at her past the edge of the page. "What, in my attic?"

She stared at him, her face slack with mock boredom.

Not a girl like he first thought, but a young woman. Late twenties, if he had to guess. Blonde and pale and slim. A rung or two below Samantha, but under all the dirt and dried blood, she was probably pretty. *For this place, anyway.*

She continued to stare without comment. He shrugged and returned to his paper with a mutter, "I guess it's just *me* who's dead."

The woman hugged herself and scooted to the front edge of the couch. "I'm hungry."

Henry gave her the same treatment she'd given him, but Adam looked over the top of his book. His weight shifted across Henry's shoulders as he pointed. "We got lots of stuff in the cabinet over there. Mostly junk, but there are also some wrinkly apples we picked yesterday."

Henry jumped in from behind his paper. "Twinkies from World War One. Some Girl Scout sugar cookies from the 30s, I think. Fairly modern Slim Jims, which I highly recommend by the way. A couple of boxes of whole milk. I didn't even know that shit *came* in a box, but it does, and you can just put it on a shelf for like, *forever*. The apples my young friend here mentioned, and two cans of New Coke from the eighties, but to be honest, I'll *never* be thirsty enough for those."

"Do you have any *real* food?" the woman asked.

Henry tapped Adam's calf and bucked his shoulders. "Get off me, kid."

"Okay. I was done with *Corinthians*, anyways."

While the boy snapped his book closed and climbed down, Henry folded the newspaper into his lap, taking his time with the answer.

Pretty or not, she's irritating the shit out of me.

Henry took a calming breath. "As duly elected representatives of the after-life, we don't really *need* to eat. Just water and sleep. Skittles and Pepsi." Henry cocked his thumb at Adam, who had moved to the desk with a box of Bri-Tone crayons. "He doesn't even get pimples. Or *cavities*. Fortunately for me, there's always the shadow assholes running around."

"The Lost," she said.

"That what you call 'em?"

She nodded, swallowing with an audible click in her throat.

"Yeah, well. Those fucking guys are everywhere. And I

can feel 'em. Their *twisted* wanting. Their despair. Some of the folks down here are just that. *People.* Looking for a way out, psyching themselves up to follow the light, but *these guys?* I can feel it in 'em. Stubborn refusal. Terror. They turned away from the choice, and now it's too late. They just take up space and try to remove the choice from everyone else."

"That's why you hunt them?"

"Well, *that.* And they taste better."

She recoiled in disgust, and Henry felt smug satisfaction. He wasn't sure why he was annoyed by the woman, but he was. He'd become increasingly agitated ever since he'd been in this damned place.

"How long have you been here?"

"I don't know," Henry said. "More than two months, less than three? Can't find a goddamn clock anywhere."

A smile flashed across her face then got lost in a grimace as if she were trying to hide it. But Henry was sure he'd seen it. She looked into the corners as if searching for something, her eyes tracking along the baseboards. Surely she'd been through some shit.

He *wanted* to give her a minute, but the back of his neck was getting warm.

"What?" he shouted.

She started, her eyes connecting with his before sliding away. "Why did you save me?"

"Why did I …?" Henry drove his fist into the arm of his recliner, and the paper fluttered to the floor. "Why *wouldn't* I? You're the first person who wasn't trying to eat us. Or kill us for our clothes. I was gonna say *normal*, but I don't know if there *is* normal in this place." His voice rose to a shout, and Henry decided to let it. "But you know what? *I* didn't even want to. The *real* reason we saved you was because Adam heard your *prayer.*"

Henry leaned over and snatched the newspaper off the floor, opening it in angry pantomime. "You were *saved*. You were *healed*. So, fuck off and take the New Coke with you. Leave the Slim Jims."

"Adam? The boy's name is *Adam*?"

"That's right."

"Is he an angel?"

Henry lowered the paper and looked up at the ceiling — rough beams and oak planking, so much like his attic office back home. He wondered if Mike Stone liked it. Sitting up there and balancing his checkbook. "I'm *literally* done talking to you. You're welcome, by the way."

"Henry?" Adam said.

"Yeah, buddy?"

"You're not being very nice."

Henry looked over at Adam, sitting with his arms crossed in severe reproach.

Amélie's face sprung into his mind. The same pouting disapproval. Longing twisted his gut, and he had to bite back the sudden swell of tears. One week, when Samantha had been down with the flu, Henry made all of Amélie's lunches. Every time he assembled the sandwiches, he put the cheese on the outside as a joke, and she put her fists on her hips. "That's *not* how it goes, Daddy!"

"Fine." Henry turned back, and the woman's face glistened with fresh tears. "What, you're crying now? Jesus, okay, you can have the Slim Jims, too."

Adam giggled, and Henry sat back, the warmth of pleasure replacing the heat of his anger. Making somebody laugh, *anybody*, was enough to make him relax.

The woman wiped at her tears with a grimy hand. "Is there somewhere I can get cleaned up, please?"

"Sure." Henry pointed his nubbin at the same cabinet that held their food. "There's a can of wipes and a mirror.

Go out the door right next to it, down the stairs, and there's a running stream smells like piss. Help yourself."

"Don't worry," Adam said. "The shadow people are afraid of us. Well, Henry mostly."

She nodded and walked across the attic like her boots were soaked in glue. She was dressed like a fantasy novel. Brown leather pants, creaking with her movement. A leather jacket belted at her waist, flaring out to cover most of her ass. Brass buttons shining out from a green flannel shirt. A battered messenger bag bouncing on her left hip, the strap crossing to hang from her right shoulder.

Henry could smell her under the dirt and sweat and blood. Not fruit and flowers, but a sweet earthiness, like baking spice.

She pried the lid off the plastic can and made a dirty pile of crumpled wipes at her feet. If she noticed Henry staring, she didn't show it. Muscles in her thighs flexed and separated through the tight press of her pants. She slid her sleeves up, and her lean forearms rippled with the movements of her fingers.

Her softness was an illusion. His imagination. This woman was hard. Strong. She made him uncomfortable, and he wanted her gone.

She kicked the dirty wipes into the corner, opened their pantry cabinet, and wrinkled her nose. She closed the door, turned around with crossed arms, and looked directly into Henry's eyes. "You're not like any other demon I've ever met."

"Oh, yeah? Out of how many?"

She shrugged. "Not that many, but I've been told about your kind."

"Told what?"

"You're liars. Cheats. Selfish and ugly. Spiritual forces of darkness that corrupt the flesh of this world."

"That is …" Henry shrugged, "unkind."

"It's the truth."

Fatigue settled over Henry's shoulders. Weeks of keeping his spirits up, for Adam, for his own sanity. Faking the smile every morning, or whatever passed for a morning in this place. Dodging every hint of any agents from Heaven *or* Hell. Always on the lookout for answers. And now it was hard to not feel like he was cracking.

"I'm tired, lady. Let me tell you some truth. I love my daughter. More than anything else … I just don't have words for how much." Samantha's face hanging in his memory, looking over his shoulder in horror as Amélie came out of her bedroom to scream his name. The cramp in his guts when he had known he couldn't save her. His life gone in a flash.

Now, I'm crying, too.

Fucking perfect.

"I couldn't save her when I was alive. And now she's in Hell. Because of *me*." He pointed to Adam. "But this boy? I love him almost as much. I'll hide him from the Devil himself. I'll lie right to *God's face!*"

He jumped from his chair, his vision turning a hazy, ugly red, her face in the center like a bullseye. He stomped and the house shuddered. Henry was losing control, but it didn't matter. He was sick of keeping it inside. Forcing it down. "And *fuck* you! I'm doing the best I can with what I have. Judging me like you *know* me. Or *him!* He's the only light in this dark suck hole, and he's all I got."

Adam ran around the table and threw himself at Henry to bury his face in his thigh, holding his leg in a fierce embrace. Henry dropped his hand on the boy's head, and the anger flowed like water to wash him clean. "He's the only thing I have," he whispered. "I'll do anything to keep him safe."

"You haven't been a demon forever?" Her voice was quiet, but it still held the defiant strength of someone who knew they were right.

Henry looked up and shook his head. "Were you a *born* a bitch?"

She shrugged. "You're probably not the only one that thinks so, but no. Thank you for saving my life."

He waved her away. "Whatever, lady."

"Aela."

"What?"

"My name is Aela."

"I don't give a shit, lady. If you hate demons so much, why are you still *fucking* here?"

She pointed at Adam. "I'm here for him."

Henry grabbed Adam's shoulder and pushed the boy behind him.

He growled at the woman, lowering into a crouch and drawing on the shadows, pulling them to him like dragging on a rope hand over hand.

The lanterns flickered and dimmed. Henry felt grim satisfaction as her face showed uncertainty. Then fear.

She took a step back, and Henry drew in a breath to roar.

"Baelzor asked me to find him!"

Henry released the breath and let go of the shadows to stand straight, spreading his arms in confusion. "Jesus Christ, lady! Why didn't you start with that?"

Adam popped out from behind Henry's leg. "You know my father?"

Aela sagged in relief, then paused. "Your father?"

Henry nodded. "That's right, lady. Adam's only *half* angel. The other half is just like me."

The boy jumped from foot to foot, clapping his hands. "Can I see him? Is my mother here?"

She stared up at Henry in a panic, but he crossed his arms. "Well? What about it, lady?"

"I don't know where he is. I was bringing him back to Solitude when we … were separated."

Henry felt a little of his good mood return. Watching her squirm was fun. "Solitude, huh? Bringing him back for what? A trial? An *execution?*"

Her eyes widened, and she looked down at Adam, an artificial smile spreading across her face. "Not exactly."

"Then what?"

"Is my father still alive?" Adam asked.

Aela put her hands on her hips and glared at Henry. "I don't know."

Adam spun and looked up at Henry. "Can we look for him?"

Henry ruffled his hair, and it fell back into perfect waves. "Sure, buddy."

Adam pumped his fist in the air and grinned, wiping his tears with the other hand. He shot past Aela and pounded down the stairs.

Probably gonna get those cowboy boots and that fucking sword.

He and Aela stood staring at each other. Henry finally nodded. "Okay. I feel like people in Solitude don't much like demons. Is that fair to say?"

Aela tipped her head, raising her eyebrow.

"There a lot of people there?"

She nodded and looked at the floor, rubbing at a spot with the toe of her boot.

"People who can protect him?"

Her eyes snapped up to his.

"People who can take care of him?"

"Yes."

"I told you. I'll do anything to keep him safe."

"They won't let you in."

18

"Yeah, but will they let *him* in?"

She nodded.

Henry laughed, and a great weight fell from his shoulders. He was no longer the boulder being pushed uphill. Somebody else's burden, threatening to roll back and crush them. Pass his responsibility off to somebody more capable and head to Hell.

Daddy's still coming, baby girl.

"Alrighty, then. Let me go get a new coffee can."

Chapter Three

HENRY STEPPED out of the cottage in a pair of canvas carpenter jeans and some heavy black work boots unearthed from a crumbling storefront. A rusty sign hung over the door, squealing as it swung in the wind: *Schuhfachgeschäft Das Handwerk.*

An eleven-and-a-half in life, these bad boys were a snug fifteen. He topped it off with a 6XLT light blue tee that had a rainbow across the chest. *Everybody's Gay!* in a script font across the bottom.

He wished he could summon Mike's body and, more importantly his normal clothing sizes, but Henry was having trouble imagining himself into human form in this place. If anything, he was feeling uglier and more demonic.

His coffee can had been a fortunate find. Still half-full of grounds from a Hill of Beans, a coffee chain known for their over-roasted bullshit. The coffee brought back memories. Sitting across from Sammy Roth and banging out a script for *Just-Right Jasper*, a cartoon about a redneck superhero that Comedy Central had passed on.

The empty can perfectly covered his nubbin, and if Henry flexed the muscles that made a fist before he lost most of his hand, that nubbin swelled to hold the can in place. Good for smacking stuff, and it kept him from seeing the ruined mess Boothe and Randall, in all their angelic power, had been unable to heal.

A big mountaineer's backpack with fur trim was strapped to his back, holding all the crap they'd collected during their weeks of hiding. Mostly useful. Matches and candles. Baby wipes. Mandyel's cell phone, only buzzing when open, faint whispering voices in the static.

All the stuff a pampered city boy thought might be useful for survival. Adam's bible, and the *Playboy* that Henry had done an interview for ages ago. It was weird the shit he'd found since coming here, especially a magazine he just happened to have been interviewed in.

The essentials.

Ten minutes of following Aela, and Henry wasn't sure where the hell they were going. The boy paced along beside him, boot heels clomping on the wet sidewalk. His sword, dark and dull, rested on his shoulder like a baseball bat.

They had found it in the back of a milk truck. Silver plastic with faux jewels in the handle, the scabbard and matching shield of dented tin. Once vibrant paint chipped and faded. "Watch this, Henry," Adam had shouted, and the toy sword became a blade of pure white fire.

He reached out and squeezed the boy's shoulder. Adam's grin shone out in the dark, and Henry hoped Aela was telling the truth. Adam deserved more than what Henry could figure out.

"Where are we going?" he asked the dark shape in front of him.

She threw an irritated glance over her shoulder. "I'm looking for the Way Home."

"Yeah, I thought you knew the way."

She sighed. "Not the way *home*. The *Way Home*."

Henry mimicked her sigh as they walked down a wide street with houses of different generations and locales oddly located next to one another. An American fifties midwest home next to a pioneer's cabin next to an early German cottage, and even more homes whose origins Henry only vaguely recognized. The only thing the homes had in common were that nobody was outside beneath the perpetually dusk sky.

Flickering lights in windows died as they passed.

He could feel the subdued fear of the people behind the glass. Not the twisted need of the Lost, just the deep fear of the unknown. The sad worry of those stuck in this dark limbo.

The street ended at a delivery truck in front of a wall of giant buildings, as if someone had plopped a sprawling metropolis at the end of a suburban street. They couldn't see past the closest buildings, as the fog only thickened around them, masking their size and scope.

Aela scraped her feet across a rough spot in the stone a few yards in front of the delivery truck's gnarled shadow. She looked up then turned in a slow circle. Henry couldn't tell what she saw in all that darkness, but she nodded with a satisfied smile and eased into a gap between buildings.

He heard the jangle of keys and the turning of a lock. The bottom edge of a door scraped through the muck on the ground, and Aela disappeared into a square of black so dark, Henry might as well have had his eyes closed. He grabbed Adam's shirt and pulled him into the doorway, turning to close the door, feeling his way up the jamb until he found the deadbolt. He threw the lock, and a candle flared behind him.

Aela held the tiny light aloft, and they stood in a room of shelves, floor-to-ceiling and packed with supplies. She used the candle in her hand to light a another set into a sconce on the wall.

"Neat." Adam rammed his plastic sword into the tin scabbard, then set the little shield against one of the shelves. Shafts of reflected light danced off the ceiling.

The glittering chains in the corner caught Henry's eyes. Gleaming and oiled, they didn't look like iron.

Stainless steel, maybe?

He crossed the room to touch them. They didn't burn. Cold and hard.

Not plain iron, for sure.

Aela stepped in next to him and lifted a latching manacle off a hook, turning it over to catch the light.

"What are these for?" Henry asked.

She snapped the manacle over his wrist and danced back.

Henry stared at the metal cuff on his wrist in a paralysis of confusion. His inability to understand why she had done it drizzling ice over his anger.

She looked at him with a haughty rise of her eyebrows. "I'm not going to present myself to my grandfather looking like this. I'm going into the next room to take a bath, and I don't want you following me. *Forcing* yourself on me."

He thought of Boothe. His half-truths that might as well have been lies. Randall's omissions that were just as bad. Mandyel's free will secrets. Angels and demons had destroyed his trust. Henry would never believe any of those fuckers ever again, but *he'd* never judge one demon by the actions of another.

But I can't fucking blame her.

If that's how he had treated people, especially women, he never would have met Samantha. He dropped his head. "I never would have done that."

Aela snorted in disbelief. She walked into the next room, shielding the candle's flame from the breeze of her passing. She closed the door behind her, and Henry stared at the floor.

"Henry," Adam said. "I can't reach."

Henry rotated his hand in the manacle and raised his arm until the chain was stretched tight from his wrist to the wall hanger. He brought his claws down in a short slash. The chain split apart, releasing him to stagger back for balance. The manacle sprang open on its bent hinge, and he tossed it into the corner.

I am a Paladin, and no chain can ... ah, fuck it.

Adam was standing with his toes on one of the bottom shelves, his fingertips brushing against a can of Dinty Moore beef stew. Looking at the stocked shelves and the organization underneath that would be capable of keeping the Way Home ready for travelers made Henry stand firm in his decision.

Adam would be cared for and protected.

What if they tried to trade him? Use him?

He shook his head and grabbed the can from the top shelf, dropping it into Adam's waiting hands.

"I can't open it, Henry."

Henry dug a claw around the edge of the can, peeling it up and folding it back. Adam dug into his pocket and pulled out the antique Swiss army knife they'd found in the attic. It had a little spoon among the tools, and Adam loved using it. Just like those cowboy boots, nothing could convince him to stop.

The boy sat down and pulled the can into his lap. He

paused with his spoon held above the quivering skin of fat. "You want some?"

"No thanks, buddy. Tear it up."

This kid.

He needed his father. His mother. He needed more than the failed parent that Henry was. Amélie's face, smiling up at the denizens of Hell, opening her arms for a burning demon's hug. Henry's payment for failing her.

These people in Solitude were the answer. Henry nodded to himself.

This is definitely the right thing.

And so what if he had to deal with a little demon prejudice? In *his* experience, demons *were* assholes. Maybe Aela had a point.

He slid the backpack off and dropped next to Adam, folding his legs underneath him. The boy kept inhaling cold stew in wolfing bites, dancing in place with pleasure. Henry reached in and grabbed the wipes, sliding one out through the slit in the lid and wiping a bit of grease off the angel's cheek.

Adam looked up, flashing another grin. "Thanks, Henry."

Henry swallowed the painful lump growing in his throat. "You got it, buddy."

The door opened. Henry and Adam looked up as one. Aela entered with damp hair spilled across her shoulders. Henry licked a glob of fat from his claw and smiled at her dawning awareness.

"You broke your chains."

"Yup."

"Why didn't you come in to molest me?"

"What?" Henry was looking at an alien. Somebody speaking a different language. "The fuck is wrong with you?"

"Demons are known to be agents of chaos." Henry bristled at that word, but Aela continued in a rush and kept him from bitching. "Demons can't be trusted to keep their word unless it's for their own gain." Her eyebrows rose in sudden understanding. "It's because you are trying to gain the boy's trust. Lull him into security, so you can betray him later?"

"Trust?" Henry said it like a word he'd never heard. He popped the snap on the cargo pocket on his right leg and slid his hand in. He pulled out Heaven's Blade, the sharp edge protected by a plastic sheath from a rusted machete he found stuck in the mud outside a moss-covered log cabin at the edges of the mist.

He gripped the sheath between his knees and freed the blade. Swirling with dark energy, like a living Damascus pattern, it hung from his hand in front of Adam's eyes. The boy kept eating, unaffected by the blade's proximity.

Henry looked into Aela's eyes, glittering with the bouncing flame. "A demon who became an angel gave me this. Won it at an auction where they sold children to the highest bidder. It can sense when an agent of Heaven is near, but it was actually made to *kill* angels. To kill *this* angel, I think."

He slid it back in the sheath. "In *my* hand, it means nothing. Adam knows my love for him will keep it away, and while I'm holding it, he knows he's safe."

Henry tossed the knife in an arc across the room. Aela caught it, and the candle in her other hand barely wavered. She hissed, holding the knife away from her with a look of distaste, her nose wrinkling as she sneered.

Adam leaned forward, his face intense. His eyes filled with dark energy, liquid black flowing to cover the beautiful blue and gold. His body tensed beside him, and Henry felt the commanding power of the angel's birthright gathering behind. The boy's lips peeled back, revealing small fangs with a demon's growl.

Henry leaned back and crossed his arms. "The demon-turned-angel who gave me that told me to kill this boy. In order to save my daughter from the eternal torture of Hell, a result of my weak self-loathing falling for his fucking tricks … In order for me to fulfill my promise to the little girl murdered at the feet of her mother, I had to kill another child."

Aela held the knife at her side, her eyes shining. "Why didn't you?"

"Because I could never face her. Saving her by killing *him?* She'd never have forgiven me, and I'd never have forgiven myself. She's already dead. And in Hell. Being groomed for service for only God knows what, but Adam is here now." Henry's voice broke. He cleared his throat and sniffed his tears up. "In a weird fucking way, she's safe for a while. But *he's* not. Please. I'm lost here, and they're gonna come for him. And I won't be enough."

Adam lifted Henry's arm and pressed his face into his ribs. He hugged Henry with a fierce embrace, tight enough to bleed the air from Henry's lungs.

Henry rested his hand on the boy's trembling head and waited for Aela to return the serve. She flipped the blade to hold it by the sheath, then tossed it back.

Henry let it land in his lap, and he leaned over the little angel to hug him back, his coffee can hand clanging off the tin scabbard of Adam'a plastic *Prince Valiant* sword.

"I was attacked by Ravagers," Aela said. "They're not usually so close to Solitude. They must have been looking for Adam. But they found me and Baelzor. Yes, I was bringing him back to stand judgment when he told me about the boy, but Baelzor never said anything about him being his son. He probably knew I would treat the boy differently had I known he was half-demon. I'll gather my things, and we'll go."

She turned, pausing at the door, the candle sending an aura around her like the sun's corona. "I'm sorry for chaining you."

She disappeared into the other room, and Henry stood with Adam still clinging to his side.

Chapter Four

THEY LEFT the Forgotten's crumbling buildings behind them.

Light from Nowhere filtered through the mist. Dark shapes moved in and out of the shadows at the edges of his vision to set Henry on edge. He hoisted Adam onto his shoulders and stared at Aela's back.

She held her gaze to the ground, glancing up every few seconds, her eyes squinting in concentration. She pulled a gold pocket watch out of her jacket. It clicked open, and she held it out in front of her, turning to face a pile of rocks at the base of a mountain, rising to a mist-shrouded height and fading into shadows.

Aela glanced at Henry. "The entry into Solitude moves every day. We should have a few minutes still." She pointed with the watch before snapping it closed and sliding back inside her jacket. "It should be right behind those rocks."

"Cool," Adam said. "A secret passage."

Henry wasn't as excited as the boy. Tension throbbed in his neck and jaw. Parched his mouth. He thought about Amélie's first day of elementary school. Samantha sat in the car, sobbing into a box of tissues. He held his daughter's tiny hand while they walked up to the big double doors, the principal standing at the top of the stairs with a sunny smile for all the children coming into her kingdom.

Amélie stopped cold at the first step. He felt her shaking, so he dropped to his knees and turned her to face him.

Her shoulders heaved from throttled crying. The stress on her face made him want to snatch her up and take her home. They could all crawl into bed and wrap themselves with a fuzzy blanket. Forget about the world.

"What is it, baby?"

"What if they're mean to me?"

"What? Why would they be mean to you?"

She shrugged. "What if they don't like me, and I don't have any friends? I'll *die.*"

A hug, a kiss on top of her head, and his promise that everyone was going to *love* her. That was enough. She nodded, drew a dramatic breath, then turned back to the steps and pulled her hand from his.

"No, Daddy. *I'll* do it."

Standing in front of the entrance to Solitude, Henry drew his own dramatic breath. There was nobody to kiss the top of *his* head, but he stepped forward, anyway. "No, baby," he whispered. "I'll do it."

Chips of rock under their feet crunched like frozen snow. Curving down, a path twisted into rocks that became boulders. Formations of stone, black and jagged. The path plunged into a withering gap, and when Henry followed Aela into the shadow, the smell changed from fetid breaths to dry smoke and wood. The light turned bright with a gas glow, cleaner than the dirty orange flicker from old candles and wet fire.

Henry turned to look over his shoulder at the sheer

face of rock behind him, as if he'd walked through it like a sheet of water. It separated into a bright cavern. A cobbled courtyard before a castle wall set into the back rise of rough stone. An iron-bound door big enough for a tank to drive through dominated the stacked block of the castle. A row of Victorian streetlights curved to the door, hurling harsh light across the lane.

A buzzing flicker at the limit of his perception reminded Henry of the LED bulbs Samantha had insisted he install all over the house.

A small group of people stood in an arc, their backs to the door. Every face turned to follow Henry and Aela's approach.

A tall man stood in the center. Broad-shouldered, but his face under the long gray hair that fell to either side was gaunt behind a long square beard. A black leather coat stopped mid-thigh, and he held a gnarled wooden cane pressed into the stone between his feet.

To his right was a dark mountain of a man. Even bigger than Henry had grown. His bald head glistened with sweat, and his bull shoulders rose and fell with his breath. His tight black tee displayed slabs of muscle. He stood on the balls of his feet, the black handle of a sword poking out over his left shoulder. Black gloves and blacker boots. Pants that were one with the night. The guy radiated a snarl-toothed menace.

A small woman stood on his other side. Dressed in a black robe with a white lining in her hood, she looked like a nun with her dark hands clasped in front of her.

They were flanked by a man on either side. Dressed the same, in rugged uniforms topped with helmets that reminded Henry of British explorers in Africa, they held spears across their bodies to angle away from the people next to them.

As he and Aela neared, the end soldiers stepped away and lowered their spears to point at Henry.

He drew Adam off his shoulders and set him on the ground. The boy brought his shield around, holding it in before him like a Spartan.

The old man's mouth twitched in a smile, his eyes twinkling with suppressed mirth, and Henry finally exhaled. That ghost of a smile burned his doubts to nothing. He felt suddenly light.

What if they want to hurt me?

It didn't matter. He knew that the old man wouldn't hurt Adam, and for now … *that's enough.*

When they were only a few paces from reaching the old man, Aela stepped out in front of Henry and spread her fingers to the side in a halting gesture. Henry stopped and reached up to scratch his nose with the edge of his coffee can. He was rewarded with that flickered smile, and he reached behind his thigh to brush his fingers through Adam's hair.

The old man looked at Aela with pursed lips. "You left without telling anyone." His deep voice trembled with emotion, a rough lilt on his words. "You left after I said you couldn't."

"Grandfather …"

"No." A single shake of his head made his hair fall forward. "I know your reasons. You yelled them at me during an argument where I said some things … for which I am deeply regretful."

"I'm sorry."

"I know. Come stand behind me now. It's not your excuses that suddenly worry me so."

"Grandfather, you don't understand."

The old man drove the tip of his cane into the cobbles,

and he threw his head back to clear the hair from his face. "Stand behind me. Now."

Aela ducked and squeezed between the old man and the nun, turning to glance up at Henry before staring at the ground.

The old man looked into Henry's eyes with a narrowed gaze. He swallowed bile and tried to keep his heart from tearing through his chest. "A demon in Solitude who is not wearing chains. What is there to say, Big Ben?"

The mountain to the old man's right burst into action, jumping forward and reaching across his body to grab the sword handle.

Henry kept still as the blade cleared the enormous scabbard on Big Ben's back with an ugly hiss. The humming blade whipped around in a blurring arc, trailing inky tendrils of power on its way to Henry's neck.

Big Ben stopped before making contact, then stepped in to hold Henry's eyes with his own. Wide and staring from a face gnarled by anger.

Henry gritted his teeth and lifted his chin from the burning blade. He swallowed, and the skin on his throat sizzled, pain lancing his spine.

Big Ben smiled. "This sword is called Demon Piercer. It's your judge and jury, but *I'm* your executioner."

Henry swallowed again. "The only thing that would make me think your penis was any smaller, was if you drove a Corvette."

Big Ben snarled and drew the blade back, his neck muscles swelling.

The old man thrust out his hand. "Ben!"

Big Ben stabbed, and Henry stood firm.

The sword bit into his chest, driving against bone.

A burst of light washed away every color, and Adam

launched from the ground, his wings blurring like a hummingbird.

The white fire of his sword met Demon Piercer, and a burst of white sparks like a fireworks finale showered over Big Ben's shocked face.

The dark blade flew through the air, its humming song pulsing as it spun.

The cowboy boots that Adam loved so much ripped apart as he dug his little black claws into the thick muscles of Big Ben's abdomen. He spun with his sword sweeping a circle. The soldiers on the end took a single step, their spears twisting in to attack.

"Stay back!" Adam shouted.

The command's power rolled out from the boy in a wave.

Everyone froze.

Big Ben rolled his eyes down to keep the terror on his chest in view, and Adam got a fresh grip. His shirt glistened with blood. Adam leaned in with his black eyes to the side of Big Ben's head, and his lips drew back from his fangs as he whispered. "Choke yourself."

The command powered against the stone, rebounding to double on itself, and Big Ben's hands crept up his chest. He groaned with the effort to stop, but they crawled like spiders until they reached his throat. The fingers closed, and Big Ben's forearms bulged.

Henry called out, "Stop it, Adam."

"No!" Adam's shout was choked with tears. "He was going to hurt you!"

"Adam, please." Henry took a step and held his hand out. Adam spun with a growl and slashed his claws across Henry's arm. Blood swelled from the gashes, and he took another step. "Let him go."

Adam leaped from Big Ben's chest, and the big man

dropped to his knees, swollen eyes staring up at the stone ceiling and veins standing out on his forehead.

Adam drove his claws into Henry's shirt right through the rainbow. Blood gushed to mix with the blood flowing from Big Ben's slice. A cold wound made by a demon killing blade. It stained the front of his shirt and poured to his waistband, trickling down the fronts of his thighs.

He pulled the struggling boy into an embrace.

Adam tore at Henry's sleeves with slashes that left weeping scrapes in his arms, screaming cries driving into Henry's ears.

Amélie had gone through a tantrum phase. Screaming and kicking. Samantha thought it was her parenting and had been terrified it had been *her* fault. Henry smothered her with love. Taking her blows and whispering into her ear over and over. *Mommy and Daddy love you.* Just a phase.

Blood from the wound in his chest filled his boots and spattered the ground. He wrapped Adam up, holding him in the same smothering embrace he had used on his daughter. Whispering in his ear.

Adam pressed his forehead into Henry's chest, and when he drew away, his face was covered in a greasy black mask of Henry's blood. His forehead wrinkled in confusion. But the anger within the boy was still building and seeking an outlet, still clawing to get away.

Henry fell to his knees, still holding Adam.

Here goes.

Henry *flared*, aiming his power into the clawing frenzy in his lap, and Adam screamed in indignant pain. The swirling power left his shocked eyes. He looked at Henry as if slapped. Betrayed and accusatory. His wings folded in, and his hand;s became pink fists, balled and ready for the next strike.

Big Ben fell over on his side, his hands still choking.

Henry didn't know what he was saying anymore. It probably didn't matter. Adam stiffened as Henry pulled him in tighter. This boy had been through a hundred lifetimes of pain. How many more to go? He murmured comfort into his ear, and all at once, Adam gasped, collapsing against Henry's bloody chest.

"Henry!" Shuddering sobs, and Adam took a quivering breath. "I didn't *mean* it. I'm sorry, Henry."

Big Ben drew a whooping breath, and the nun rushed to his side, dropping to her knees beside him.

The old man stepped back with his hands ushering Aela behind him.

Henry watched the pool of his own blood spread beneath him. The big bastard's sword had dug deep. The perfect weapon against a demon's skin.

Henry closed his eyes, feeling himself sink into the ground. Darkness closed in on him. He had been trying to teach Adam a lesson about … something he couldn't remember.

The darkness below him opened into fire as he fell. Heat from the flames burned the air from his lungs. His skin bubbled and burned.

Finally.

Henry was on his way to Hell.

I'll find you, baby girl. Daddy's coming.

Chapter Five

A FACE HOVERED in front of him.

Dark and cracked like an old boot. Eyes squinted in their inspection, the old brow wrinkled in concentration.

"I got a booger on my lip or something?" Henry asked.

The face jerked back in surprise. An old woman in black robes rocked back in a chair next to his bed. Her small hands fluttered up to her chest like birds. Her white-lined hood flew back to expose gray hair in tight curls.

"Oh my," she squeaked.

She pulled her hood back up and folded her hands in her lap. "You must forgive me. I've never seen a demon up close like this."

Henry stretched and sat up, throwing the sheet back and swinging his feet over the side. His claws clicked off rough stone. "And what do you think?"

"To be honest, I'm rather unimpressed."

Henry laughed at the ceiling. He looked back down, and she was joining him with a smile of her own. He gave his head a rueful shake. "You and my first prom date, Sister."

She sobered and pointed to a white ewer on the stand next to the bed. "The boy said you'd be thirsty. After he laid hands on you, your soul came back into your body in a rush of light, and your wounds closed. He healed you sure as I'm breathing."

Henry grabbed the pitcher and tipped it up eagerly, then stilled when he saw the wall at the head of the bed. Clocks covered every inch of the white plaster. Ticking silently. Hands marking off seconds. Animated eyes darting back and forth. Pulsing LED dots. Nixie numbers glowing in tubes.

He drank the water with his eyes scanning every face, all of them moving in perfect unison. *7:05 am.*

"I've never seen a soul fall to Hell, before."

Henry dragged his eyes away from the time. He finished the water and set the pitcher down with a gasping breath. "Huh?"

"Or to be pulled back. It's something I'm glad I lived to witness."

He flashed back to Adam's claws slashing in his fury.

Henry shook his head. "I don't follow, Sister."

The nun leaned forward. "Usually when somebody dies here, they simply cease to be. No Heaven or Hell for the souls that are trapped. Not without passage. But a savage fire opened beneath you, and the flames licked up to consume your flesh."

Henry swallowed his disappointment. To be alive here instead of in Hell felt like betrayal. Like Boothe asking him to kill a sweet little boy.

A boy with a fucking temper.

Henry raised his eyebrows in mock disbelief. "No shit?"

"Yes. And that's why I think Abraham brought you inside. The fires of Hell are reserved for the punishment of *humans.*"

40

"That's some shaky logic."

She smiled. "I thought so, but he leads us. Who am I to argue?"

"That's right. Who *are* you?"

"Sister Gladys Hines."

Henry stuck out his good hand. "Henry Black. Pleased to meet you."

Her eyes moved from his hands to his face. She set her jaw and took his hand in a firm grip. One pump, and she let go, snatching her hand back to her lap.

Good enough for me.

"So, where's Adam?"

"He's by the Dreaming Tree. Big Ben is teaching him how to hold his sword correctly."

A stab of jealousy rose into Henry's throat, but he swallowed it down. "He is, huh?"

Sister Gladys stood, pushing off the arms of her chair with a grunt. "He'll never apologize. You should go see him. Abraham has closed off most of Solitude to you, but he wants you to see the tree."

"Why?"

"Aela told him about how you saved her life. That can't go unpaid. Now, get dressed. I'll be in the hall just outside."

The door clicked shut behind her, and Henry looked down to realize he was naked. Next to a nun.

And she was unimpressed. Fuck.

His backpack was leaning against the wall behind her chair. He dug through it and pulled out some fresh clothes. He was going to miss that T-shirt, but he had more, and for the hundredth time since learning he could, Henry thought about taking his Mike Serafino form. Dress him in some decent clothes. Maybe impress the nun.

He shook his head and finished lacing his boots. He slid his scarred nubbin into the coffee can and stood.

The train's gotta slow down some time.

Then I can get off.

Henry stepped into the hall, and Sister Gladys smiled up at him. Several nuns passed with their heads down, carrying bundles wrapped in white cloth. Nuns walking in the opposite direction with empty hands. He looked up, and his jaw fell open. Clocks hung from the ceiling, running from one end of the hall to the other. Pendulums swinging. Second hands sweeping.

"The fuck is with the clocks?"

"To those who have waited thousands of years for salvation, time is very important."

"Salvation from what?"

"From this place, Henry. We are all souls hidden from His sight. We can't make the journey to be by the Lord's side until we escape."

Mandyel's words came to him. "He plants His seeds in difficult climates, ones that might in fact *kill* them. That way, they will not trust in themselves, but rather in God."

She looked up at him from the edge of her hood. "That is just so, Henry. But it has been a long, long struggle."

The end of the hall opened onto a towering room filled with the twisted trunk of a massive tree. A thousand yellow flames in ornate fixtures made the room into a park beneath the noonday sun. Henry skidded to a halt, nuns scattering to get around him.

The air above was full of branches, twining through the leaves of other limbs, heavy pods drooping at the tips. A spiraling raceway ascended to the ceiling, nuns scurrying up and down in long files. They pulled the pods free, spreading the heavy wrapping of leaves aside to expose the interior crop.

Clocks. Books. Food. Guns. Each item went into a clean white cloth, and the nuns carried their bundles away.

Sister Gladys pushed a hand against his back to get him moving, and Henry stumbled into the room with his mouth open, turning in a circle as he walked. The top of the tree was lost in the shadows, and he couldn't tell how tall it was.

"This is the Dreaming Tree," Sister Gladys said. "When God rested on the seventh day, He dreamed about Solitude, and it sprang forth as you see it. A place *outside* of time, where the people who were born from His dreams lived in peace."

"Then what happened?"

"His third gift to us."

Mandyel's words again. "His first gift was His form. His second was His will."

"That is also just so, Henry." Her face crinkled into a surprise smile.

"So, what was the third gift?"

"Entropy!" The old man's deep voice echoed out from behind the tree.

That must be Abraham.

He walked as if he didn't need the cane, but he stumped it into the floor anyway. "Or as *we* understand it, *time.* Or maybe more to the point, the *passage* of time. God woke, for His work was not yet done, but his dream continued on."

Big Ben's hulking form edged past the tree with Adam's bouncing frame right behind him.

"Henry!" Adam cried, and he was off like a shot, jumping across the roots without looking, skipping across the room as if flying.

Henry dropped to his knees to catch the little guy, rocking from the impact and laughing into his hair.

"I'm sorry, Henry."

"Me, too, but you were kinda out of control. You were hurting people who didn't necessarily deserve it."

"But he was gonna *kill* you."

"I know. He kinda *did*."

Adam pulled back with his lower lip quivering. "But I said I was sorry."

"I heard you, but one of these days, that might not be enough anymore."

Adam's brow drew down. "What do you mean?"

The vertigo of memory washed over Henry, and he nearly fell over. Amélie looking up at him with that exact expression. Pouting confusion. "But I said *please,*" she had whined.

"Yeah, because that's what you're *supposed* to do, and that was very nice, thank you. But sweetie, that doesn't mean you get what you want just because you said please. Sometimes, the answer is still *no*."

He pulled Adam back and looked into his eyes. "That's no excuse for losing your shit like that. And it was no excuse for me to use him to get to Hell."

"Is *that* what you were doing?"

"Kinda. But I wanted you to learn something, too."

"What?"

"I don't really remember, buddy."

"You were trying to get to Amélie, weren't you?"

"I think so, yeah."

Adam stepped back and put his hands behind his back. "Do you forgive me, then?"

"Of course I do."

He grinned and reached up to put his hand on Henry's forehead. His little face smoothed into a look so serious, that Henry wanted to pull his head away from the child's touch, unsure of what was coming.

"I forgive you, too," Adam whispered.

Henry felt like he had been doused with freezing water. Adam dropped his hand, and Henry panted until he caught his breath.

I'm done crying.

"Thanks, buddy."

Adam pulled his plastic sword from the metal scabbard and brandished it in Henry's face. "Big Ben showed me how to stab. He said if I catch a motherfucker in the nuts with this, it'll stop 'em cold."

Henry barked laughter, and Big Ben rocked onto his toes, rolling his eyes up to look at the branches of the Dreaming Tree.

"We'll save your daughter, Henry."

"I know we will, buddy."

He stood and looked over at Sister Gladys. Her eyes shone with unshed tears. "An angel's forgiveness is no small thing."

"Neither is a demon's, Sister."

Her face crinkled into that sweet smile that Henry was falling in love with. "I'm beginning to think so."

Abraham stepped over a root and came level with Henry, dropping an arm across his shoulders. "Adam's been telling us quite a story."

Henry felt the power in the old man's arm and smiled to himself.

This old man is not as old as he wants everyone to believe.

"Yeah, well, only the parts where I was awesome are true."

Abraham's smile didn't quite reach his eyes. He raised his head to look up at the tree, lifting his cane to point. "What do you think of our tree? Our Dreaming Tree?"

"It's a tree, all right."

"It's a *magic* tree, Henry."

The old man's false joviality grated against Henry's nerves. "So, what's it do?"

"It creates whatever we dream about."

"So, it's not just a clever name."

That unamused smile again, and Henry wanted the old man's arm off of his shoulders. "All of Nowhere is full of magic like this, but you are standing on the very spot where God rested his head."

Henry looked down at his feet. "And I'm allowed to just walk all over it?"

Abraham dropped his arm and stepped back with a smirk. "It's just *rock*, Henry. No, the sacred thing in this room is not the *room*. It's the *tree*."

Abraham walked to the trunk and placed his palm against it. "Those born here, they dream the things they need. Those who wander in from the Forgotten, they *remember* those things. The tree grows them, and we harvest those dreams. Even you yourself may have a cocoon growing something just for you."

He turned and regarded Henry with a penetrating stare. "And I wonder what that thing might be. I'm very interested."

Henry shrugged. "Couldn't tell you. I *did* see some guns come out. Like little black peas in a holy pod."

Abraham nodded. "They're not reliable. Complicated technology tends not to work, except for the clocks, and we don't really know what drives *them*. It's not like we have someone running around winding them all up. We have some steam power and coal fires, but nothing more complicated than a sawmill."

"Like the start of a renaissance fair, huh?"

Abraham smiled and nodded like Henry had told him

something from a book that he'd already read. "Yeah, but here's the thing. This is why time is so important to us. We're running *out* of it, you see?"

"What do you mean?"

Abraham crooked a finger, urging Henry to follow. He turned and stumped around the tree.

Henry took the same path, passing in front of Big Ben close enough to feel the bull's breath wash across his face. He heard Adam's skipping steps, and the boy ran around with his plastic sword in front of him, heading an imaginary charge.

Henry felt the change in the air on the other side of the tree. A faint mustiness. A dimming of the light.

The farther from the trunk he walked, the darker the wood became. At the limits of the branches, where they touched the walls, the leaves were black and curled. The pods wrinkled and shrunken.

"The most fertile ground in all of Nowhere was under the Dreaming Tree. But our tree is dying, and the Forgotten has succumbed to the rooting nightmares. Most of the twisted city above us is given birth by the pain and fear of those incapable of moving on. They can't even find *this* place, and we've had to close our doors, lest we are overrun by those souls so sick … We couldn't possibly care for them all."

Henry reached up and touched a blackened limb, and the slick skin gave way under his finger.

Abraham closed his eyes and lowered his head. "The tree does not bear the fruit it once did. *We* will die when *it* does. And its death fast approaches."

Adam lowered his sword and looked up at the sick branches. "Can I help?"

Abraham looked at Henry from under his brows, his

gaze intense through his hanging bangs. "Well, I don't know. Would you like to try?"

Adam turned his face to Henry. "Can I?"

"Sure, buddy."

He grinned and walked to the trunk with his hands held out in front of him. They touched the bark, and he closed his eyes. His breathing slowed, and Adam bowed his head.

Henry looked at Abraham, but his eyes were fixed on the boy's back. Henry shrugged and looked back at Adam, and the child jumped back with a relieved sigh. He spun and whipped out his sword, slashing at the air with gusto.

After several swings, he slowed, noticing everybody's stares. "What?"

Henry threw his hands up. "That's it?"

"Yeah." Adam grinned and pointed over his head. "See?"

They all looked up. The black was turning to green. Leaves spreading out and filling in. Pods swelling. The disease tracked back toward the trunk and in moments the tree was healed.

Henry took a deep breath of the pure air, and pale flowers blossomed overhead, covering the tree in a bloom of brilliant white.

Sister Gladys fell to her knees, her hands clasped in front of her breast, wide eyes tilted up in amazement.

Adam danced up and put his hand on Henry's thigh. "I dreamed about ice cream last night. I can't wait!"

Chapter Six

ABRAHAM RUSHED through the halls of Solitude, his cane striking the ground and echoing off the ceiling and walls. The city's residents scattered in front of him, then recoiled in horror when they saw Henry following with Adam perched on his shoulders, holding onto his horns like reins.

Big Ben pulled even with the old man. "He shouldn't be in here."

Abraham waved him away. "He's no danger, Ben."

"But you said he would stay with the tree."

"I know what I said." Abraham careened around a corner, narrowly missing a woman pushing a cart full of pies. She jumped back with her hand to her throat. Henry came around right behind him, and the woman sagged against the wall with a squeal.

Henry waved as he passed. "Howdy."

Big Ben turned to walk backward so he could face the old man. It was clear Abraham wasn't going to slow down. "We can't have him just running around like this. There are women and children in these halls."

"Dammit, Ben. I don't *care*. This is more important than your concerns. Times they are a-changing!"

Sister Gladys ran by like a pigeon running for bread-crumbs, her robes held up with one wrinkled hand. She jabbed up a finger. "Close your everloving mouth and stop being a *fool*, Benjamin. Can't you see what's happening?"

Big Ben turned and slowed his pace. "I see a couple of ignorant old geezers too caught up in what a book says instead of paying attention to what's right in front of their noses."

"That's *enough*, Ben!" Abraham had the tone of a man continuing a tired argument that he no longer cared to win, like a parent saying, "because I said so," when all other reason failed to sway a child.

Henry smiled.

Suck it, Benjamin.

Abraham slid to a stop in front of an iron door. He dug through his pockets, and came up with a giant ring of keys. He closed his eyes, ticking off keys as he spoke. "The Sanctum. Wine cellar. Armory. Jessica's room. Ah, yes!"

The key turned with a deep clang, and Abraham swung the door. Henry flinched back from the wash of emotion billowing out from the other side. Dark thoughts of hunger and despair, and the air smelled like a dirty stable.

Abraham stepped aside and waved everybody through. Henry pulled Adam from his shoulders as he crossed the threshold into a wide stairwell. The door shut behind them, and they came into a long room lit by soft flames in the iron chandeliers hanging from the center of the ceiling. Both sides of the room were lined with bars. Holding cells for Solitude's criminals.

Aela sat behind a desk through a doorway off to the right. She looked up at the group as they passed, and

Henry gave her the same wave he'd given the pie lady. She charged out of the office, blonde hair flowing out behind her, and Henry nearly choked on laughter when she passed Big Ben to keep pace at *his* side.

"What is my grandfather doing?"

"Fuck if I know."

"Henry," Adam shouted, "Pick me up. You're going too fast."

Henry scooped the boy up and planted him on his shoulders where the boy took hold of Henry's horns like a steering wheel as they reached the end of the room.

Abraham stood panting in front of the final cell. He pointed to its interior. "Well?"

Henry shrugged. "Well what?" He turned, and one of the Lost threw itself against the bars, reaching out to grab whatever fell into its grasp. "Holy fuck!"

Abraham stood in front of Henry, addressing him and Adam in turn. "I don't think these people are truly *lost*. It's not a fair name. They're not beyond redemption. They're not castoffs. Don't you see?"

Sister Gladys laid her hand on Henry's arm. "They're *sick*. Like the tree."

Adam leaned forward, and twisted his gaze down, trying to see into the cell.

"Can I, Henry? Please?"

Henry sighed. "Sure, kid. Why not." Adam squirmed until Henry let him down.

Henry extended his hand to Abraham. "Give me the key."

"Abraham?" Big Ben said.

The old man looked over, and the big man shook his head. "Don't."

Abraham dropped the key into Henry's hand.

Big Ben's jaw bulged, his lips lifting in a snarl. He spun on his heel and marched away.

Abraham put his hand on Henry's back, urging him forward. "Don't worry about him. He'll get over it. He always does."

Henry nodded, stepping forward to the limit of the Lost's seeking fingers. "Cover your ears."

He didn't look to see if they complied. He drew in a deep breath and roared.

The Lost leapt back in terror, and Henry's vision wavered from the steam rising up from his breath.

Henry jumped forward and slotted the key into the lock. He twisted and pushed, and the door swung in with a metallic groan. The Lost cowered in the corner.

It was a female. Her tattered clothes shook with her panting breath. Adam stepped out from behind Henry for a better look, and when she saw the boy, her eyes widened. She launched from the corner, her filthy hands twisted into claws.

Henry swung the coffee can up and bashed her in the side of the head.

She dropped to the floor, dazed but not out. She struggled to all fours, shaking her head.

Henry bent and wrapped her in a crushing hug. She wailed and thrashed, and he held her head in a tight grip so she couldn't twist free and bite him or Adam.

"Get on it, kid! Careful of the mouth!"

Adam crept up and lifted his hand to her face.

She gnashed her teeth, biting the air.

Adam pulled his hand back, and his face hardened. He placed his hand to her cheek and closed his eyes. Like before, he stepped back with a smile, clapping his hands.

The Lost sagged against Henry's chest. He opened his arms and she fell to the floor, catching herself with her hands. Henry stood, pulling Adam behind him while she dropped to her hip, turning to squint up at the people standing outside her cell.

"Where am I?" she whispered, her skin tone going from grey to a healthier pale, her voice ragged from screaming.

Sister Gladys rushed in, falling to her knees next to the woman healed by an angel's touch. She looked at Adam in awe as she passed.

Abraham lowered to one knee and pulled Adam into a hug. "Thank you," he said into the boy's hair. "But can you do it one more time, son?"

The boy looked up for permission, but Henry was already nodding. "Let's do it, kid."

Abraham stood and turned to the cell directly across from them. A shirtless man lying on a metal cot was breathing in shallow breaths, his skin turning black from tendrils of darkness bleeding under his jaw.

Abraham took the keys back from Henry. "We've never captured a Ravager alive before. They always turn black and burn away, sometimes taking whole buildings with them." He threw the cell door open and walked up to the dying man to stand looking down into his face. He wrinkled his nose and waved a hand in front of his face. "Just like the rot in the Dreaming Tree. If we can find out where they are coming from, maybe we can fix them, or extinguish the threat."

Henry followed with Adam trailing along. The man on the cot was a giant, with thick arms much longer than the rest of his frame might suggest. Thick stumps of legs splayed apart, the pointed toes of his boots aiming out to either side. Henry's eyes swept his body, and when they reached the tattoo on the Ravager's chest, he snarled and flung himself back. The thorny *F* and *C* surrounded by the viney *O*.

A member of the Order From Chaos cult. Here in Solitude.

"Fuck this!" His eyes skated over the dark runes crawling from the main symbol. Then Henry closed his eyes. "No. You're not doing this." he opened his eyes and pointed. "You're not healing that fucker, I don't give a shit."

Abraham looked on with confusion and concern at war on his face. "Henry, we need information. This man may know something of importance."

"I don't give a shit! Adam's not gonna get his hands dirty on this … Adam?"

The boy had stepped around him, his face slack with curiosity. Before Henry could stop him, he laid his hands on the man's shoulder, and the Ravager bucked under his palms, groaning in pain.

Adam threw himself back, shaking his hands as if trying to get feeling back in his fingers. The Ravager settled, and the black traveled down his arms, the skin blistering as it spread.

Henry pushed Abraham aside, and the boy slid his toy sword free. It burst into white fire, and burned an arc into Henry's vision as Adam swung it down with a cry of effort.

Flames splashed down the Ravager's chest, and the blade passed through his neck into the cot's metal frame. The head sizzled as it rolled away, and Adam pulled the blade free. Just a shiny piece of plastic. The black faded from the Ravager's skin.

That's one way to heal a guy.

Adam slid the sword back into its tin scabbard and held his arms up, his face twisting with tears.

Henry pushed past Abraham and picked the boy up.

Adam pressed his face into Henry's neck and cried. After a few hitching sobs, Adam leaned back and wiped his eyes dry. "I know where my father is."

Henry pushed a stray hair out of the boy's face. "Well, let's go get him."

Chapter Seven

HENRY HELD his pack open with his dented coffee can hand and stuffed a rolled-up tee into the bottom next to Adam's bible and a box of Peacock matches. He looked to the side for the next thing to pack, but the shirt had been the last. He closed the pack and studied the clocks above the bed.

Adam bounced on the bed behind him, the squeaky springs substituting for the silent passing of seconds.

How long have I been here?

Time passed differently in Nowhere. Slower, and with no turning calendar. Where was Samantha? Had she married Mike Stone? Were they trying for a baby as hard as she and Henry had?

Henry was sure Pastor Owen was still looking for the boy, and with time moving at full speed on Earth, he was more steps ahead than Henry could count.

Adam dropped to his butt and scooted next to Henry, lifting his red arm over his head to lean into Henry's ribs. "Do you think he'll still remember me?"

"Will *who* remember you, buddy?"

"My dad. Do you think he'll like me?"

Henry slid the boy to the floor and turned him toward his eyes. Blue and gold, swirling with power, brimming with tears. His silvery hair nearly to shoulders that were a couple inches taller than when they met. Regret squeezed Henry's heart.

Stop growing, kid. Stay just the way you are.

"Of course he'll like you," Henry said. "He'll *love* you. The same as me. Only more, since he's your dad."

"Really?"

"Absolutely. Besides, homely as you are, you'll need all the love you can get."

The boy giggled music. Like sunshine on Henry's face. "I'm not homely."

"Oh, you're hideous. Breaking mirrors and shit."

"Sister Gladys said I was a flower."

"Yeah, but she's old. Probably half blind."

"Yeah. I bet she's like *fifty*."

A throat cleared and Henry snapped his head up. Adam dropped into a crouch, his small hand reaching for a little toy sword.

Aela leaned in the doorway with her hands hidden behind her back, smiling and shaking her head. Hair tumbled to either side of her face like Abraham's, and light from the hallway beamed through it like a halo. "I've got a surprise for you, Adam."

The boy stood up straight, his face opening with an anxious smile.

She pulled her hands around, and each one held a small cowboy boot.

"My boots!" Adam bounced forward to take them from her hands, then wrapped her right thigh in a hug, pressing his joyous grin into her hip.

Aela smiled and ruffled his hair.

He dropped right to the floor to put the boots on.

She shrugged. "One of the Sisters found a pod dangling right off the floor, and those were in it. We all knew who dreamed them."

Adam stood and stuck them out one at a time, like a little awkward model. "Can I go show Abraham?"

"Sure, buddy."

He squeezed past Aela and shot down the hall, his boot heels sounding like the old man's cane. Once he was out of sight, she turned back and crossed her arms. "How long have you been a demon?"

"I don't know. About a year, maybe."

She dropped her arms and walked to the chair in front of him, her leather outfit creaking with every step. She sat and pushed the hair away from her face. "How did it happen?"

Henry sighed and tossed the pack into the corner next to the door. "I used to be famous. Rich. Had millions of fans all over the world. That's why they targeted me."

For a second, Henry figured they were burglars. They were dressed the same, in black pants, shirts, and gloves. Except they wore no masks. Immediately, Henry wished he'd not let Sam talk him out of buying a gun. Now he was standing at the top of the stairs, helpless.

"To feed the chaos. Another little piece of ground in their fight against Heaven. So, they killed my daughter. Shot me in the back of the head. Raped my wife right there on the cold tile. I wanted carpet, but Samantha really liked the look of natural stone."

"You killed my daughter. MotherFUCKER!"

"Your daughter?" Peterson's face fell in thought, only to brighten with memory. "Henry Black? The comedian?" He laughed and slapped his knee. "Mr. Punchline, his very self? Sorry, that wasn't me. But I did show up soon after and put my cock in your wife's bum while you bled out on her feet."

"I was so *pissed*. But, I was pissed for *me*. They had taken everything from *me*. When a demon in Nowhere offered me a chance at revenge, he told me I could see my family again. But he never told me how. And I never asked." Henry shook his head. "My daughter dead. My wife an alcoholic. And still, I was pissed because *I'd* been tricked. I killed everybody in my way, and those souls taken in retribution were traded for the soul of the demon's lover in Hell. I was selfish, and for my selfishness, my daughter was sent to Hell in that woman's place."

Henry closed his mind to the memories and sniffed back his tears. He made his hand into a gun and pointed it at his face. "And this is my punishment. The form of a demon. This monster." He lowered his hand to his lap. "Then I met Adam. The man behind the Order? The man that betrayed my family? He was looking for that boy to give him power over God. How can you even imagine something like that?"

Again he shook his head. "To not only find out that Heaven and Hell are *real*, but then discover that you're in the middle of a war between them? All I could do was ask *why me*? Even after the demon who tricked me asked me to kill Adam. Gave me that blade I showed you, and for a second … I thought that if I did it, I'd go to Hell and maybe I could find Amélie."

The tears came anyway, and Henry let them fall. "That's why I deserve to be a monster. Thoughts like that prove I *am* one. Might as well look like one, too."

He looked up, and her face was impassive, the muscles in her jaw bunching under her temples. Henry shrugged and spread his arms. "But what are you gonna do, huh? It is what it is, right? Everything happens for a reason and all that bullshit?" He chuckled and wiped his cheeks. "So, what about you? What made you become a bitch?"

Her eyes narrowed and she tipped her head.

Holy shit. She's actually gonna tell me.

The door frame creaked, and she snapped her head around, her eyes wide.

Henry followed her gaze, and Big Ben leaned through the doorway, a meaty hand on either side holding him up. "Abraham wants to talk to us before we leave. Let's go."

Ben pushed off and left without seeing if they followed.

Henry opened his mouth for a joke about finishing too fast, but Aela was already up. She turned into the hall, and Henry closed his mouth with a snap.

He grunted as he stood, then grunted again when he bent over to pick up the backpack. He cast a final look at the wall of clocks over his bed, and walked out without closing the door behind him.

Aela stood with her arms crossed and her hips cocked to one side.

Big Ben squatted next to a black bag, sliding supplies in with exaggerated care.

"You know," Henry said, "we can do this on our own."

"No, the boy told Abraham that if we helped you all, then he promised to come back and help us heal the Lost or whatever else Abraham thinks will save us all."

"Oh, did he?" Henry asked, annoyed that Adam was making deals without consulting him.

The two spear men from the other day stood to the side, leaning on their weapons with a lazy competence that made Henry want to polish his coffee can.

Whooping laughter from behind the Dreaming Tree.

Abraham jogged out with Adam on his shoulders. The boy held the old man's cane above him. Abraham jumped the last root and lifted Adam over his head then set him on his feet. He stood with his face flushed and his eyes bright.

Aela smiled and crouched to her bag, digging through it like a woman in need of distraction.

"Well," Abraham said, clapping his hands. "Gifts. I want to give you all a small token before you leave Solitude. Before you leave me." He reached out, and Adam handed him the cane. Abraham smiled, and he looked at Sister Gladys as she emerged from the hallway holding a small bundle of something.

Abraham took the bundle and pulled the corners of the cloth to the side. Six glowing bulbs, like miniature ornaments. Twinkling blue. "These are Dream Lights. Made from the sap of the Dreaming Tree collected by our very own Benjamin. Distilled using the mist that surrounds the Forgotten. They won't light your way, but they *will* repel the Lost. We have seen that they are truly lost souls. Sickened by nightmares. Let us steer these wayward children back into health, and not to the point of a knife. The Sisters of Solitude make the lights, and they should do their job for a time."

Sister Gladys took them one at a time and delivered a light to each of them, starting with Aela. Henry came last. A brown leather thong let it hang from his neck. Henry wondered if the people here dreamed about cows to make leather, or just the skin and meat.

Faint blue, the Dream Light pulsed into his palm, and he slid it over his head. The strap tangled on his horns, and he heard Big Ben snort laughter while he puzzled out how to get it on. Henry finally got it figured out, and dropped the light behind his shirt to rest against his chest. A tiny point of heat over his heart.

"Good," Abraham said. "I don't like the idea of letting this boy go ..."

"We've been over this," Big Ben said.

Abraham nodded and held his hand up. "Yes, and I

agree. The children of Solitude and Solitude itself are more important, but I just wish … perhaps we should send more people with you?"

Big Ben shook his head. "We've been over this, too. A smaller group can stay hidden. *I'm* going with them. Kasey and Solomon are going. Aela can handle herself." He pointed at Henry. "And … this guy's got jokes."

Hey, fuck you!

Big Ben sliced his hand at Adam. "And you've seen what *he* can do. I think we're safer with him than he is with *us*."

Abraham leaned on his cane. "I know all that, Ben. I just can't help believing that we're not doing right by this child." He gave his head a weary shake, his hair falling forward. He walked to Aela like a man who *needed* that cane and stood looking down into her eyes.

Tears on both faces.

Abraham rested a hand on her shoulder. "This quest may mean more to our people as a whole, but you have the most to lose. Like the others *born* here, if you die, you will never receive passage to Heaven. Your mother was able to find the path to Salvation, but until Solitude is back in His grace, you will never be offered the light of redemption."

"Maybe. But you're assuming I deserve it."

"Aela, my dear granddaughter. Of course you deserve it. That's why I have tried to keep you in these walls. To protect you until the roll is called."

Big Ben chopped his hand at her. "You should stay here with Abraham."

She shrugged out from under her grandfather's hand and stepped back. "No. I'm sick of everyone else making my decisions for me. I'm making my own choices from now on."

Henry laughed. "That's what *I* said."

She sent a poisonous glare over her shoulder, then she spun around. She stopped to snatch her bag from the floor and stomped away.

Abraham looked at Henry through his tumble of hair, that knowing smile on his lips.

Adam broke the awkward moment by running over and pawing through the bag at Henry's feet. He found the bible then ran to Abraham. He held it up to the old man. "I want you to hold onto this while I'm gone, okay? You can read it, but don't spoil it. I'm only on Galatians."

Abraham took the book with a shaking hand. Adam wrapped his leg in a hug and pressed his cheek into the old man's thigh. "Thanks for everything, Mister Abraham."

Abraham pulled Adam away, and he squatted down so their eyes were level. "No, son. Thank *you*."

Adam stepped back. "You are a person like a tree planted by streams of water, yielding fruit in season. Your leaves do not wither, and whatever you do prospers."

Abraham staggered to his feet, pressing the bible to his chest. He nodded, lifting his hand in an absent wave. His dazed eyes tracked across the room until they spotted Sister Gladys. He held his hand out, and the old woman ducked under his arm. They supported each other as they left the room.

Henry looked at Adam's shining smile. "What did you do?"

"I blessed him."

This fucking kid.

Henry looked up, and Big Ben stood with his arms crossed over his barrel chest, his eyes narrowed in thought.

Henry didn't like that look at all.

Chapter Eight

THEY WALKED out of Solitude and through most of the Forgotten without incident, but the closer to their destination they came, the darker the emotions rolling off of the rocks. The Dream Lights kept the Lost at bay and gathering hordes at a distance. It was only a matter of time before the lights would fail them, though.

Henry could tell Big Ben felt it, too. The set of the giant's granite shoulders, lifting with the tension. His footsteps becoming a driving rhythm in the dirt. Henry didn't like the fucker, but he was still glad to have him around.

They had walked all day. Buildings became smaller. Older. With more distance between them until eventually they were walking through tall grass and tumbles of stones bigger than Henry and Big Ben combined.

Miles from the crumbling city lay a graveyard for misfits. No order or reason to the headstone placement. Hills and valleys with markers jutting into the air like crooked teeth. A dark rise of earth at the distant border, and over the scraping wind was the whisper of trees, brushing their leaves as they swayed.

Even Adam was subdued. Sitting on Henry's shoulders and whispering to himself, words too low for Henry to hear in a sing-song. Like poetry. Henry strained to make out the words, and then, in his silence, he heard.

"I will guard the feet of the ones who are faithful, and I will shroud the wicked in darkness, for the might of man will not prevail against me. My enemies will be broken into pieces. Against them, I will send my thunder. I will not fear, though thousands come from every side, and from my hand will come deliverance. My hand will be with them, keeping them from pain and free from harm. I will shield them with my glory, and hold their head high. I will guard the feet of the ones who are faithful ..."

Not a prayer, but a promise.

Henry had only been to two churches in his life. St. Bartholomew's in Cincinnati, Ohio, and the Burg Spires Church of Hope. One for his grandmother. The other for Samantha. He wasn't big on prayers, and his recent first-hand experience with God's Word wasn't changing his mind. But the little angel's words sent a shiver down his spine.

Adam wasn't talking to God.

He was talking to *himself*.

Big Ben lifted a fist to bring them to a stop. He squatted down and fished the Dream Light out from under his shirt. Its wan light cast a tiny spot on the ground. Henry felt rising emotion in the dark. Sharp pain from the Lost as they drew nearer.

Big Ben inspected the stone under his feet, and he turned to look up like he was sniffing the air. He headed off the path and into the cemetery. Winding his way through rocks and broken stone, he paused every few yards to consult the ground with the small blue light which was growing dimmer over time.

After several of those stops, a row of leaning mausoleums bloomed from the shadows. Big Ben tracked to the third one, cracked and grown-over with sickly brown moss. He motioned Aela to his side, and she slid a ring of keys from her bag. She worked the lock open, and Big Ben bent to the door, placing his hands against it, his white teeth shining out of his dark face with effort.

The door grated open enough for his big body to barely fit. He stepped aside and waved them through. Henry lifted Adam from his shoulders and filed in behind the rest of them, turning to add his shoulder to Big Ben's. The door inched closed, seating against the warped frame with a deep clash of stone.

A candle flared to life. Big Ben turned to clap Henry on the back. "Thanks."

That must have hurt.

Henry nodded and shrugged his backpack off, dropping it by the door.

Aela handed Henry a candle, lighting another from its dancing flame, and she turned to sit on a stone bench. "This is the last Way Home before the forest."

Henry looked at the full shelves. "Who stocks all this shit, anyway?"

Big Ben leaned Demon Piercer into the corner. "The Sisters of Solitude."

"What, they just walk around with an armload of food and clothes and shit?"

Aela nodded. "Their vows make them invisible to the Lost."

"Okay, but what about the Ravagers?"

Kasey slapped Solomon on the shoulder on his way by. "That's what *we're* for."

"Fine, then why are the Way Homes *here*?"

Big Ben rolled his eyes as Aela doffed her boots with a

sigh. She crossed her foot over her thigh and leaned over to massage the sole. "My grandfather believes the Lost can be led back into Solitude. He thinks they can all be saved, and I think now that he's seen Adam heal one, he won't stop until they're all within his walls."

"But you don't believe it?"

She glanced at Adam, who was looking up at Big Ben in fascination. "I'm not sure. I've seen the terrible things they're capable of. Just because we found one that we could bring back doesn't mean they *all* can be saved. Or that they *deserve* to be. That's what all this is for. It's so the Lost can become the Found, and they can use the contents of the safe houses to find—"

"The way home," Henry finished.

Big Ben clapped his hands with a grin. "Sister Gladys told me there was a cellar beneath us. And that it may or may not be stocked with beer."

"Very good." Kasey jumped up and headed through the low doorway behind Big Ben's shoulder. Solomon followed, and Adam ran over to put his hand on Henry's leg. "Can I go?"

"If it's okay with Big Ben, sure. Just don't drink too much."

He rolled his eyes. "I'm not allowed to drink. I'm just a *kid.*"

Big Ben swept his arm out. "Come on, little man."

Adam ran through the door, and Big Ben looked Aela with raised eyebrows. "You coming?"

"No, I think I'm going to stay here with Henry."

"With Henry?" His eyes narrowed. He pursed his lips and nodded, the muscles in the back of his neck flexing in angry spasms. Then he turned without another word and disappeared into the back of the mausoleum.

His footsteps pounded down the stone stairs, and

Henry cleared his throat. "Remind me to sleep with my eyes open around that guy."

"No, he's … fine."

"What, are you two a thing?"

"He thinks so, but I just … I'm not ready for another one."

"Why not?"

She put her foot flat on the floor and leaned forward, elbows to knees. "Do you believe in redemption?"

"I kind of *have* to, don't I?" he said, waving his stump over his ugly mug.

"But what if you did something bad? Something so bad …"

He wanted to touch her. Put his hand on her shoulder and tell her it was okay. But he was ugly. A monster.

"What did you do?" Henry asked.

She leaned back with a bitter smile. "Never mind. I'd rather you saw me as I am now. Not what I *was."*

Wouldn't we all.

"So, what's in the trees?"

The bitterness left her smile, and she sighed in relief. "We don't know. Nobody's ever come back. Until Adam looked into that Ravager's mind, we just thought, I don't know. Dragons? It could have been anything."

She looked up to stare at the ceiling. "Nowhere is big. Endless. But no matter which direction you go, you come back to the Tree that holds up a sky that changes from sunlight to shadow after you see it for the first time."

Henry nodded. "Like an open house working for buyers."

"And past the Tree is the mist that hides the Forgotten. Like the drain of some cosmic sewage system. We *need* community. Yes, many of the people in the Forgotten, and in Solitude, were criminals. Many of them still are.

And being born in Nowhere doesn't make you free from sin. Far from it."

The bitterness twisted her face again. Henry had to stop his hand from rubbing her arm. An unconscious gesture that usually made Samantha feel better.

"A lot of the Lost have no place in the Forgotten. Running from their pasts. Hiding from the angels that gather souls for ascension. The demons that troll for souls that belong in Hell. All those people should count for something. They ought to be able to live out their lives here without judgement."

She laughed, glancing at Henry in embarrassment. "Anyway, the Fortress that Adam saw? Nobody's heard of it. And that frightens me. If Nowhere is endless on the outside, how deep does it go in here?"

"Well, I guess we'll find out tomorrow."

She stood. "I guess you're right. I'm going down to see if there's any beer left. You coming, too?"

He waved her off. "No, I think I'll just stay up here. Out of the way."

Her face fell. She knew what he was saying.

I don't want to fuck up your good time with my presence.

"This may be your last chance," she said.

"I've got more to regret than missing out on one last party."

He watched her leave, and he lowered himself to the floor in front of the door. He curled up on his side, his hand under his head as a pillow.

A fortress inside an unknown city in the trees. A forest where nobody has ever gone. Adam had seen where the Ravagers took his father, and Henry couldn't help but wonder at the convenience of finding the one guy who could tell them where Baelzor was. Just waiting for the one person who could find it.

He imagined Mandyel lifting his drink in a toast. A thousand moves ahead.

Henry heard laughter drift up the steps, and he closed his eyes with a smile, hoping Mandyel was half as brilliant as everyone seemed to think.

Maybe then they could survive this and he could get his daughter out of Hell.

Chapter Nine

"Henry, I miss the sun."

"Me too, buddy. We still going the right way?"

"It's always straight ahead. Where it's darkest."

The dirty light of Nowhere, like a perpetual black cloud, seemed bright compared to the shadows under the trees. Wet leaves and mud squelched underfoot. A marshy reek of rot was ripe in air that hung like a fog.

The branches above them swept back and forth in a restless rhythm that made Henry think of a great beast blowing its breath on his body.

The wide path through the black forest twisted and turned like a riverbed. Like walking into a tunnel, the way ahead disappeared into darkness. Henry felt thoughts breaking between the trees around them. Emotions turning from hesitant fear into hunger and purpose.

He grabbed the Dream Light hanging from his neck, but it was cool.

Rasping laughter from the shadows to his right.

By the way Big Ben's head whipped around, Henry knew that he'd heard it, too.

Henry shook his head. "Abraham was right. We should have brought an army."

"Quiet," Big Ben said.

Kasey crept up to Henry's left. "I don't think it matters anymore. They're all around us."

"How many do you think there are?" Solomon called from the front of their line.

More laughter, and Henry saw flitting movement.

Kasey spun toward the sound. "They're everywhere."

Henry dialed his thoughts away from the fear, tuning into the hunger surrounding them. "Adam, I think you better draw your sword."

"No," Big Ben said in a harsh whisper. "It'll draw attention to us."

Aela lifted the pale glow of her Dream Light overhead. "Henry's right. It's like they've been following us. Waiting for something."

Big Ben shook his head. "They're just waiting for the Dream Lights to die. The end of the trees is right around the next bend in the path, and we'll be in the open again."

Henry shook the incredulity from his head. "How the fuck do *you* know? You got a map or something? Why'd you bring us out here all by ourselves, anyway? I thought you didn't know what to expect, and Aela told me nobody ever comes in here. Adam, draw your sword. It's time to get mad, buddy."

The toy sword became a white beacon, and Adam rose into the air on buzzing wings. Henry shrugged out of the backpack and peered into the trees.

Glittering eyes hid at the edge of the light on both sides.

Henry caught Big Ben's glare over Aela's head, but before he could say anything, the air split with the screeching of attacking Lost.

Pouring out of the gaps between the trees, they headed straight for Adam, staring into the flames of the sword he held over his head. Henry roared and jumped forward, his boots sliding in the muck.

Adam swung the sword, and one of the Lost fell, its head spinning into the dark.

Teeth sunk into Henry's forearm.

"Fuck!"

He smashed the coffee can down onto the top of a gray head, and the teeth crumbled as they tore free of his flesh.

He lost sight of Adam behind a swarming mass of twisted bodies, clawing and biting. Henry dropped into the shadows and hurled himself through the dark, bursting into the glow of light from Adam's sword.

He swung his claws, and the blood streaming from his arm mingled with the splashes painting the snarling faces around him.

Adam screamed in pain, and Henry's vision turned red.

Rage exploded into his brain, and all the sick passion of the Lost fell away. Time slowed, and Henry saw the attacks before they happened. Their intent painted across the canvas of his anger, he drove his claws into everything in reach.

Adam's sword dimmed as he collapsed to the ground.

The souls of the Lost glowed red inside their bodies like road maps of energy, pulsing with their heartbeats. Henry stood with his legs spread, one foot planted on each side of the little fallen angel, and the bodies piled in a circle that grew with each swing of his claws.

Each bite.

Each punch of his ruined left hand, the coffee can splintering and tearing from the force of his blows.

Their life force swirled into his nostrils.

Instead of letting it drain into the ground, he inhaled.

And Henry *burned.*

Another group of the Lost spilled out from the trees. Sticks as weapons. Dirty stones and rusty knives. Henry roared into their midst, and they broke around him, slashing and beating. A spearhead drove through the neck of a thin female in a rotting wedding gown.

Kasey spun into the next target, and Henry tore the arm off a Union soldier brandishing a fractured flintlock rifle.

Aela at the edge of his vision, stabbing her knives, her lips drawn back in a grim snarl.

To his right, a flash of a tattered butcher's apron covering the wasted form of a male swinging a pitted cleaver.

Henry struggled to stay put, over Adam's shuddering body beneath him.

Henry caught the blade in his thigh and felt it grate against bone. The butcher toppled with his guts splashing through the slices in his abdomen, and Henry inhaled another soul.

A sharp stick tore through the skin under his arm, breaking off as the Lost fell against him, biting into the meat over his ribs.

Henry tore the point free and drove it into the Lost's eye. It burst, squirting fluid and blood over Henry's fist. Its scream joined the others.

A rock smashed into his knee, and his leg folded in with a ripping that roared over everything else. Henry snarled as he spread his arms to catch the wiry male driving into his chest.

He spun to land on the twisting body and thrust his face into the Lost's neck. He tore the throat out with a bite that scraped against the Lost's spine, and blood flooded his mouth a split second ahead of the trapped soul's energy.

He pressed into the bloody mud and stood with his weight on his good leg.

He spit the flesh from his mouth and raised his claws for the next one. But there were no more.

He gasped, hot breath steaming from his mouth. The red left his vision. The last of the life energy he had absorbed worked on the torn ligaments of his knee. The bleeding wound in his side. He growled as the pain of healing seared through him, and he looked down, then spun with his eyes wide in panic.

Where's Adam?

The question left him cold. His demon vision darkened, and he realized everyone was covered in blood and dirt. Lost in the dark.

"Where's Adam?" he shouted.

"He's here," Aela cried.

"I'm here, Henry."

His little voice flooded Henry with joy. It didn't matter that it was dark. Henry couldn't see through the tears, anyway.

He followed the voice to their shapes on the ground.

Aela sat with Adam in her lap. Blood and grime covered her face and hair. Adam's white outfit was nearly black.

Henry fell to his knees, skidding through the mud, splashing bits of filth into the boy's face. Adam reached up, and Henry scooped him into his arms. The sobs left him breathless. He could only rock him back and forth, thanking a God he hated that the boy was okay.

He felt Aela's hand on his shoulder, and he looked into where her wide eyes shone from her filthy face. "Are you all right?"

"Just a few scratches, and I'm lucky. They all went straight for Adam."

"Not *all* of them." Big Ben's voice strained from pain and effort.

Solomon's arm was slung over Big Ben's shoulder, and his feet dragged through the mud. Henry started to rise, but helping meant letting Adam go.

Kasey came limping out of the dark, pushing against Solomon's other side, taking the burden from Big Ben and easing the wounded man to the ground. "He's hurt pretty bad."

Aela slid over to join him, bending to examine his injuries.

Big Ben slid to the ground with a grunt, his breath in ragged gasps. He laid Demon Piercer across his thighs. It glistened with blood from handle to tip. Blood dripped from his fingers and pattered to the ground.

Henry held Adam away from him, inspecting his body for damage. "Are you hurt?"

"I was," Adam said, his voice dry and cracking. "I got stabbed in the stomach. It hurt so bad, but I killed that motherfucker, then I healed myself." He turned to look at Solomon. "Can I heal *him*, Henry?"

Big Ben said, "No. You've been through enough. Kasey will take him back to the Way Home, and we'll move on. I just need a little rest."

Aela spun to face the big man. "You need more than a *little rest.*"

"I'll be fine, woman."

"No," Henry said. "We'll *all* go back. All the way to Solitude maybe."

"No, Henry," Adam cried. "You said we would save my father. You *promised.*"

"I know, buddy, but you're *hurt.*"

"No, I'm not. I just need to rest like Big Ben."

Big Ben pointed behind Henry. "He might be right. Look what you did."

Henry turned and froze in disbelief. The Lost lay piled and scattered, torn beyond recognition. Henry barely remembered the frenzy — just enough to feel a swelling wave of satisfaction and pride, both of them sick.

He turned back, and Big Ben looked at him with that measuring expression he'd given Aela in Solitude. Henry opened his mouth to ask the ox what his fucking problem was, but Kasey broke his concentration.

"I think Solomon's gonna be all right. He's cut up a little, with a lump on his forehead the size of my fist. But he's breathing okay."

Big Ben nodded. "What about you?"

"I'm banged up a little, but I'm doing better than *you.*"

"He's got a point," Aela said. "Maybe *you* should take Solomon back and wait for us at the Way Home."

"*Hell* no. What if there're more?"

Henry nodded. "Then we all go back."

Adam wriggled out of Henry's arms. He tried to stand, but sat with a splat, and his head dropped to his chest. "You promised."

Henry felt the kid's pain. Exhaustion crept into his shoulders.

Big Ben raised his hand. "All right. *I'll* take Solomon back, but you people get into the trees and hide. I'll be back as soon as I can, and then we'll keep going."

Henry shook his head, but he extended his senses out, spinning the dial in his head. There was nothing out there but darkness. "Okay."

Adam smiled and climbed back into his lap.

Big Ben slid Demon Piercer back into the scabbard on his back. He stood with a grimace, and walked over to

Solomon, his boots squelching into the mud. He bent and put Solomon's arm over his shoulder. He got a tight grip on Solomon's wrist, took a whistling breath, then stood with Solomon draped behind his neck. Demon Piercer's handle looked like it dug into the man's ribs, but Henry thought he wouldn't mind.

"I'll be back as soon as I can." His shape disappeared into the shadows leading out of the woods, and Henry wondered if they'd see him again.

Adam's soft snores rose from his lap, and Henry shook his head. "No fucking way. This is insane. I don't care how mad the little guy gets. We're going back."

Aela reached up to grab Kasey's hand as she looked at Henry. "Are you sure?"

"Fuck yeah. Something is wrong about all this. I can't put my finger on it, but yeah. I'm sure."

Kasey released Aela's hand and whispered, "Do you hear something?"

Aela crouched down. "What is it?"

"Voices."

Henry strained his eyes into the dark, staring down the path. He heard nothing, but a glow grew between the trees. Bobbing light, as a lantern held out in front of someone walking over uneven ground. He quested out with his mind, searching.

No dark emotions. No hunger or *need*. Just the light coming closer, and the whisper of voices in the distance.

"Into the forest," he hissed.

Kasey stooped to grab his spear, and Aela lifted her knives as they eased through the mud. Henry pushed through the wet brush on the side of the path, holding Adam against his chest to soften any vibration that might wake him.

He wove through the trees for several yards, but the

sticks and leaves were dryer the farther from the path they went. They were making too much noise, so he stopped in his tracks, spinning and dropping to his knees. Aela and Kasey crept to his side, making much less noise than *his* big ass.

Aela dropped her hand on his forearm, reassuring Henry with a squeeze. He sat back to wait.

The light came closer, sending yellow shafts through the trees.

Chapter Ten

THE LIGHT WAS a square lantern held above a man's head.

Like Paul Fucking Revere or something.

The man wore jeans and a white tank top. His arms were colorful tattoos clear to the knuckles. A silver chain hung from his belt.

His face was dominated by a hooked nose over a mouth of crooked fangs poking out of his lips in every direction. An aluminum bat cocked over his shoulder. Slick blond hair hung above his glinting eyes.

He was followed by a slop of shit whose belly sagged beneath the bottom edge of his red tee to hang over the crotch of his khakis. In one hand he held a long fire axe. In the other was a dripping sandwich. He pressed the sandwich into his face and took a wet bite, wiping his mouth on his forearm. The light washed over the pile of bodies, and Sloppy pointed with the axe. "What the fuck is *this?*"

If dumb had a voice, it would sound like that guy.

Slick held the light higher and shrugged, making the shadows dance. "I don't fucking know, man. These creepers are *out* there."

"Ravagers," Aela whispered in his ear.

Henry's heart charged. He locked his muscles to keep from leaping out of his skin.

He slowed his breath and leaned forward to listen.

Sloppy took another bite. "I ain't never seen nothing like *this*, though."

"Fuck yeah, man. Happens all the time. Like once, me and Chester was walking the walls, and a bunch of creepers come up. I nicked one with an arrow, and when they smelled the blood, it was like chum."

"What's chum?"

"That shit they put in the water to attract sharks. You ain't got the Discovery channel?"

"Hey, excuse the fuck outta *me*, man."

"I'm just saying. You should watch more TV. Maybe you learn something."

"Whatever." Sloppy crammed the remaining third of the sandwich into his mouth, stuffing the last bit in with a fat finger. His cheeks puffed out while he chewed, and he looked around with a bored expression.

"Wha we *onna oo?*"

"The shit did you just say, you fat fuck?"

Sloppy swallowed, and his eyebrows drew down. "I'm not fat, okay? I just got a slow metabolism."

Slick turned to hold the lantern over Sloppy's head. "It's faster than anorexia, that's for sure."

Henry tipped an imaginary hat.

That wasn't bad.

"Fuck you," Sloppy shouted. "I said, what are we gonna do?"

"I don't know. What do you wanna do?"

"I don't know. Nothing?"

Slick dropped the light to his thigh, and the underside of their faces lit like Jack-O-Lanterns. The shadows stretched to give them evil leers. "If we say something, they'll just make us clean this shit up. If we don't say *nothing*, then when the Watch comes through, they'll find it, and then *they'll* have to clean it."

Sloppy grinned with rotten teeth and nodded like his neck was a broken spring. "Fuck yeah! I only got a week left, anyway. I don't wanna spend it cleaning creeper blood outta my fingernails."

"Then let's head back and tell Thompson there's nothing to report. Fairies or some shit."

They walked back the way they had come, their jokes and laughter fading into the distance.

Henry looked into Kasey's confusion. "What was that?"

Kasey shrugged.

"What's anorexia?" Adam asked.

Henry looked down and stifled his laughter. "Don't worry about it. How you feeling?"

"Better. I took a nap."

"Not *much* of one."

Henry set Adam on his feet and smoothed his hair. It was crunchy with dried blood. The boy ducked away from his pat, knocking his hand away with annoyance. "I dreamed about my mother."

"You did?"

"Yeah, she misses me."

"I'm sure she does, buddy."

Adam pressed his knuckles into his eyes and sniffed. Henry felt his own throat close, but he swallowed and took a deep breath. "So, what should we do?"

Aela stood and slung her bag around to rest in the small of her back. "I say we follow them."

"I don't know. Those guys may be dumb as paint, but we have no idea what's at the end of that path."

"Then let's find out. We're going that way, anyway."

"Yeah," Adam said.

Henry looked over, and Kasey shrugged again. "Let's just take a look."

Adam grinned and spun to run through the trees. Henry reached out to pull him back, but the boy was too quick.

Goddamn it!

Henry jumped to his feet and followed as silently as he could, but he still felt like he sounded like a blind moose crashing through a forest made of plastic bags.

Adam stopped at the edge of the carnage, then bent down and drew his plastic sword from the mud. He turned, his eyes widening when they fell on his shield. He straightened with it hanging from his arm, again ready for battle.

Henry slowed when his feet hit the mud. He stepped over a gray corpse, stabbing his toe through the gaps in body parts as he made his way to his backpack, then leaned forward the last few feet and hooked a strap with one claw. He teetered when he pulled the pack to his chest, threw his other arm out for balance, and retraced his steps until he was clear of the bodies.

He stuck his arms through the straps and seated the pack across his shoulders. Saw them waiting for him, their eyes sparkling in the dark, and sighed. "We might as well get this over with."

Henry kept his head swiveling, and his mind dialed to its limit. But he saw, sensed, and heard nothing. Just a walk under the hidden stars.

It was several minutes before he fixed on the glow in the distance, growing until it lit their path. He slowed and motioned for them to get to the edge of the trees.

Big Ben had been right. They were almost out of the woods. The path opened into a clearing, the mud and rocks edging up to a line of asphalt. A cracked road with a faded double yellow line down the center.

A faint growl of machinery, the reek of diesel. It reminded him of walking down Stanton Avenue when the trucks were delivering the papers to the news stands out front of the capitol building.

Henry squinted through the last of the trees. At the edge of the road, a guard shack made of plywood and corrugated metal, full of flickering light, sat facing a smoking contraption that was rumbling like a freeway. "It's a generator."

He turned and waved the rest of them forward. They crowded up to look over his shoulder, Adam peering past his thighs. "You need to get one of those in Solitude," Henry said. "Pretty soon you could even have the Internet. So much porn."

Kasey snickered.

Henry inspected the guard shack. It looked like someone was sitting with their feet propped out the window. "Is that Sloppy?"

Aela leaned forward, squinting like Henry had. "Who?"

"The fat bastard that was with the guy holding the lantern. Slick."

"I can't tell."

Kasey nodded. "That's him."

"You sure?" Henry said.

"Oh, yeah. And he's asleep."

"Where's the other one?"

"I don't see him *anywhere.*"

Henry drew Heaven's Blade from his pocket. He let the sheath slide back as he raised the knife to his face. "Let's go make sure he *stays* asleep."

He turned to Aela. "Stay here with Adam."

She shook her head, her face clouding with anger.

"Henry's right," Kasey said. "If the other guy's around, you can send us a signal."

"What *kind* of signal?" Her voice dripped with scorn. "You want me to send up a *flare*?"

Henry shrugged. "You got one?"

Aela bent down and picked up a rock the size of a chicken egg. "If I see something, I'll throw this rock. And trust me, I'll try *really* hard to hit you."

"Fair enough."

Henry spun and ran toward the guard shack in a crouch. He heard Kasey's soft steps on the blacktop behind him, and as he got a closer look, he could see that it *was* Sloppy.

He's asleep, all right.

The grumbling generator covered their approach. They walked right to the open window. A mound of crumbs covered the front of Sloppy's shirt, and an empty pack of Pinwheels danced on his chest, rising and falling with his snores.

Henry peeked around the edge of the guard shack. Small blue globes that looked like the Dream Lights Abraham had given them stretched in a haggard line from the shack to the base of a log fortress built right over the road a half-football field away. Like Old West settlers protecting themselves from Indians. A fortress to a child.

Spiked walls lashed together with chains, and the road ran through an opening in the front blocked by a train-crossing gate. Light from inside the fort washed out. Flickering flames and pulsing colors.

Henry thought he heard the faint notes of a raucous pirate song.

A rickety tower at the front corner had a small roof over it, like the builder had plunked another one of the guard shacks on top of a teepee of logs. A spotlight hung off the side, facing the ground.

The generator sputtered, chugging to catch up, and the lights in the guard shack flickered. The row of blue bulbs dimmed and buzzed. The generator revved, and the lights brightened before settling back to normal with the regular laboring engine's cough and bellow.

Sloppy's snort broke rhythm, and he pulled his feet out of the window, sitting up and rubbing his eyes. He scraped crumbs from his stained T-shirt, knocking the empty wrapper to the ground.

Henry stood and leaned through the window. Sloppy froze and looked up at the demon hanging over him.

"Howdy," Henry said. "You guys still serving breakfast?"

Sloppy twisted his jiggling flesh to reach behind him. Henry shot his claws out and grabbed Sloppy's hand before he could drop it on a big red knob that looked like the Staples Easy Button.

Sloppy barked a desperate snarl and reached his other hand under the arm in Henry's grip. But his bulk was too much to overcome. He couldn't reach the alarm with his other hand.

Kasey's spear entered the window, creeping through the air. Sloppy froze, and his eyes tracked the tip of the blade. They rolled down to keep it in sight as it poked into the bubble of flesh under his jaw.

"Where's your buddy?" Henry asked, releasing Sloppy's hand and leaning his elbows on the edge of the window. "The one with all the teeth and the oily hair?"

Sloppy's brow creased in concentration. "Who, Slick?"

Henry choked on his laughter. "No fucking way! That is really his name?"

"What?"

Henry flapped his hand. "Never mind. Where is he?"

"He's takin' a shit."

"Nice. How long's he usually take?"

"Like, forty-five minutes. I think there's something wrong with the guy."

"So, we got some time together, just you and me, and Kasey makes three. Tell me something, Sloppy. What's going on over there in Fort Irony?"

"I ain't telling you nothing."

Kasey leaned into the spear, and it pierced the flap.

Black blood poured around the blade under Sloppy's chin. He sucked in breath, and tears rolled down his red cheeks. "I don't know nothing," he whined. "I'm just supposed to hit the button if anybody I don't know comes out of the trees, man."

"That's it?"

A snot bubble burst under Sloppy's nose. "Sometimes, me and Slick go into the Forgotten, and we have a little fun, you know?"

"This isn't a confessional, Sloppy. I just need to find a guy. A *demon* that came through here a couple of days ago. Maybe you've seen him?"

Sloppy's eyes widened, and he shook his head. He winced when the spear cut deeper. Then he groaned, his eyebrows rising in comic despair. "I don't know what you're talking about, man."

"Yes, you do, Sloppy. I can see it in your pudgy dumb-fuck face. Just tell me where he is."

Kasey twisted the spear, widening the hole, and Sloppy squealed. "I don't know I don't know! He kept trying to get away. They had to move him, but I don't know where to. I swear to God."

Henry grabbed the shaft of Kasey's spear. "Well, the joke's on you, Sloppy. God ain't listening."

He pushed the spear into Sloppy's throat and felt Kasey lean in.

The blade pushed out the back of Sloppy's neck. The Ravager's spirit was strong. It didn't want to let go, even as he drowned in his own blood. Henry snatched the life force out of the quivering frame of dying meat, and he breathed it in.

Sloppy slumped with a final gurgle, and Kasey jerked the spear free, splattering black blood down the front of Sloppy's shirt.

A shout of alarm rose up from the fort. Henry looked into Kasey's shocked eyes. "Did he hit the button?"

"No!"

"Then what the fuck?"

A whistling behind him, and Henry spun to catch the fastball of Aela's rock on the point of his collar bone. It bounced off with a crack, and a buzzing tingle shot down his arm. He slapped his hand over the point of impact and squinted into the gloom.

Aela jumped up and down, pointing frantically at the road in front of the fort.

Henry stuck his head around and saw the silhouette of a lone figure sprinting down the center of the road. A crowd of Ravager's filled the opening, pressing against the train gate. It snapped under their pressure, and they poured out into the road to give chase.

The spotlight in the tower snapped on, tracking across the grass at the edge of the road before finding the runner. It lit a wiry man in an orange shirt covered in daffodils, his blue work pants wrinkling and fluttering with his pumping legs. Light broke through his wild hair and scruffy beard, and he waved both hands at Henry as he passed.

"Get the fuck outta here!"

No more questions. Henry lowered his head and took

off, digging his claws through the soles of his boots as he pushed off.

A few steps from the tree line, and the fort blew up.

Pressure and sound slammed him in the back. He stumbled as yellow light painted the woods with his shadow. The roar rumbled through the ground, and Henry crawled into the cover of trees with flaming debris raining around him.

The forest and grass caught fire, burning with a greasy flame that dumped black smoke into the air.

Henry felt hands under his arms, and he let them help him up. The guy in the loud shirt slapped him on the back and watched the inferno with open-mouthed glee. "I set their gas on fire! They had barrels of it just stacked up, leaking all over the ground. You shoulda seen it."

Henry pointed to the burning fort. "I *did* fucking see it!"

The man draped his arm over Henry's shoulders. "I've been working these guys ever since they took me, and this guy Thompson, he *loved* me. Thought I was hilarious. Gave me a cigarette, and I don't even *smoke*."

Burning forms ran from the fire. Aimless and waving. Screams rising into the sky with the smoke. Flames spreading deeper into the trees.

The guy pulled his arm back and waved smoke from his face. "Don't worry. The mist'll put the fire out eventually." He stuck his hand out, and Henry took it.

That gets me every time.

"Baelzor," the guy said. "Frank Baelzor."

"Henry Black."

His face brightened. "Like the comedian?"

"Yeah, that was me before," he pointed at his horns.

"Hey, I saw you in Tucson."

"Daddy!"

Henry turned and almost raised his arms to catch the angel in a hug. Disappointment twisted in his gut when Adam leapt into his father's arms instead.

Frank held the boy close for a squeeze. He pulled him back and looked into Adam's face. "Hey, champ."

"We were coming to save you."

"You were?"

"Yeah, but we got attacked in the woods."

"Yeah, you'll have that."

Frank slung Adam over his shoulder. The boy squealed laughter as they headed down the path, and Henry lowered his head. Kasey finally caught up.

"What the hell was that?"

Henry was going to explain, but then shook his head, "Ask them."

Chapter Eleven

KASEY HAD EYESIGHT OF LEGEND, so he stayed behind, hiding in the trees next to the path. He was watching for a group to come out of the burning fort. A fresh squad of Ravagers who might give chase. He'd run ahead of them until he caught up to Henry, and then they'd all haul ass to the Way Home.

Frank Baelzor led the way, carrying Adam on his hip and listening to the boy's tales of adventure with Henry. Holding a flickering torch in the air, he walked while nodding and making all the right noises at all the right places, yet seeming to listen with only half an ear.

Henry was impressed with Adam's storytelling. He recounted many details that Henry thought were too subtle for such a young mind, but he had to remind himself that Adam was special. He wanted to pick the boy up and tell him how proud he was, but the boy was in his father's arms now. Just like Henry promised.

"It sounds like you got the same bad luck as your old man," Frank said.

"Yeah."

"Every time I tried to save your mother, something always got in my way. Like somebody was keeping me from her on purpose. But *just* her."

"Where is she?"

"Well, she's in Hell right now."

"Why?"

"She rejected the will of God so she could give birth to *you*. A beautiful boy that's gonna change the world."

"She's in Hell because of me?"

"No, she's in hell *for* you. There's a difference."

Henry tightened his hand into a fist, his claws digging into his palm. "My daughter is in Hell *because* of me."

Aela laid her hand on his arm, warm and smooth. He didn't push it away. "She was put there for somebody I killed, but she's *still* there for somebody I *refused* to kill. There's a difference to *that*, too."

Adam squirmed out of Frank's arm and dropped to walk on the path. "He's talking about me, Dad."

Frank glanced over his shoulder. "He is, huh?"

Henry nodded. "God wanted me to kill him."

"He doesn't want him falling into Satan's hands, right?"

"No, he doesn't want him falling into his *own* hands."

Frank stopped and turned around. He switched the torch to his other hand. "What is that supposed to mean?"

Henry opened his fist. Blood glittered in the light like gemstones. "Heaven wants him removed as a chess piece altogether. No one gets him, but more importantly, he doesn't get to grow up to become something that either side can use."

"So nobody gets him. Big deal, right?"

Henry growled. "Order From Chaos."

Adam jammed the point of his sword into the mud.

The boy's hair was clean, laying to either side of his head in silver waves. His outfit was white. No splattered mud on his boots. His father's white Chuck Taylors looked new.

Henry thought of Boothe's blood resistant suits. Charlie Mara jumping into the hallway in front of Adam's cell. All shiny and new.

How do they fucking do that?

Frank nodded. "That's who tried to hold me in that fort. Bunch of assholes."

"Not on Earth," Henry said. "They're fucking brutal. Loyal. They have the support of the whole fucking city. And Pastor Owen has the perfect cover."

"I never really liked that guy, but I'm not big on church people."

"You know him?"

"Oh, yeah. He presided over me and Marisol's wedding."

Henry's knees buckled, but he locked his legs and stayed on his feet.

"Daddy. That's the man who killed Henry's daughter."

Frank stepped back and wiped his brow. "Oh, *shit.*"

Henry jammed his nubbin into his right hand, like a baseball player conditioning his glove. "And the man chasing Adam."

"He wants to kill my son, too?"

"No, he wants to use him to become the independent third party in this fucked up election. Pastor Owen wants to be God and Satan at the same time."

"Huh, that's probably why he kidnapped me."

Henry spread his arms. "You think?"

Frank grinned, then he reached behind his waist, like an undercover cop pulling his badge. He looked at Aela, holding a knife wrapped in cloth. "Here you go."

He tossed the knife and she caught it, just like Heaven's

Blade back in the Way Home. Its handle was black, and when she unwrapped the blade, Henry saw the power flowing along its dark edge. Felt it buzzing against his senses.

She wrapped it back up and stuffed it into her bag.

"What is that?"

Frank smiled. "It's what your girlfriend there stabbed me with while trying to drag me back to Solitude. I was just looking for a way to find my boy. Had a friend send me a message. Told me he was on the way down."

"What's it do?" Henry turned to Aela. "Does it kill demons? Were you just gonna kill him right there on the fucking spot?"

"Nah," Frank said. "It just shows you the demon's true form."

"Oh, yeah?" Henry waited for her to look at him. "And what did he look like?"

She pointed at Frank. "Like that. Just like that."

Henry took in the demon's islander shirt and blue pants. The Converse sneakers and fashionably messy hair. "That's your *true* form?"

"I don't *have* a true form. My real secret is that I'm a shape-shifter. That's why I'm so good at my job."

"Henry," Aela said. "I was going to bring him back to Solitude, but we were attacked by Ravagers. And I think he showed his true form when he sacrificed himself for me."

"What do you mean?"

"They had a knife to my throat, and they were going to rape me, but Baelzor … a demon … he fought them. It allowed me to escape, but it meant he wouldn't find Adam."

"So you treated me, the next demon you met, like shit?"

She shrugged. "Yeah."

He wasn't going to get tears and apologies from her and didn't want either. "Yeah, well. I probably deserved it."

Frank twirled the torch in a circle over his head. "Shouldn't we get going?"

Henry raised his hand. "Hang on a second. You just said being a shape-shifter made you good at your job. What *is* your job?"

Frank gave a modest shrug. "Oh, you know… I sneak into places. Sneak through them. Procure certain items for certain people."

Aela rolled her eyes. "You're a thief."

"Yeah, but I'm *really* good at it."

Henry crossed his arms. "Can you get into *any* place?"

Frank narrowed his eyes. "Most any place, yeah?"

"What about Hell?"

Frank shook his head. "No way."

"What if somebody else got you in? Could you sneak through? Procure certain items, maybe?"

"Like what kind of items?"

Henry uncrossed his arms and looked down at his claws. "Like a couple of angels."

"Your daughter?"

Henry nodded. "And your wife."

Frank looked up like he was thinking about it, but he was already nodding. "Yeah, I think I could find them. If we can get into Hell."

"I think I know a guy. Kind of the religious type back on earth. We'll probably have to persuade him."

"Between the two of us, we should be good."

"We just gotta get there."

"There's a guy down here I used to know. Plays chess. Smart guy."

Henry growled and looked down at Adam. "I don't think he'll be very happy to see us."

Frank looked at his son and realization dawned on his face. "That son of a bitch. *Boothe's* the one who wanted you to kill my boy?"

Henry nodded. "He doesn't know you know, though. Maybe that's how we get him to go along with our plan. I hide out with Adam until you convince him to send you back to Earth. We all hitch a ride, and then next stop?"

Frank grinned. "I guess I'll see you in Hell."

"How many deals are you going to make, Henry?" Aela asked.

Henry glanced over without meeting her eyes. "As many as I have to."

"Then what about me?"

Henry opened his mouth to answer, but footsteps slapping in the mud had him spinning around with his claws out.

Kasey came running out of the dark. "We gotta move!"

They broke into a run. Frank bent down to scoop Adam into his arms, but the little angel scurried to Henry, climbing up his body to drop on Henry's shoulders. Frank grinned with a shake of his head.

"How many?" Henry asked.

Kasey shook his head, Frank's torch behind him hiding his face in deep shadow. "Too many to count."

"Should we stay on the path or break into the trees?"

Frank pulled even with Henry. "Can't you just take him away? Teleport or something?"

"Nope. Something about the weight of destiny?"

Frank looked up at Adam. "You got a champion? Henry's your champion?"

His voice floated down from Henry's shoulders. "No, he was promised to another."

"Then who is it?"

Henry felt Adam's shrug.

"Well, shit. You think we'll make it?"

"If you shut up and *run*," Kasey shouted.

Frank shut his mouth with a snap of teeth, and they ran.

Chapter Twelve

HENRY GLANCED OVER AT AELA. The bouncing torchlight made her face swim in and out of focus.

They'd been running for almost an hour, but she and Kasey were keeping up step for step with two demons whose feet were fueled by a different kind of calorie.

Henry hated running. Humans were made to *walk*, and recline in La-Z-Boys.

Samantha never judged him. Never seemed to notice his weight at all. He found it damned hard look at himself in the mirror, though, and it pissed him off that she hadn't hated it, too. He grew jealous once they started living together. She stayed fit and trim with seemingly little effort. He complained that it was easy for her. "I just look at a *picture* of an Oreo and gain a pound."

So he decided to try and lose weight. Joining her for a single yoga class changed his mind quickly. Those women were hardcore. Sweating, panting, and trembling with effort. Five minutes in, he tapped out. He never complained about her looking better than him again, and like always, Samantha never judged him.

Henry faced front, and the gray light of the Forgotten filled the space between thinning trees. The ground dropped away in a gentle angle. Roofs of the tombs scattered at the edge of a misfit cemetery poking out of the swirling mist.

He threw a glance over his shoulder. Orange lights flickered in the dark distance inside the forest. He turned and saw the Way Home mausoleum nestled in a group of similar stone structures. Energy flooded his lungs. They were going to make it.

He looked behind them again, and the lights bobbing through the trees had tripled.

Goddamn it!

He ducked into line behind Aela as they wove their way through the headstones.

Their pursuers pounded into the mud like thunder.

At the corner of the Way Home, Aela jumped in front of Kasey with the ring of keys. They crowded around as she unlocked the front door, and Henry bent his shoulder to the wood. Adam jumped to the ground and leaned against the door beside him.

Henry again marveled at Big Ben's strength and wondered how the man had managed to open the Way Home hampered by his wounds. The door slid back with a groan, and they piled inside. Henry spun to close them in, leaning into the opening to check on the progress of their pursuers.

Dirty shapes in the mist poured out of the trees and crested the hill, burning torches and the flash of weapons held high. Breaking into the open must have spurred their excitement. The thunder of their steps drowned in the wave of their shouts, and Henry shut the noise out with a final push.

They sat in the dark with their panting breath filling

the emptiness. Heavy treads up the stone stairs, and they turned to wait for Big Ben's candle to illuminate the room.

He ducked his bald head through the doorway and straightened with confusion on his face. "What are you doing here?"

Aela grabbed a candle from a shelf and held it out for a light. "We're hiding from the Ravagers."

Big Ben held his own candle overhead, making no move to bring it to Aela's reach. He indicated Frank with a tip of his chin. "Who's that?"

Frank jumped forward with his hand extended. "Frank Baelzor."

Big Ben looked at the demon's hand, disgust twisting his mouth. "I'm not gonna shake your hand. Get away from me."

Frank shrugged and put his hands behind his back. Henry took a step with his hands up. "Chill the fuck out, Mongo."

Big Ben's eyes widened, and he reached over his shoulder in a blur. Demon Piercer rang against the scabbard as it cleared his back. "*You* chill the fuck out, Punchline."

Henry froze. Aela threw her hands up and shouted at Big Ben, but Henry barely heard her voice. Didn't understand her words. He looked into the hate in Big Ben's eyes, and another betrayal clamped over his heart. "What did you call me?"

Big Ben narrowed his eyes. "What?"

Henry cleared his throat. "What did you call me?"

Aela held her hand up. "Let's calm down."

"No!" Henry dropped the pack from his shoulders and kicked it into the corner. "You called me *Punchline*. Why?"

Big Ben shrugged. "Because you think you're funny. I don't."

Henry shook his head. "No, fuck that. The men who killed my daughter called me that. Because I'm a comedian. A lot of people called me that before I died. Like a nickname."

"Yeah, so?" Big Ben lowered his stance. A tension in his knees and shoulders.

"I only said I was famous. I *never* said I was a comedian." Henry took another step forward, and Big Ben pressed himself into the doorway. "Back in Solitude, you said I had jokes."

Big Ben set his jaw, and a smile pulled at the corner of his mouth. "I don't know what you're talking about."

Henry dropped into a crouch and roared. The candle held over Big Ben's head flickered and danced in the hot wind of Henry's breath.

Aela flinched back and looked from Henry's face to Big Ben's. "Ben?"

Big Ben shrugged. "He's just trying to trick us. I *told* Abraham to keep him out of Solitude, and now he's trying to turn you against me."

Red haze filled Henry's vision, and Big Ben's life energy pulsed into existence as if Henry's anger had flipped a switch. He had to concentrate on the words before he could force them out of his mouth. "Why did the Lost attack Adam? Why didn't the Dream Lights repel them like Abraham said they would?"

"How should I know?"

Aela held up a finger. "My grandfather said *you* collected the mist for the distillation of the Dreaming Tree's sap. What did you do, Ben?"

"Don't point your finger at me, woman."

Kasey pulled his spear around and planted the end between his feet. "Where's Solomon, Ben?"

Big Ben set the candle on a shelf next to his shoulder,

then scratched the stubble on his chin. "He's in the cellar. You can go down and see him if you want."

The herd of Ravagers declared their presence with a swelling rumble of feet. Henry couldn't tell if they were right outside or one row over.

Either they're running in a circle around us, or there's a thousand of 'em.

He looked back at the door and caught Adam's frightened gaze. The boy was pressed into a corner, his sword held in a desperate grip. He stared at Big Ben with wide eyes. Shock and terror.

Henry turned back, and showed Big Ben the murder in his face.

The big man's eyes flew wide, and he leapt forward, thrusting the sword at Henry's chest.

Henry saw him as slow as a man moving through water. He stepped under the thrust with ease, moving to the outside of the big man's left arm.

Big Ben's eyes were focused on the space where Henry had just been. Henry threw his head back and laughed, driving his claws into the meat of the muscular shoulder.

Big Ben howled as a pound of flesh flew away, exposing the shining knob of his shoulder joint. Blood splattered along his neck and the side of his face. His lunge ended with him driving his good shoulder into a shelf of blankets, crushing the wood into splinters and scattering wool across the floor. Demon Piercer stayed in his hand.

The Way Home shuddered, thrumming like a stone drum. Henry's rage rattled the bars of his confusion. Dust fell from the ceiling in a grey cloud.

Big Ben rose with his bloody arm dangling. He gritted his teeth and looked up, edging back toward the doorway.

Frank dropped to his knees and pulled Adam against his chest.

The thunder of feet grew, and Ravager voices rose in a frenzied howl.

The ground shook underfoot.

Another smashing beat of the drum, and the walls of the Way Home tilted.

The corner split.

Churning bodies and grinning faces in the opening.

Shouts of victory, and the Ravagers drew back for another run.

A chunk of the stone ceiling sheared off and crashed into Aela's shoulder.

She screamed and fell to her knees. Blood welled from her forearm.

Henry turned with his arms held out to scoop her up, and she screamed again.

Her eyes were as wide as they could go. Whites all around, the speck of a candle in her pupil glowing as a shadow grew. Then three feet of black blade burst from his chest, the tip stabbing into Aela's leather jacket, scraping against her arm to tear through the seam in back.

Her face turned black with the splash of his blood.

Cold spread through him, radiating from the sword grinding against his ribs. He couldn't draw a breath to cry out, and the red haze left his eyes altogether.

Henry heard Adam scream from far away.

The blade drew out, and Aela collapsed against him. Blood burst into his throat, and the remaining air bubbled out of his lungs. He shivered from the cold as ice formed in the pit of his stomach.

Henry fell from Aela's arms, and his face smashed to the floor.

The door fell away, washing the gray light of the Forgotten across his face.

Adam's scream fell into a lilting rhythm. Henry

couldn't make it out. Soft and beautiful, he heard the fear and panic beneath it, but there were no words. When he recognized the song of the Trackers, Henry didn't have the energy to tell the boy to stop.

You're delivering yourself into their hands, kid.

Stomping feet on the floor of the Way Home. Shouts and clashing steel.

I'm not fucking worth it, buddy.

Amélie's face hung in front of his closing eyes. She looked so much like Samantha. Pushing her hair away from her forehead. Just like her mother.

Lucky she didn't take after… the monster.

Gold light broke on the other side of his eyelids. He didn't have the energy to look.

Sleep now.

Suffer no more.

The booming voice chased Henry's thoughts into darkness.

Chapter Thirteen

HENRY OPENED HIS EYES, expecting fire.

A cracked plaster ceiling. Vaguely familiar. A soft bed holding him up. A rough blanket scraping against the edge of his bandaged chest.

Movement over his head, and he flicked his eyes up.

Clocks.

Henry drew breath for a sigh, and pain lanced up into his neck. He coughed, and blood filled his mouth. The gagging spasm continued, and his mind filled with panic. He was drowning.

A warm hand on his arm, and the coughing slowed. Eased. Henry swallowed the blood and took in clean air. His pounding heart slowed, and he drew sipping breaths, afraid that a deeper inhale might invite the cough.

He turned to see who was touching him. A large hand carved from pearly granite. A rusty cuff on the wrist below a bulging forearm. Henry followed the arm up and smiled.

Ramiel sat in the chair that Sister Gladys had occupied the last time Henry woke in Solitude. The Tracker. His guardian angel.

They had met outside Adam's cell under the Viazo Grand.

The Tracker reeled back, and the sword dropped from his hands. He caught his balance and dropped to one knee. One fist over his heart, the other pressed into the ground in front of his feet.

I swear fealty to you.

"Hey, Remmy," Henry whispered. A dry croak of noise.

"Hello, Henry." Ramiel's deep voice, warm and comforting like his hand on Henry's arm. Washing over him and pushing him deeper into the down. "Sleep now."

Suffer no more.

HENRY WOKE WITH A JAW-CRACKING YAWN.

He stretched with a painful pulling deep in his chest muscles, rolled over with a groan, throwing the blankets aside and touching a tentative finger to the wound under the crease of his right pec — a hard ridge of scar tissue like bone.

He looked down, and his lips curled in disgust. The width of his hand, a hard rise of skin, black and puckered. Tendrils of darkness radiating away from its center, like the rot that consumed the Ravager in the wake of Adam's touch.

Henry dropped his hand and sighed.

He reached for the porcelain ewer of water on the bedside table, but instead of healthy fingers grabbing the handle, his twisted nubbin bumped it and sloshed water over the rim. He drank the water in a few desperate gulps and waited to catch his breath before returning the pitcher.

A soft knock from the hallway.

Henry pulled the blankets over his lap and looked at the opening door.

Sister Gladys poked her head through. She smiled when she saw Henry, and she threw the door wide, entering with another pitcher of water.

She turned the handle to his waiting fingers and sat while Henry finished another gallon. His belly swollen with liquid healing, Henry nodded as he set the pitcher next to the first one. "Thank you," he said, his voice the deep rumble he had gotten used to in recent months.

She smoothed her robes beneath her legs as she sat. "You're quite welcome, Henry."

"So, what's happening?"

"Oh, same old, same old."

Henry chuckled, but he saw the tightness around her eyes. The hollows of her cheeks. "How long have I been here."

"Three days. The angel came to the gates with you under one arm and Aela under the other."

A hard anxiety twisted his guts. "Is she okay?"

Sister Gladys grinned. "She's fine. A broken shoulder and blood loss. Exhaustion. The angel healed her once he was inside Solitude." She pointed at the scar on his chest. "He did the best he could by you, but his power had limits."

If Ramiel healed me, then Adam must be ...

"Where's Adam?"

"They took him, Henry. The other Trackers took him away."

That painful twist in his guts again, and Henry doubled over, tears squeezing through his eyelids. "Ah, fuck," he gasped.

In his mind, Adam's face floated up beside Amélie's, and they each had the same sad smile.

I failed them both.

"How was I supposed to save them?" Snot dribbled onto his lip. Tears dripped into his lap.

I couldn't do it.

"I'm just a fucking *comedian*, for shit's sake."

Her small hands on his shoulder were like twisted steel, digging into the base of his neck. She pulled him into an embrace, and even through his pain, a nun of Solitude comforting a demon pushed his sorrow aside with awe.

He held her against him and cried into her shoulder.

"No, Henry. Don't blame yourself." She rocked him. Like Samantha had rocked him. Like he had rocked Amélie.

"He's dead."

"No, Ramiel says he's *not*."

Henry shook his head and pushed her away. He wiped his nose on his forearm. "How does he know?"

"Because Adam was *taken*. If the Lord's true intention was for Adam to die, they would have killed him right then."

Relief brought fresh tears, and he nodded with a smile. "I guess that makes sense."

"It does." Sister Gladys smoothed her robes and drew her hood back over her head.

Henry pointed to a glistening smear on her shoulder. "Sorry about that."

She looked, and a sad smile that reminded him of his daughter spread across her lips. "You're not the first person to cry on my shoulder today."

Henry scrubbed at the tears with his knuckles and sat up straight. He took a deep breath. "What's happening?"

She shrugged. "War has come to Solitude." She leaned forward and patted his knee. "Get dressed and come out to the Tree. Someone has been asking about you almost non-stop."

"Who?"

She would only smile as she eased the door shut behind her.

His wrinkled and stained backpack sat empty in the corner, its contents neatly stacked next to it.

I guess people don't leave other people's shit alone in Solitude.

He didn't bother with the boots. Somebody had cleaned them, but they were torn and the soles were pulling loose. Black canvas jeans and a black tee. The dark color seemed morbid, but they crowned the pile.

Out in the hall, he threaded his way through the line of bustling nuns. Instead of avoiding him, they moved to include him, and he even saw the flash of a smile accompany a wave or two.

Progress.

In the chamber that housed the Dreaming Tree, he stepped to the side and watched the activity. What looked like a frenzy soon settled into a pattern, and in the center stood Aela. Guiding and pointing, leaning into the ear of a nun, both of them pulling apart with a nod once she delivered instruction.

He leaned into the wall and crossed his arms, content to look at her while she worked. The lines of worry that had creased her forehead were gone. Her jaw still firm, set with the fierce determination that flashed in her eyes, and despite everything that had happened, she appeared oddly satisfied.

As if noticing his scrutiny, she paused as if she were listening for an echo, then turned to greet his eyes. Her grin hit him like a fresh breeze, and he barely got his arms open before she was against him with her cheek pressed to his chest.

Her scent rose up, that earth and spice that reminded him of fresh bread and pumpkin pie. He filled his lungs.

She stepped back, and he kept his nubbin on her shoulder, pushing the fall of her hair from her face with his other hand.

She grabbed his forearm, hanging onto it like she was dangling from a branch. "How do you feel?"

"Like shit."

She laughed, and her breath parted the dark hair hanging across his forehead. "To be honest, you *look* pretty bad, too."

He shrugged, pulling his arm out of her grasp. "Well, you can look good for the both of us. What's going on?"

She frowned. "My grandfather won't let me outside. He sent me here to organize the harvest instead."

"What are you harvesting?"

She turned and led him to the trunk of the Dreaming Tree. "Mostly what everyone had been dreaming about lately. Weapons and medical supplies."

"Sister Gladys said war had come to Solitude. The Ravagers?"

"And more. Henry, there's so much more."

She took his hand and led him from the room. The activity continued unabated, and Henry realized she had just been filling a role required by Abraham. No matter how much she resented it, she had been pleased to follow orders.

Maybe for the first time in her life.

He felt foolish following her, being led by the hand down stone hallways, ducking under clocks and through doorways. No scandalized gasps and old ladies recoiling in horror, but there were more than a few raised eyebrows. Looks from the side of an eye.

They came to a wide stairwell spiraling up into a broad tower. She slid her hand from his and charged up the steps taking them two at a time. He tried to follow with the same zeal, but two flights later found him leaning on the stone rail with spots swirling in front of his eyes.

He couldn't get a deep breath and he tasted blood. He forced himself straight and continued his ascent with a more measured pace.

Aela came back down, running at an angle, her face shadowed with concern. He waved her away. "Just a little out of shape, that's all. Gimme a minute."

"Oh, Henry. I'm sorry. Do you want to go back down?"

"Fuck, no. I'm *this* far. Lead the way. I'll make it."

He focused on his feet slapping flat on every step. His hand sliding along the rail.

The air cooled, and the light turned from the orange of warm fires to the gray of mist surrounding the Forgotten.

The rail fell away, and Henry almost fell without its support. His feet thought there was another step, but the floor extended into a wide landing. His knees locked, and he waved his arms for balance. Aela slid up under his arm, and he leaned on her as she led him through a doorway that opened onto a view of the crumbling city.

At another railing, Henry bent over and planted his elbows on the top. Three bright lights swelled in the darkness of the mist below him.

The structure that was Solitude spread out in every direction. Like a thousand different parts of a thousand different cities.

Below him, the three lights swelled, and Henry heard the beating of powerful wings. Mist parted under the air, and the lights were revealed as angels. Three Trackers hovering, armed and armored. Black blades and shields, but the one in the center held a sword that Henry remembered.

Ramiel.

The mist continued to swirl away, uncovering a line of Ravagers and demons looking up at the angels in fear.

A clang drove a vibration into the floor, and Henry looked behind the angels to a giant door that slid open on the clank of a giant chain.

"They go from one hidden entrance to the next," Aela said. "Rotating with them as they open."

"Almost like they know where they are, huh? Like they're being led to 'em?"

"Yes."

So, Big Ben's still alive.

Through the door poured a neat file of soldiers. Men and women of Solitude, armed with spears and swords. Arrows bobbing over their shoulders. Abraham ran at the head of the line, a sword in his hand instead of a cane. Kasey ran with him in lock-step, his spear held against his chest. The soldiers followed to form a line below the angels' feet.

The wings cleared more mist, and at the edge of the courtyard stood a row of cultists from Order From Chaos. Long robes glowing with power. Hoods obscuring their faces in shadow. They lifted their hands in a gesture that Henry remembered from outside the Viazo Grand when Pastor Owen sent a fireball bursting down the hill.

That was probably what killed Ezra.

Their hands glowed with growing power, and they raised their fists. Colored flames burst from their fingertips, and a wall of fire rolled above the dark army waiting to attack.

Trackers unfurled their nets. They spread to join each other, snapping together to make a single shield that caught the fire before it could hit the walls of Solitude. The cultists raised their hands again, and on some unheard cue, the Ravagers and demons charged, their screams ripping into Henry's ears.

The soldiers of Solitude rushed forward as the wall of fire boiled in the air, growing as it neared the smoking nets above the Trackers' heads. Henry turned before the two armies met. "I need to get down there!"

"You can't be serious. You barely made it up *here.*"

"You don't understand. I need to *feed.*"

Realization dawned in her eyes, and her disgust bobbed to the surface.

He grabbed her arm. "It's what I am. I'm not asking you to accept it. I'm just asking for a little goddamn *help!*"

Aelsa set her jaw and nodded, then reached under the back of her jacket. Two blades appeared in her hands with a hiss. She turned to lead the way back down the stairs, throwing the occasional worried glance over her shoulder.

Henry couldn't blame her. By the time they made it to the bottom, he was bent nearly double with pain, every breath tearing at the scar in his chest.

Aela drove her shoulder under his arm, and they hurried down a hallway with a heavy door set in the end. The sounds of battle raged on the other side. He could smell the fear and desperation from Ravagers and soldiers of Solitude alike.

His mouth watered, and he wept with relief when she jammed a key into the lock and drove the door open with her hip.

A Ravager died at his feet as he entered the courtyard. An arrow through his wide mouth, the man's eyes rolled up to meet Henry's as his soul sank through the dirt. Henry dropped to his knees, snatched the life-force into his mental grasp, and breathed it in like he inhaled Aela's scent.

The energy burst through him, spreading to the tips of his fingers. Colors brightened. Action slowed.

Men and demons dying all around him, and Henry fed with glee, banishing his guilt as he grew swollen with power.

Pain split his chest, driving between his shoulder blades. The tunnel dug through him by Big Ben's betrayal closed with a searing hammer blow, and Henry turned his face to the gray sky and roared.

It felt so fucking good.

He pulled the shadows at the base of the wall around him and flung himself into the darkness, riding the waves under the troughs of light faster than thought. He burst into the middle of a pile of Ravagers hacking at a squad of pike men, and they perished in the blur of Henry's attack.

Like in the forest when the Lost had swarmed, Henry's heart beat out a rhythm faster than the actions of the lesser beings on the battlefield.

He stepped in front of each slash and every blow. Spinning and clawing, he danced toward the robed cultists at the top of the rise, pulling more power into his soul with the passing of every enemy.

A final wall of flame lit the courtyard as it screamed over his head, and the cultists stepped back one by one, disappearing into the wall as if were made of water.

The entrance is closing!

Henry dove into the shadows and launched himself at the last cultist, his robes swallowed by the stone. Henry thrust his hand out. It sank through the stone and caught a fistful of fabric, his claws sinking into flesh. The liquid became solid, and the stone closed over his hand, capturing both he and the cultist in the wall surrounding Solitude.

Henry screamed in frustration, lifting his feet to plant them on either side of where his hand plunged into the stone. He bunched his muscles in preparation, and *flared* as he pulled.

His fist exploded from the stone in a shower of rocks and powder. The cultist flew out, swinging overhead and hitting the ground with a splat.

Henry dropped the soaking handful of shredded flesh and bent to the cultist's twisting lump of a body. He pulled the sinking soul of the dead cultist into him, wiped the blood from his claws onto his pants, and looked up at the nearing line of soldiers.

He stepped back with a growl, his ass pressing into the rock behind him. Ramiel and the other Trackers hovered in the air, their light shining in the eyes of the men and women of Solitude. Tears on their faces and blood on their hands. Henry dropped his claws. And then he heard it.

Applause. Cheers.

They were clapping for *him*. Henry Black.

He almost took a bow.

Chapter Fourteen

THE CHEERING quieted as light filled the area between Henry and his new fans. Ramiel descended with his wings spread, his armor charred by Order From Chaos fire. His feet touched the bloody ground, and Henry rushed forward to greet him.

Ramiel dropped to one knee, his fist to his heart. The soldiers of Solitude hushed, the only sound now the scraping of their boots.

Before the angel could plant his other fist on the ground in salute, Henry grabbed it and pulled him to his feet. He wrapped the Tracker in a hug as enthusiastic as Adam's had been, and the soldiers erupted in shouts as loud as the Ravagers preparing for the charge. An angel and a demon holding each other in brotherhood, fighting for Solitude together.

"I feared for you," Ramiel said in his ear.

They separated, and Henry shook his head. "I hate myself too much to let me off the hook *that* easily."

He saw Aela's grandfather over the angel's shoulder. Henry stepped to the side to catch his eye. "Abraham!"

The old man nodded, bowing his head and looking away from Ramiel.

Henry made room for Abraham and pointed at Ramiel's chest. "That's a little bright. Can you dial it back a little?"

Ramiel laughed, but his glow diminished to a point over his heart, pulsing and spinning before winking out. Abraham came into their group, rocking with the same good-natured blows to the back and shoulders that had fallen on Henry and Ramiel. The crowd still cheering.

The glow from the other two angels filtered through the crowd as they joined their brother. The soldiers split apart as they stepped up, their own lights dimming to nothing.

A man and a woman. Cast in stone no less perfect than Ramiel's, the man a creamy brown agate, the woman a shining onyx.

Ramiel indicated the woman. "Angelique avenges murderous lust." He tipped his head to the man. "Bariel ushers the tides against his enemies."

Abraham shuffled his feet and looked at the ground. "To stand among such as these."

Henry leaned over and bumped him with an elbow. "Imagine how *I* feel."

Something hit him in the back hard enough to rock him forward a step. He spun, and Aela lifted her hand for another blow. He let it fall and crossed his arms. "Hi, Aela," he said with a bright smile. "What's up?"

"Damn it, Henry! You could have been killed."

"So could you."

Abraham's brow drew down in consternation. "Why are you away from the Tree?"

Hands on her hips, Aela said, "I was helping Henry."

Henry turned to the angels over his shoulder. "She's an independent woman."

Ramiel and Bariel looked nonplussed, but Angelique grinned, her brilliant teeth shining out from her dark lips.

Henry turned back, and Aela was drawing a breath to argue. Abraham was bracing himself for the storm. Henry jumped between them, hanging an arm across each shoulder and turning them to walk back inside. "Shouldn't we be getting to the next place they'll attack?"

"No," Abraham said. "We have about eight hours before the next entrance thins at the south tower."

"Is there any other way in here?"

"Perhaps scaling the cliffs or bridging the river, but they'd lose more with that kind of assault than just waiting for us. The mists will turn them away, and that's even without the help from Heaven."

"We are not *technically* from Heaven," Ramiel said.

Henry looked back with a smile, even though Ramiel appeared sick from admitting his transgression. "Oh, off the reservation, huh?"

The angel nodded. "A Tracker can only penetrate the mists when assigned or called. We were waiting just on the other side of the border when the boy began his song."

Angelique clanged her sword against her armored shoulder. "There was a dispute over who would get to answer the call."

Aela stayed pressed into his side, but Abraham slid out from under Henry's arm. "They combat the magic of the priests while we attack demons and Ravagers on the ground."

"They're not priests," Henry said.

"Maybe not as *you* see them."

"They're just plain old cultists. Sick fucks who want to hurt little kids."

"Do they all do these magics?"

"Well, no, but that doesn't mean anything."

"It means they have ascended through the ranks high enough to *learn* these magics and to command an army in battle."

"Fine. What's your point?"

"Just one of perspective. I like to teach."

"You do seem to like to talk. I'll give you that."

Abraham looked at Henry through the fall of his gray hair. "This is only the second time an angel or a demon has walked through Solitude, and I wonder what is next."

"Yeah, I wonder the same thing. What *is* next?"

"We will prepare for the next attack, and you and Aela will pack your things."

Henry and Aela stopped in their tracks. A few steps later, Abraham stopped, too. He looked around as if he couldn't find them, finally spotting the pair behind him and turning around. His eyes twinkled above his smile.

The soldiers broke around them as they stood in the center of the hallway. Kasey came into view, breaking from the stream. He stepped in front of Abraham. "Sister Gladys says their work was much easier this time. Says to do whatever you did the next time, too."

Abraham guided Kasey around him with a hand on the spear man's shoulder. "We'll do what we can, son."

Henry dropped his arm and watched Kasey jog back into the thinning rush of soldiers. "What is this bullshit?"

"What's important to you, Henry?"

"What?"

Abraham nodded and raised a finger to his chin. "Let me tell you what's important to me. My granddaughter is important to me. The people inside these walls." He spread his arms and spun in a slow circle. "These walls themselves. The Dreaming Tree."

"What are you getting at?"

"What I'm getting at, Henry, is that I don't give a *shit* about what *you* think is important."

Henry slumped in confusion. He looked at Aela, but she stared at her grandfather as if he had sprouted a tail.

Abraham moved in and put one hand behind Aela's neck. The other he put behind Henry's. He drew them into a circle, pressing their foreheads together. "I know now that the only thing that matters is Adam. The boy who can heal Solitude and its people. The city has been waiting a long time for his arrival. Many of these people even longer than I have, and what does time mean to someone as young as the both of you?"

He dropped his hand from Henry's neck, and Henry stood while Abraham drew his granddaughter in closer. The old man closed his eyes and kissed her cheek. "Your twenty-seven years is gone in a breath. I've been in Solitude for over a thousand years. They are both equal in this equation if the boy doesn't survive."

Henry lifted his hands in a helpless shrug. He turned to Ramiel, but the angel was nodding. "He is right in this, Henry. We must find the boy. His existence is too beautiful for me to go on as I have."

"But what about Solitude?"

Angelique leaned against the wall, crossing her arms. "No Sister of Solitude will suffer for my absence. I will stay."

Henry pointed to Bariel. "What about him?"

The angel didn't speak for himself. Instead, Angelique threw herself off the wall and draped her arm over his shoulder. "He will stay, too."

"Fine." Henry turned. "Let's suppose I don't know where to look."

Abraham stepped back from his granddaughter, tears shining on his face. "Is that really true?"

Henry thought of the Dreaming Tree. Then he thought of the Tree on the other side of the mist. A chessboard at its base.

Fuck.

Henry slumped in defeat. "Yeah, I know where to look."

"Good." Abraham pushed the hair from his face, exposing his smile. He looked at Aela with a tilt of his head and turned away. "Goodbye, my dearest one."

The old man raised his hand in a final wave then turned the corner.

The angels shuffled into a circle. They held hands, their heads bowed as if lost in prayer.

After a few moments, Henry realized it was exactly what they were doing. He felt embarrassment rise into his face, like he'd been intruding. He shook his head and turned to Aela, but she was gone, turning the opposite corner as her grandfather.

Fuck!

He lurched into a run, racing to catch her.

The angels can find their own way.

Chapter Fifteen

Henry edged up next to Aela.

She marched down the corridor with her hands balled into fists at her sides, driving her boot heels into the floor.

He thought better of saying anything, following in silence as she took turn after turn. They reached a door, and she threw it open to stomp inside. He hung on the threshold, and she bent to the side to retrieve her messenger bag from the back of a chair.

"Already packed, huh?"

She grabbed the door. "It's *always* packed. I'm going to take a bath to get the blood out of my hair. You can either wait or find your way back." She slammed it in his face.

Henry waited.

He looked down at the dried blood flaking from his skin. His nose wrinkled in disgust, and he leaned his head back with his eyes closed.

Mike Serafino sprang into his imagination, and Henry wondered if he could bring the man's likeness to fruition. Instead, he pushed the image away to stand as the demon he was. His nubbin, twisted with swirling scars. The black gnarl of skin on his chest and under his shoulder blade. Dark hair swept back from his forehead, neat and tidy. *Maybe a little shorter?*

Black boots beneath the cuffs of his black jeans, and the black tee, new and dry. The *Hill of Beans* coffee can seemed a bit much, but he kind of liked the look. Like jewelry. Besides, it was funny. The Henry of his imagination nodded, and he opened his eyes.

I'll be damned, I did it.

New clothes and a new coffee can not dented or stained with blood. Unfortunately, he couldn't imagine a fresh new hand.

Aela's door flew open. She froze when she saw him.

"Sorry for slamming the door in your face."

"That's okay. We both had some things to think about."

She slung her bag over her head and pushed past Henry into the hall. He followed with a smile so wide, he thought his cheeks might cramp.

They found Ramiel at the base of the Dreaming Tree. Sitting cross-legged on the floor, he sipped from a tiny cup, staring up into the leaves. When they stopped at his side, he said, "I can see the boy's hand in this tree."

"Yeah," Henry said. "He's fucking special."

Ramiel rose and offered his empty cup to a passing nun with a bow of his head. She returned his bow as she took the cup from his hand. Ramiel turned with a smile. "Shall we?"

"Yes, please," Henry said.

Aela shifted her weight and looked from the demon to the angel and back. "Where are we going, exactly?"

Henry smiled. "To the Tree of Life outside the mist."

"How are we going to get there? The Ravagers' army is outside every door."

Henry's smile became a grin. "We're gonna fly."

"I thought the mist would turn everybody away."

"It does," Ramiel said. "But always to the Tree."

"Oh." She swallowed and turned her wide eyes to Henry.

Ramiel turned and walked through the halls with a spring in his step that was practically a contagion.

Ready to rumble.

At the base of the tower that had nearly beaten Henry earlier, the angel stepped aside and swept his hand toward the stairs. "After you."

Aela took a deep breath and slung her bag higher up onto her shoulder. She jogged up the stairs, and Henry followed.

He hit the top without effort and shielded his eyes from the light growing from Ramiel's breast. Like the sun, it flared whenever he spread his wings. "Come to me, children."

Show off.

Henry pressed up against him. Aela jumped forward, clinging to the angel's side with her eyes squeezed tight. He had been in the angel's net throughout his first flight. The second time he'd been almost dead. This time, Henry's heart pounded with excitement.

A single beat of his wings and Ramiel lifted from the balcony. Then they were airborne.

The mist swirled around them as they soared away from Solitude, the Forgotten shrinking behind them.

Henry's stomach rose into his throat as they dropped, and the mist disintegrated to a broad plain yawning before them, the Tree rising into the shadows of roiling clouds.

Ramiel brought them in gently, and Aela jumped to the ground, opening her eyes and clutching her jacket in pale fists. Henry stepped away, and Ramiel extinguished his light. Henry turned to Aela and grinned. "On the wings of angels."

She grinned back and turned to Ramiel. "Thank you so much."

The angel bowed with a grin of his own. "It is my pleasure."

"Well, I ain't getting any deader." Henry turned and walked toward the tree. He heard their footsteps following, and he nodded to himself.

Let's get this over with.

In a space between the roots at the base of the ancient tree was a stone table topped with a chess board. Round and set with three backless chairs, only two people sat at the game. Randall had his back to the tree, but his opponent was a woman rather than Boothe. Voluptuous in a tight white dress, black hair falling in broad curls past her shoulders. She leaned forward with her face set in concentration. She was familiar. It tickled Henry's mind like a gnat buzzing past his eyes. Bumping through his hair.

He shook his head and stopped at the edge of the table. "Howdy, Randall."

The fallen angel reached for his knight as Henry's shadow descended. He moved it to claim one of the woman's pawns. He didn't look at Henry, instead leaning back to cross his arms while waiting for her next move.

"Don't ignore me, Randall."

Randall ignored him.

Henry snapped his fingers in front of the angel's poker face. "Don't fucking do this."

Randall looked away.

Henry kicked the base of the stone table, and the board slid off, dumping pieces on the ground. "Talk to me, Goddamn it!"

Randall jumped from his chair. "Henry! I *can't* talk to

you. Trackers are nearby, and I'm required to alert them to your presence."

Ramiel growled, and the color drained from Randall's face. The Tracker stood at Henry's back. "You will *not.*"

Randall nodded and reclaimed his seat. "Of course I won't."

"Henry?" Recognition spread across the woman's face, and she jumped up, bending to grab his hand.

Henry drew his head away and rolled his eyes down to keep her in sight.

She pulled away and looked up, her eyes wet with unshed tears. "Thank you for what you did for me." Her Spanish accent fit her throaty voice in a sexy blend that surely reduced men to putty. Demons, too. Henry knew he'd heard her voice before. "I can never repay you," she gasped. *"Que Dios siga tu bendiciendo."*

Aela cleared her throat. "And what did you do for her?"

"Fuck if *I* know."

The woman stepped back, smoothing her dress and tossing her hair back. "He saved me from an eternity in Hell."

Henry rocked back as if she had slapped him.

Boothe's wife.

"Maria?"

Henry stopped, looked back, and saw the fog parting, lit by brilliant light. And from that light, walking in a glide so light across the grass she might as well have been floating, was a woman with long dark hair. She was beautiful. And judging from the way she looked down at Boothe, and then up at Henry as if he were a monster, he knew in an instant who she was.

Henry spun, his eyes darting into every shadow and hiding place. "Where the fuck is he?"

Randall sighed. "Pouting."

"What do you want with my husband?"

"I want to rip his dick off. How's that?"

"Why would you want to do this?"

"Oh, I guess he never told you how I *saved* you?"

Her eyebrows drew down. She looked over at Randall, but he shook his head and looked away. "He said you sacrificed. You became a monster in exchange for my freedom."

"My daughter is in Hell because of him."

"No, Henry." Randall drove his hand through the air like a knife. "Your daughter is in Hell because of *you.*"

"Still giving me that old bullshit? He fucking tricked me, and you know it!"

Maria's hand rose to her throat, eyes widened in horror. "He *tricked* you?"

"You're God damned right, lady."

She turned to Randall. "He tricked him?"

Randall's shoulders lifted into an uncomfortable hug. "That's not *entirely* accurate."

"Ooh, that *man.*" She sneered in anger. She straightened her shoulders and smoothed her dress. Her face grew cool, and she raised an eyebrow before turning around and striding away. Her bare feet barely denting the brown grass.

Randall swept his arm at her departing back. "You should probably follow her, Henry."

He jumped to it, jogging to catch up, and heard her muttering under her breath. Henry kept his distance. She dodged around a growing collection of dry bushes.

They had begun to form a pattern. Lines and curves. The grass became neat stone pavers, and Maria led him through a gap between a row of hedges that extended away to either side. They entered a sheltered garden, and

Boothe stood facing the corner with his hands behind his back.

Ramiel and Aela crowded in behind him. Henry slowed to a stop next to Maria.

Maria stepped to the side and tipped her head at her husband's back. "There he is."

Henry wanted to charge over and drive his claws into the angel's kidneys. Pull his head back and tear out the asshole's throat using only his teeth. Grab him by the—

No. I fucking need him.

"Boothe," Henry said. "I hate myself for even thinking it. For not coming over there and tearing your fucking arms off, but I need you. Goddamnit, I need your help, and it makes me sick to my fucking stomach."

Boothe didn't answer. Maria sighed in disgust. "*Hace como que la virgen le habla.*"

Henry shook his head. "What?"

"He is ignoring you."

"No shit, lady."

Boothe shifted his weight, but he didn't turn around, remaining silent.

Maria crossed her arms. "*¿Ya estamos otra vez?*"

Boothe shook his head. "*Lo siento.*"

She looked at Henry, cocking her hip and pointing at Boothe's back. "*Tiene una hueva que no puede con ella.*"

"What?"

"He's *lazy.*"

Boothe spun around. "*¿Te puedes tranquilizar, por favor?*"

Maria squared herself and put her hands on her hips. "*¡No me grites! Todos los hombres sois iguales.*"

Henry looked from one to the other and threw his hands up. "What the fuck is going on?"

"They've been doing this for months," Randall said.

Henry looked at the fallen angel squeezing between the dry hedge and Ramiel's shoulder. "Why?"

Randall shrugged. "That's just what their love looks like."

Boothe spread his hands. "*¡No puedo creer que pienses eso!*"

Maria nodded. "I do. I really do."

"*¿Es que no podemos hablar de esto como adultos?*"

"Did you trick him to save me?"

Boothe threw up his hands and looked at Henry. Begging for help. Searching for any way out.

No fucking way, buddy.

Boothe dropped his hands and his shoulders fell forward. "Yes. I tricked him. It was *the only way* to save you."

"Then no. We can't talk about it like adults." Maria turned and marched toward the garden entrance. They each slid out of her way, and Boothe's love disappeared into the mist.

"I *like* her," Henry said.

Aela grinned. "Me, too."

Ramiel nodded like a sage. "A strong woman is a blessing."

Boothe raised his hands. "All *right*. All right. What do you want with me?"

Henry smiled. "Just one last thing."

Chapter Sixteen

BOOTHE PLACED a hand against the Tree while keeping the one hand in his pocket. His head hung in defeat. "Adam and his father are in Heaven's custody."

Ramiel stood looking into the sky, his sword across his shoulders. His wingtips dug trenches through the dirt as he turned side to side, scanning the horizon. Randall and Maria continued their game. She had his queen on the run.

Aela sat nestled in the twisted roots, looking at the Forgotten swelling out of the mist, bag hugged to her chest.

Henry crossed his arms. "So, let's go get 'em."

Boothe sighed. "We can't just 'go get 'em,' Henry."

"Why not?"

"Because … The father is going to Hell. Adam will be killed following a hearing."

"Let's get there before that, then."

Maria clucked her tongue. "They're going to kill that poor boy, Walden?"

"*Walden?* Your name is *fucking Walden?*" Henry laughed.

Boothe ignored Henry, twisted his head to look at his wife under his arm. "He's not a *poor boy*, Dear."

"Fuck that!" Henry shouted. "He *is* just a boy. He's the sweetest, most gentle—"

"Tell that to people he's killed," Boothe interrupted.

"Oh, I guess *you've* never killed anybody."

Boothe turned and put his hand over his heart. "But I'm not a sweet, gentle little boy, am I?"

Randall slid his queen behind his bishop. "He is a weapon. *Not* a boy. He has the weight of destiny upon him, and he is a danger to God and all of reality."

Maria's knight moved to trap Randall's queen in the corner. "A small boy has the power to kill God?"

Boothe waved her question away. "Of course not. It's the man he will become that has Heaven worried."

"So, *teach* him," Henry said. "Keep him in custody and show him the right way to live."

"It's not that simple."

"Why the fuck not?"

"Because there are other forces at work here, Henry. This isn't just a parent trying to shout louder than MTV."

Randall took Maria's bishop. "Prophecy has a way of coming true."

Maria pushed her rook across the board with a smile. Randall's queen went into her pile. He clutched his hands into fists and growled in frustration.

Boothe pinched the bridge of his nose, squinting in pain. "Henry, I am so sorry."

"Finally," Maria said. "An apology."

Boothe ignored her barb. "You have every right to be angry, Henry."

"*Angry?*" Henry shook his head. "I don't even know what angry looks like anymore."

"Be that as it may, you must understand that I didn't

know you when I made the deal to turn you. To trade one soul for another."

"You didn't trade one soul for another. You traded my *daughter's* soul for another."

"But to the ledger, it doesn't matter. It was a wager. And you were a pawn."

Maria slid a pawn of her own forward, exposing Randall's king to her queen waiting in the wings. "Check."

Randall balled his hands again, wincing with a hiss.

Maria smiled in satisfaction and looked up at Boothe. "What *is* the boy's destiny?"

Boothe spread his hands. "He is supposed to go to Hell to save his mother."

"Why is his mother in Hell?"

"She broke the rules, Maria. She fell in love with a demon, and they had a child. Patently against the rules."

"Why is love always against the rules."

"It's not the love. It's the product of love."

"Sex?"

"No," Boothe groaned. "The boy, Maria. A child was created with the power to tear Heaven apart. If he falls into Lucifer's hands by rushing in to save her ..."

"So, get his mother out of Hell."

"What?"

"If his mother is not in Hell, the boy has no reason to go there, and he won't fall into the wrong hands."

Randall avoided Maria's queen by sliding behind his remaining rook. "That is probably something they have already considered."

She bombed his rook with her other bishop, then leaned back with her fingertips hovering over the board, tapping out her excitement. "That's Mate." She looked up at Boothe from under her eyebrows. "Is it?"

"Yes, it's Checkmate."

"No, silly. Is it something you've considered?"

Henry stood bathed in shock.

How could I have missed that?

He looked into Boothe's eyes and pointed at his own chest. "I was gonna take him there."

"What do you mean?"

"I was going to take him to Hell to rescue his mother. Him and his father."

"You were going to take that shape-shifting liar and his demon spawn son into Hell?"

"They were going to help me find my daughter, you fuck! That's all I've been doing since I met you. Making *deals*."

"It doesn't matter, now. I can't get you into Hell."

Henry nodded with half a shrug. "I didn't know you ever *could*. Besides, I know somebody else who can get me there."

Randall jumped from his stool. "It *is* Checkmate." He threw his hands up and stomped off, shaking his head. Maria smiled and lowered her hands into her lap.

Boothe narrowed his eyes, ignoring Randall's outburst. "You were going to convince the pastor to send you through a portal?"

"Maybe."

"Henry, they've positioned themselves since you've been gone."

"Positioned themselves, how?"

"Pastor Owen has moved into the Lucius estate as the mayor's official clergyman. The Burg Spires Church of Hope has closed, and they have moved an army into the Forgotten."

"How?"

"I don't know, Henry. But his power has grown."

"All the more reason to save Adam."

"All the more reason to kill the boy and keep him out of the pastor's hands!"

Maria slapped her palm on the chessboard. "Enough!" She pointed a perfectly manicured finger at her husband. "Walden Boothe. You *will* help save this child."

Boothe looked at the ground. "Even if Henry's idea wasn't fantastically insane, *I* can't get to Earth anymore, either."

Henry wanted to punch the defeat right off the angel's perfect face. "Why not?"

"I guess you could say, I'm on probation."

"Better demon than you are an angel, huh?"

"Henry, it is *your* fault that I'm in trouble in the first place."

"Oh, give me a fucking break!"

Aela shot to her feet and spun to face them. "This is ridiculous!"

She pointed, taking both Henry and Boothe in with a wavering finger. "You two are the vilest, most disgusting … cheating, pathetic liars I've ever seen. Who cares who tricked who? Who's in trouble and who's *angry?*"

She tugged her bag over her head and slung it to the ground. Tears spilled from her eyes, and Henry's guilt rose to choke him. He wanted to crawl away. To get out from under her accusing stare.

She pointed to the Forgotten. "My grandfather might be dead. My city overrun with Ravagers while they kill everybody I've ever known. Betrayed by a man I might have once loved if things had been different. And I saw that little boy look at Henry with *love*. Not calculating or complaining. Not trying to make a *deal*. He loves you, Henry. And you're sitting here arguing over who's been cheated more?"

She shook her head. The ugly disappointment in her eyes appeared to be dancing.

"That boy healed the Dreaming Tree. The thing that keeps the city alive and gives its people hope. If it had died, we all would have gone with it, and there would have been nobody to receive us into Heaven. When somebody from the Forgotten passes, they're simply *gone*. Don't you understand how terrifying that is? When you walk across the very stone where God slept, and you realize you'll never get to sit at His feet, that you'll just cease to exist as if he woke up and forgot all about you? That's *worse* than Hell."

She sighed, spread her arms, then let them clap against her thighs. "Everything my grandfather ever said, and Adam was the first thing that made me believe that salvation was possible. Adam and Henry." She wiped her eyes and bent to retrieve her bag.

"Sister Gladys always told me men were too dumb to hear reason when it came from a woman's mouth." She pointed at Maria. "I never believed men were that simple, but this woman just gave you the solution to everything. Get to earth. Make the pastor send you to Hell. Save Adam's mother and Henry's daughter. Leave Adam here with us so he can heal Solitude. Maybe even all of the Forgotten. Why would you deny any of that?"

Henry felt proud, even though it wasn't his place. Abraham had raised a good woman, and Henry was pleased to know her, even if he was just, in Sister Gladys's words, a dumb man. He turned to Boothe and spread his hands. "How about it?"

"I told you, I can't get back to Earth. They let me get you, then you took off with the kid, and that was it, I was put on probation."

"Where *can* you get to?"

Boothe raised his eyes to the sky and tipped his head. "I can get you to Heaven."

Maria smiled from behind her hand. "Checkmate."

Chapter Seventeen

HENRY STEPPED through the portal and bumped into Aela as she froze, staring up at something with her open mouth. Henry couldn't blame her, but he still grabbed her by the upper arms and moved her out of the way.

Ramiel followed behind him, his face impassive. Maria came through next, then Boothe, stepping out and releasing the portal's energy to sizzle away in a swirl of white fire.

Aela looked at Boothe, her face slack with awe. "This is Heaven?"

A broad set of white marble stairs led up to a building of glass that rose into the clouds. Golden light from a bright sun beaming through the gentle fog at their backs gleamed off the mirrored windows. Pearlescent veins ran through the stone, twinkling with reflected light.

Boothe ran up the steps and turned with his hand on the tall glass front door. "Not exactly. This is the lobby."

He opened the door, and Henry pushed Aela up the stairs. Resisting feet made her stumble, but Henry held her steady.

Just the sun is probably enough to blow her mind.

He stared up at the floating clouds, their reflection rolling down the glass to merge with the swirling fog behind his silhouette. Horns poked above the head of his shadow.

He thought of standing on the Burg-Heartstone bridge. He expected the falcons, Chelsea and Leo, to descend in a screaming dive. Approaching his reflection with the clouds at his back was like falling into the bay.

Henry followed Ramiel through the door, pushing Aela's resisting body into the bright interior. Maria's heels clicked off the floor behind him, and the door swung shut on a silent hinge, blocking the wash of sunlight that sparkled off the granite floor.

"Okay," Henry whispered into Aela's ear. "I guess I *definitely* know how you feel."

A counter on the far side of the room was blocked by a snaking line of … beings. Demons and angels. Humans and golls. Fairies flitting above the heads of everyone shuffling forward with their heads bent. Looking at the floor between their feet and keeping to themselves.

A glass wall over the counter with windows sliding back and forth, angels in matching yellow polos leaning out to wave over the next in line.

Henry shook his head. "Is this where the DMV got the idea?" His voice rang out to echo against a ceiling that seemed to be as high as the sky, and he ducked his head and covered his mouth in embarrassment. A demon with a gut and an ogre's face lowered his book to gaze at Henry with raised eyebrows.

Henry waved. The demon shook his head and went back to his book. *Cooking with Booze.*

The clash of a lock boomed out, and a door opened on the side wall. Three angels in shiny business suits emerged, crossing in front of Henry without a glance. Groomed wings folded back like the shining parts in their hair. A female rushed out behind them, overtaking her male counterparts and leading the group across the lobby.

Henry looked back as the entry door behind them opened, and the lobby glowed with another dose of sunlight to dazzle Henry's eyes. Aela turned to watch a Tracker glide through with a human held in front of him, hands chained behind his back. Henry followed her astounded gaze, and the Tracker's feet skimmed the shimmering floor as he ushered his human to the counter.

"This *can't* be how it really is," Aela said, her voice a choked whisper.

Boothe tipped his head in apology. "We're in a bit of a transition."

Henry swept his arm across the lobby. "Transitioning into what?"

Aela pointed at the black velvet rope. "Should we wait our turn over there with … the rest?"

Ramiel shook his head. "No, we won't have to wait much longer."

Another lock echoed across the lobby as it unlatched. Henry looked at the door where the angels had already entered, but this was a different door. A tidy angel in a gray suit with black checks stepped out with an open leather binder crooked in his arm. He read from a paper and looked up with a bored expression. "Walden Boothe?"

Boothe straightened his jacket and extended his arm. Maria laid her hand on his wrist, and he led her around the line toward the door.

Henry mocked Boothe smoothing his jacket, and extended his arm, bowing over it in sarcastic enthusiasm. Aela fluttered her hands at her throat and ducked under his arm, draping it over her shoulders as though it were a mink.

Henry had no perspective. If this was all the result of a bad trip, then he was on some *very* excellent shit.

Ramiel's stone face wasn't enough to dampen his humor. Henry smiled as he followed Boothe and Maria deeper into Heaven.

The angel led them down a carpeted hall. Dark wooden walls and formed plaster ceilings. Angels passing to the left, many with brass Antioch phones pressed to their cheeks. Sharp suits and neatly knotted ties. Sleek skirts and button-front shirts. At the end of the hall, a bright elevator invited them with open doors. Gold and mirrors. Walnut and marble. No buttons or numbers, just a clunking hiss as the doors closed, and a harp to fill the silence as they rose.

Aela's fingers dug into Henry's ribs like claws.

The elevator doors opened into a bright room filled with desks, each one with an angel bent over a pile of papers. An angel pushed a coffee cart between the rows, and another angel followed, handing out folders and papers with efficient repetition.

Down the right-hand side and into another hallway. Same as the first. The angel who escorted them from the lobby kept a brisk pace, and at the end of the hall in front of a grand window, he stepped to the side of an open door and tipped his head toward the interior. Henry looked out the window over the angel's shoulder as he passed. It looked down on a glorious campus filled with clouds and lights. A giant park surrounded by buildings that stretched into the distance. And the Tree in the center.

I finally found out how tall the thing is, I guess.

He was the last into the office, tearing his gaze from the gorgeous gardens and following the angel inside. Five chairs crammed into the corner in front of a desk covered with papers and files from one edge to the other. Henry really got a sense of his own size when he tried to wedge himself between Ramiel and Aela. He closed his legs and twisted one knee over the other, his coffee can hand dangling over his feet.

The angel sat and laid his paperwork down, tracing words with a forefinger. A framed picture of a church under construction hung on the wall over his shoulder. Flowing script covered puffy clouds in the bottom corner. *But someone will say, "You have faith and I have works."*

The angel flipped over a page and looked at the group with a sigh. "My name is Sariel, and I've been assigned to your case."

Henry looked down the line. Aela's shocked face, pale and still. Boothe and Maria sitting nearly in each other's laps. Ramiel's polite boredom.

Henry shrugged. "So, how's it look?"

Sariel tipped his head with a sigh. "After speaking with Mr. Boothe about your intentions, I have to be honest. It doesn't look good."

"What, our chances?"

Sariel chuckled. "No, Mr. Black. Your chances haven't even entered into it."

"Then, I don't understand."

"Adam and his father, the demon Baelzor, are being held pending a hearing. That hearing *will* find in management's favor, and Baelzor will be sentenced to Hell as *Receptorum.*"

"And Adam?"

Sariel spread his hands. "He will be executed."

"How can you just *say* it like that?"

"It's the way it has to be. Without a champion, he is unrepresented."

"I'll do it."

"You *can't*. You are already a champion to another, *and* you've been named Paladin. We haven't had a Paladin for over a thousand years."

"I don't even know what that means."

Sariel leaned back in confusion. "How can you not know?"

"It's not like there's a fucking *manual*. The last thing I did worth a shit was this bit about getting caught on the subway watching a video of two dogs fucking. Now, all the sudden, I'm a *Paladin?*"

"But you were able to destroy a holy relic in defense of the Elioud."

Henry lifted the coffee can from his lap. "And I lost my fucking hand in the process."

Sariel tipped his head. "And if you'd like to file a formal complaint, I can help you with that. But Mr. Black, by virtue of your holy appointment, you are one of the most powerful beings in existence right now."

"Fine, then let the kid go."

"You're not *that* powerful. There are *rules.*"

"Maybe, but nobody seems able to tell me what they are. Look, if the boy is supposed to go to Hell to save his mother, just pull her out. Problem fucking solved."

Sariel sighed and leaned back, looking at the ceiling. "It's not that easy."

"Then make me understand all this mess. Because if *that* won't work, let *me* go to Hell to save her."

Sariel spread his hands. "He's already in custody, Mr. Black. There are very few agents who can change that."

"Like who?"

"Well, if a champion declared himself, maybe *that* agent could affect a change in the boy's position, but allowing that there is nobody of sufficient power to do it, my hands are tied."

Henry took a breath to shout, but a voice from the doorway nearly stopped his heart. "I'll be the boy's champion."

Henry dropped off the edge of his seat to one knee. He craned his neck around to look into the hallway. He had always been taught that a modern man pushed everything down. Tamping the feelings deep into the most private recesses of his soul. But when he saw Mandyel leaning against the jamb with his hands in the pockets of his wool suit, his compressed rage and joy and regret and fear burst out of him in a wordless shout.

He sprang from the floor and was in front of Mandyel in a single breath. He wrapped the angel in a smothering hug, shouting broken questions and words of relief in a jumble punctuated by Mandyel's grunts and chuckles.

Henry stepped back and wiped his tears away, the coffee can clanking off his horns. "What the fuck, man? You know I can't take this shit."

Mandyel smiled and squeezed Henry's shoulders. "I'm truly sorry, Henry. It was the only way."

"But *how?*"

"Through a golem."

"The fuck is a golem?"

"It's a loophole, Dear Henry."

"I see now," Sariel said. "I'm very sorry sir, but I wasn't prepared to receive you."

Henry turned, and Sariel was looking at the floor at his side.

Mandyel waved the angel's concern away. "Don't worry about it, pal. Your plate's full enough."

"No, that's not good enough." Henry shook his head and pointed at Mandyel's chest. "I want a straight answer."

Sariel gasped. "Mr. Black! You are addressing an *arch*angel. Please, show him the respect he is due." He looked up from the floor, lifting his scandalized eyes to Henry's gaze. He whispered, "You *touched* him."

Mandyel strode in and stood next to Serial's desk, turning with his arms crossed to face Henry and his companions. "We're old friends, Sariel. Probably older than even Henry would believe."

Sariel looked back to the floor. "Such a thing ..."

Mandyel shrugged. "I'm not *technically* allowed on Earth. I created the golem to represent my interests outside my domain. When our friend Ramiel killed me, you only saw the destruction of my vessel. A construct built for the sole purpose of presenting options to those who might be ... instrumental in my cause."

Henry caught Ramiel's eye before the Tracker turned away with an expression of broad innocence. "You fucking knew?"

Ramiel looked back with a sheepish nod. "I suspected."

Henry threw up his hands. "Well, that's just fantastic."

Mandyel shook his head. "Henry, after so much, you still don't understand. Starting with Boothe's instructions, such as they were, all the way to joining my golem to get you closer to the boy, there was always one important thing."

Henry looked around. A normal looking office full of cabinets and files. His companions sitting with expectant faces. His friends?

Maybe.

Boothe, a being he once hated but decided to forgive.

Ramiel. An angel he decided to free at the urging of a beautiful boy that reminded him of his daughter.

Aela. A woman he decided to save.

Maria. A woman he realized held no special power over him, but one he decided to allow into the privacy of his weird and terrifying life.

Henry nodded. "I had to *choose*."

Mandyel grinned. "That is exactly right."

"Isn't it supposed to be easy to choose the right thing, though?"

"No, Henry. Sometimes, it's the most difficult choice you can make."

Henry crossed his arms and looked up at the ceiling.

Either in his head or right beside him, Amélie yelled, "Don't do it, Daddy!"

Everything else in the universe, including every cell inside him, screamed for Henry to tear the fucker's face from his skull.

Patrick grinned.

And in that grin, Henry's life with his family flashed before his eyes. From the moment Samantha found out she was pregnant to the moment Amélie was born, to a hundred other tender moments. They all flew by even faster than they had in real life. Gone and never to happen again because Patrick Harrison and his stupid fucking cult had ended everything.

Henry's hand shook around Patrick's throat, even as he squeezed tighter.

"Tell me why. Why us?" he said.

"Please, Daddy," Amélie said, now standing beside him, tears streaming down her face. "Please, just come with me."

Patrick stared even as his face began to turn purple, staring at Amélie, and all Henry could do was remember that this was the last man who had touched his daughter. The man who had murdered her.

He gritted his teeth and screamed, "Stop looking at her!"

"Daddy!" Amélie cried out as Henry's fingers shot through the bastard's throat, killing him in an instant.

Amélie screamed again. But her scream was cut short.

Henry spun around. But his baby girl was gone.

An easy decision in the end, but at such a cost …

He looked at Sariel, ignoring Mandyel's look of pride. "I choose not to kill that boy. I *choose* it."

His vision brightened with his red rage. Heat swirled from his mouth. A swelling of power rose in his chest. The weight of his words sweeping promise into reality, pressing against the demands of an absent God who didn't want to kill the boy, either.

This was all part of His plan.

Mandyel turned to the desk, his eyes swirling with white light. The corner of his mouth curled into a smile. "Me and a couple of the boys are going down to Solitude. We'll be taking Adam and his father with us."

Sariel looked up, squinting into the light. "But Hell will come for him."

Mandyel nodded. "I believe Lucifer will *empty* Hell for a chance at that boy."

"Then there will be war."

Mandyel bared his teeth. "I do so hope."

Henry stepped back in shock. "Oh, shit. That means we can save Adam's mother."

Mandyel pulled back with shock of his own. Light swirling in his eyes reflected off of the unshed tears, like diamonds on velvet. "Henry, you have thought of another before thinking of yourself."

Henry shook his head. "I don't understand."

Mandyel gripped his shoulder, and heat drove out of the angel's hand. "You will *also* be able to save your daughter."

Henry slumped into Mandyel's touch.

Finally.

Sariel shook his head and slipped a pen from his inside pocket. "I have seen *such* things today." He bent over his paperwork, scrawling on page after page. "The boy will be remanded to the custody of Archangel Mandyel. The demon Baelzor will be handed over to Paladin Henry Winston Black."

He snapped his portfolio closed and clicked the pen before sliding it back into his pocket. "Your intentions of entering Hell are not officially sanctioned, and no succor will be given. In the event of capture or failure, I suppose I won't have to worry about my next review because this is likely the end of everything."

Mandyel straightened his tie and buttoned his jacket. "You've made an excellent decision, brother."

Henry threw his head back and roared laughter. He slapped Mandyel on the shoulder before walking out. "You're certainly the one to know."

Chapter Eighteen

HENRY STARED at the clouds rolling away from the steps. Golden light rippling through like reflections from a pond.

Boothe stepped into his periphery, buttoning his jacket with a flourish. "I've never been inside Solitude. I was never permitted through the mists."

Henry chuckled. "Nervous?"

"Perhaps."

"You know where you're going, right?"

"I do. Ramiel gave me his memories of the place."

"That's was nice of him." Henry looked down at his feet, lost in the fluff swirling around his ankles. "When this is over, and I've saved Amélie … when we're through with each other, are we gonna be *done?*"

"I truly hope not, Henry."

"Yeah, me neither. Kind of."

Boothe reached out and traced a circle in the air. The path of his finger flared into bright white flames, and the image of the Dreaming Tree filled the portal.

Aela's fingers gripped his, and he stepped into Solitude with her at his side.

Abraham stood to the side with his back to their arrival. Bent over a table surrounded by soldiers — men and women in mismatched armor.

The Sisters of Solitude froze as Maria and Ramiel followed Henry through the portal. Abraham stood straight as Boothe stepped through and released the energy, the opening now closing with a rush of rolling flame.

The nuns continued with a collective shrug. Abraham turned, leaning on his cane as if he actually needed it. A bloody bandage on his right hand wrapped his knuckles. His sunken cheeks and hollow eyes brightened when he saw Aela, and she let go of Henry's hand to throw herself into the old man's arms.

Henry stepped up behind her. Abraham pulled his face from the top of her hand and dropped a hand on Henry's shoulder.

Henry grabbed Abraham's forearm, squeezing the same way he had Aela's hand in his when they walked through the portal. "How goes the war effort?"

"Surprisingly well, but there has been a development."

Henry felt Boothe come near then stepped back to indicate the angel with a wave. "This is Boothe and his wife, Maria."

Abraham's eyes narrowed. "We met at the base of a different tree a long time ago."

Boothe nodded. "That's correct."

"As I remember, I refused your offer."

"That is also correct."

Aela pulled herself away from Abraham's embrace. Abraham looked down at her with a smile, then back up at Boothe. Henry recognized the old man's polite amusement. "You are welcome in my home."

Boothe bowed his head. "Thank you."

Abraham nodded and turned to Henry. "It would seem that you've come just in time to answer some questions."

A portal opened behind the old man's back, and Mandyel's light poured out.

Henry pointed. "Maybe you should ask *him.*"

Mandyel stepped through the glowing circle, pulling his wings in to clear the sides. Adam rested on his hip, his head leaning against the angel's chest. Mandyel's feet hit the stone of Solitude and his light dimmed. The boy jumped from his arms and launched across the floor.

"Henry!"

Henry dropped down to receive the little angel's hug, closing his eyes and inhaling the boy's scent. Adam broke free and turned to Aela. He shouted her name and jumped into her arms. Abraham got the same treatment. He finished with Ramiel, then back on the floor, the boy looked up at Maria with wide eyes. "Hello."

"Hello, little one."

"You're beautiful."

Maria laughed, filling the room with her sultry voice. "That is a very sweet thing to say."

"I'm Adam."

"And I'm Maria." She tipped her head toward Boothe. "I am his wife."

Adam's eyes flicked over to Boothe, and his face scrunched in disgust. "I don't like him."

She laughed again. "Sometimes, I don't either, but he's actually a very good husband."

Boothe dropped to one knee to meet the child's eyes. "Adam, I'm very sorry for what I tried to get Henry to do. I'm going to try and save your mother to make up for it. Is that all right?"

Adam narrowed his eyes and looked at Boothe down the length of his nose. "You mean it?"

"I really do, yes."

Adam nodded. "I forgive you, Mr. Boothe."

Boothe rocked back and wavered to his feet as if to keep from falling over. "Thank you," he whispered with a breathless rasp.

Henry hid his smile as he looked back at Abraham and barely kept from cringing into a corner at the sight of twenty giant angels with hard faces standing behind Mandyel. Males and females covered in golden armor. Swords and shields. Flails and maces.

"We are here," Mandyel intoned, "at the behest of those in need. Is there such a one who requires the Army of the Lord?"

Abraham dropped to one knee and bowed his head. "I do not fear those who can destroy my body. Rather, I fear those who can destroy my soul."

"Then we are God's servants for your good."

"Then through God's grace, I will destroy my enemies that they shall know peace."

Mandyel drew a breath and shouted, "Nay, do not think I have come to bring peace!"

The angel pulled a blazing blade from his back, sizzling with the same fire swirling in his eyes. "I have not come wielding peace, but a sword!"

Mandyel and the angels rose from the floor with a single beat of their wings that resounded with thunder. The nuns fell to their knees, staring into the brilliant shimmer of holy light. Henry followed, lowering his eyes to the floor.

Now, that's a fucking entrance.

He looked back up at Mandyel. The rest of the angels stood as if waiting for flapjacks. Smug smiles and boredom. Mandyel sheathed his sword and bent to pull Abraham to his feet. "Let us prepare for the defense of the Children of Solitude, my son."

Abraham nodded as he stood. Mandyel turned him to stand at his side, an arm draped across the old man's shoulders. "And this is where it ends, Paladin Henry Black, for though we both now serve the Lord, our paths shall diverge."

Henry shook his head. "No, I can't … I don't know what to do."

Mandyel smiled, and Henry saw the amused glint in his eye. "Come on, pal. Even though you trust in the Lord, don't walk into battle unarmed."

"What does that mean?"

"Rest and prepare. Let Hell send its armies to this place. Let the pastor send his priests. Give them the time to look away, then strike in His name."

"What, am I just supposed to party?"

Mandyel glanced down the line of angels. "Do you really think you have something to offer in the coming fight."

"Maybe."

Abraham looked uncomfortable under Mandyel's arm, his eyes shifting from the floor to the glowing hand hovering over his chest.

Mandyel chuckled. "You've thought of others enough. Take a moment for yourself. Sleep. And prepare for your task." He turned to go, halting when Henry spoke again.

"But … Will I see you again?"

Mandyel shook his head. "Only if we fail."

Abraham cast a panicked look over his shoulder as Mandyel and his angels ushered the old man and the soldiers of Solitude into the corridor.

Frank Baelzor had been standing behind them, hidden from view during the exchange. His head bobbed back and forth as each angel passed, and when the last one left, he clapped his hands and stepped forward with a grin. "That was pretty cool, right?"

Henry turned and walked down the hall toward the room where he'd stayed the last time.

Time.

Mandyel had said to take time for himself. Every minute he took for himself was what?

A day for Amélie? A week?

He made it to his door and threw it open. He wanted to rip every Goddamned clock off the motherfucking wall. Flip the bed over and tear the sheets apart. Tip the lanterns over and set the whole place on fire.

For a guy making his own choices, I feel like I don't have a say in anything.

Pastor Owen's face sprung into his mind. So understanding. So *forgiving*.

The door opened, and Henry spun around with his claws up. Boothe stepped inside and closed the door behind him. He walked across the room, moving like an old man, dropping into the chair next to the bed with a weary grunt.

Henry leaned back against the wall, crossing his arms. "What's your fucking problem?"

"The portals, Henry. They take a lot of energy."

"Poor fucking baby. Suck it up."

Boothe shook his head. "Why do so many people *like* you? I've never understood it."

Henry sighed. "To be honest, I don't really know, either." He dropped onto the bed, stretching out and driving his head into the pillow. "Tell me, doctor. Am I like this because my mommy never loved me?"

Boothe chuckled. "No, you're like this because you are constantly fighting your nature."

"The fuck does that mean?"

"You must feed, Henry. There are demands on your energy of which you're not even aware. From moving through the shadows to your heartbeat. From basic thoughts to the skills of a Paladin."

"Like what skills?"

"I don't know, Henry. I've never seen a Paladin. But I've seen many demons."

"Yeah, so?"

"Demons are made for one purpose. That purpose may exhibit in different ways. Charlie Mara's speed. Frank Baelzor's shapeshifting. My silver tongue. Still, that purpose is to transport souls to Hell. Either those of the recently deceased or those you have ended yourself."

"I've tried not to kill that much, but sometimes it's really fucking hard."

"Of course it's hard. You're *supposed* to kill. Those who deserve it. Those you're ordered to finish. *That* is our purpose."

"Pastor Owen always told me not to kill. Made me promise."

"And why do think he would do that?"

Henry remembered the pain of his hunger. The nagging feeling that something was missing. That he was forgetting something. The struggle to keep that promise. "He did it to keep me weak. To keep me from gaining the strength that might rain shit in his garden. He wanted to keep me on the sidelines."

The chair creaked as Boothe stood. "I believe that is the reason, yes. You have made great strides, Henry, but you must strive for more. Don't deny what you are."

"That's just the thing, though. I *do* accept it. I just fucking hate it."

Boothe sighed. "I need to rest, Henry. I will see you in the morning. We shall get started then."

"Whatever."

The door closed with a soft click. Henry crossed his forearms over his head, covering his eyes.

The door whispered open, and Henry shook his head under his forearms. "I don't wanna talk about it anymore, okay?"

As the door clicked shut again, the bed shook with freshly settled weight. Henry snatched his arms from his eyes, and Aela dropped onto his chest, pressing her face into his neck and sliding a knee across his waist.

"What are you doing?" His voice cracked, and he cleared his throat. Her scent hit his palate, and he lowered his arms to drop a hand on her back. And then he froze. Her earthy musk mingled with the memory of Samantha's jasmine, and his breath became trapped in his chest.

He raised his arms overhead and stared at the ceiling. The lanterns' flickering flames casting dancing shadows across the cracked plaster.

Aela took a deep breath and slid down his body, rising on her knees and crawling backward off the bed. She turned and locked the door, then shrugged out of her leather jacket.

There are nuns right outside in the hallway!

He didn't stop her.

She kicked off one boot. The other.

Your grandfather's going to war with a bunch of angels!

He let her continue.

Aela loosened the laces on the front of her shirt, crossed her arms to grab the tail out of her waistband, then slid the shirt off, her bare breasts rising with her hands over head. She pulled the shirt away, and her hair tumbled in a spread, falling to brush the skin above her nipples.

Henry's breath left in an explosive sigh, along with his objections. His growing erection pressed against his jeans, and he was afraid to move, but also afraid to stay still.

She loosened her belt and released the clasp under her belly button. Then Aela bent forward and slid her pants down over the swell of her hips, turning so he could see her ass as it popped free. The leather creaked, and her lips parted as she stood.

Heat flooded his crotch. Burst into his cheeks.

She stepped forward, resting her hand on the footboard post.

Henry cried out as he swung his legs over the opposite side and curled over the fist he drove into his own gut. "No, not like this."

Aela gasped. "What?"

"This," he said, waving his hand over his entire wretched monstrous body.

Henry jumped to his feet and turned around with his back to the wall. She stood with a hand over her mouth, the other pressed against her stomach. Yellow light gleamed off the ridges of a light but muscular body. Solid power under soft compassion. Pouting lips and a face full of quiet sorrow. Henry had to drag his eyes to the floor.

He thought of Mike Serafino. As if he were a Sunday outfit. Aela gasped in shock, and he looked up, seeing Serafino reflected in her wide eyes.

She stepped back, hugging herself to cover her breasts. The lines of her abdominal muscles ran all the way down into the swell of her pubes.

Henry wanted to punch his stupid penis back into flaccidity.

He spread his arms. "This is what I *want* to give you. This man that I've pretended to be over and over … like a costume. But he's not me."

He thought of good old Henry Black, and she took another step back as his form changed to the balding frump that only one woman in his whole life had been able to love. "Or there's *this* guy. But he's not me either."

Then Henry thought of his true form. The demon with the horns and scars and a missing hand. The murderer. The monster. Without clothes his erection sprang up, bobbing with his heartbeat, and he was glad his skin was red enough to hide his embarrassment. Bare in front of her, body and spirit. At least she'd see how much his *body* craved her.

"But this is all I got." He lowered his eyes. "And it's not what I want to give you. You deserve so much more."

"Henry," she whispered.

Still, he refused to meet her eyes. His dick finally got the hint, deflating as he shook his head. "I don't know why you would want this. Why *anybody* would. "He held his hand out to forestall any response. "I don't want to know."

Henry cleared his throat. "But I want you ... I really do ... I just *can't*."

He hadn't heard her come to the bed, but he did feel her breath on his chest. "Look at me."

Henry lowered his arms and shook his head, looking over her shoulder instead.

"Look at me." She reached up and put a hand on either cheek, forcing his face even with hers. Tears welled in her eyes, but she smiled. Henry sighed in relief.

Hate how I look, just don't hate who I am.

Aela shook her head. "If you could only see what I do." She dropped her hands, wiping her eyes and sniffing. "Let's get some rest. We'll talk another time, okay?"

Henry slumped in relief, and he nodded in dumb agreement.

Aela walked around the foot of the bed, pausing to

bend over as she gathered her clothes. She glanced to see if he was watching, and they both burst out laughing when he jerked his eyes up to the clock wall.

Henry wished it was dark, and the lanterns guttered out. Aela hissed. "Did you do that?"

"I think so, yeah." He could see her in the blackness. Like the glowing face of an irradiated watch. A tiny glow surrounded her body as she stretched her hand out to find the edge of the bed, her eyes wide.

He dropped onto the bed, sliding under the sheet and rolling away from her. The bed swayed as she crawled in and pressed up against his back, sighing into his hair. Her warmth spread through him, and he tried to stay still as he cried.

Her hand crept across his ribs, and instead of wiping his tears away, he put his fingers over hers. He stared into the darkness as she fell asleep, wondering about the fairness.

Because now Henry was afraid of losing Aela, too.

Chapter Nineteen

HENRY AND BOOTHE stood at the top of another tower in Solitude, leaning out and watching the battle below against the latest incursion.

Mists above the city had turned to black smoke, swirling and twisting as if alive.

Fire erupted from the ground, lava pluming into the air. White flames from an angel's burning sword shot out to meet it. The sparking clash sending a shower of coals into the upturned faces of humans and demons. Ravagers and cultists.

Colored fireballs of energy crisscrossed the courtyard. Thundering explosions of dark power. In the middle stood Mandyel and Abraham. The archangel's holy fire spreading in deadly arcs. Abraham's glowing cane full of righteous streams of blue light. Sap from the Dreaming Tree splashing out to shower Solitude's enemies with nightmares.

Demons clawing at the sticky liquid covering their faces, screaming in terror and tearing at their own skin.

Adam's bright light flitting around, swiping with his Prince Valiant sword. His shield ablaze on his arm.

He's probably safer there than anywhere he's been so far.

A rallying call and the soldiers of Solitude poured from the gate with Angelique and Bariel leading the charge. The clash exploded up the tower in a rush of noise and light, and the combined armies of Hell and the Order were driven back.

The demons melted into the ground in retreat. The cultists' priests stepping back through the curtain of rock as the entrance to Solitude closed again. A cheer dying on the beating of wings as two dragons with liquid fire dripping from their gaping maws loomed over the walls.

Mandyel's angels rose, their nets extended to catch the jets of fire belched into the thick air. Mandyel himself shot from the bloody earth to decapitate one of one of the beasts in a stroke. The other dragon reared back and turned tail. Flying back into the dark mist, the smoke hardening into the barrier that hid Solitude from the rest of the Forgotten, and the cheer rose anew.

They were safe again. For now.

Henry pushed back from the rail and turned to Boothe. "You feel good about leaving them?"

"No, but we must."

"Fuck, I just wish there was something we could do."

Frank knocked the stone with his knuckles. "Did you see those dragons? They were badass!"

Henry spread his hands and looked at Frank with a growl.

"What?" Frank said. "They were *cool*. I'm just saying."

Henry shook his head and turned back to Boothe. "Do you know where Aela and Maria are? I'd kinda like to leave before the next volley."

"I believe they were gathering a few final things before setting out."

"Girl stuff, huh?"

"God help us."

Henry glanced over at Frank, but he was staring at the aftermath with an open-mouthed smile. Henry leaned toward Boothe and lowered his voice. "Aela came to my room last night."

Boothe frowned. "Why tell me that, Henry?"

"I don't know, but there's nobody else to tell, so suck it."

"Fine, Henry. You see, when a man and a woman love each other very much …"

"God damn it!" Henry shouted, then he noticed Boothe's smile. "Fucker."

"Were the advances unwanted?"

"Yes … well, no. Kind of? I … pushed her away. Look, I don't know. It just seemed like a weird time to get all hot and bothered, you know?"

"Why is it a weird time?"

"Fucking look around!"

"Was there opportunity?"

"Well, yeah."

"And desire?"

"I guess."

"Then the time was right. Why did you fight it?"

"Because, dammit. *Look* at me."

"Maybe you should look at yourself."

Frank tapped Henry's arm. "He's right, you know. You're not so bad for a demon. You're actually pretty cool looking."

Henry sneered with a shake of his head. "Who the fuck asked you?"

Frank raised his hands. "Whoa, dude. Just trying to help."

Boothe sighed. "It's not his fault, Henry. In fact, it's probably Maria's."

"How?"

"She was a fertility goddess. A minor Iberian deity. Prehistoric and quite powerful before the rise of Jehovah. She thrives on conflict resolved by the power of love."

"Kinda like Huey Lewis?"

Boothe sighed. "She's a matchmaker, Henry. It's what got her into trouble over a thousand years ago."

"Trouble you got her out of?"

"More like trouble she got me into."

"What happened?"

Frank leaned in. "Yeah, what happened?"

Boothe looked at Adam's father. "I made a deal very much like Henry's. And it turned out very much the same."

"Only you *saved* the one *you* loved."

Boothe ducked his head and looked at Henry. "And I would do it again and again. Such is her hold over me."

Henry looked down at the courtyard, now clear of combatants. Dark and empty.

Would I do it all again?

Knowing what I know now?

He looked over at Boothe, and the angel's face was tight with worry.

Henry chuckled. "I probably would, too."

Light flickered from the stairwell. Footsteps clapping off the stone.

The three of them turned to watch Maria and Aela enter the balcony in front of Ramiel's angelic glow.

"You know," Frank said. "Marisol's a bitch."

Henry twisted to look at him, but Frank just nodded.

"No really. Sometimes, I hate her. Like this deep ache that twists my guts up, and I just want to spit her out, but I can't. I'm gonna leave my son in the middle of Armageddon. That sweet, amazing boy. That shining fucking light that is the only truly beautiful thing I've ever seen, except for Marisol. Except for that woman, that angel. I'm gonna leave him in the hands of the ones who have been trying to kill him his entire life. Go back to Hell. And not to save her … just to see her. If I can't bring her out, just seeing her again before I die will be enough."

Frank swiped his eyes with the backs of his wrists and sniffed. He grinned with a shrug and clapped his hands. "I'm *hooked*."

Henry looked at Boothe, but the angel's eyes were on Maria. Henry followed his gaze, eyes passing over Maria to light on Aela's face. Back in her leathers, messenger bag on her hip. She grinned at him, and Henry's breath hitched like someone had splashed his face with icy water.

It hurt that the sight of her made him feel so good.

And Samantha has Stone. Stop whining.

Boothe extended his hand, and Maria took it with a smile. He turned with her trailing behind him and traced a circle in the air. Now, granted permission by Heaven, Boothe was finally able to bring them back to Earth. White fire spiraled a bright window into existence, and Boothe held out his hand, inviting them to walk through.

Henry took Aela's hand and walked forward. He saw Frank offer his hand to Ramiel, but the angel declined with a curt shake of his head. "Suit yourself," Frank said.

Henry laughed as he entered the light.

Boothe's apartment hadn't changed a bit. Well, except that the destruction and mess he'd left were now cleaned up. New items replacing the ones he'd destroyed.

Henry felt like he was finally home, but a nervousness

gnawed at his gut as he wondered who'd cleaned up the place. Maybe someone else had moved in, and —

Then he smelled cigarette smoke before seeing it swirl away from the open hand coming at his face.

His head rocked back from Nadia's slap, and he stepped into Aela, keeping his body between the two women.

"You son of a bitch!" Nadia shouted. "Where have you been?"

Charlie Mara jumped up from the couch, his black ponytail flying out behind him. His small eyes were wide, wrinkling his eyebrows up into his hairline. He grabbed Nadia's hand, dragging her back. "Hang on there, girl."

Henry spun and wrapped Aela up, holding her hands at her sides. Both fists were full of steel, demon-killing energy swirling from the blade's razor-sharp edges. "She's a *friend*."

Ramiel and Frank came through the portal. Frank's face brightened. "Charlie!"

Charlie smiled back. "Hey, Frank." Nadia's hands turned to black scales, claws springing out to slice Charlie's black work shirt, drawing dark blood to flow down his arm. "Oww, holy fuck!"

"Let me go, Henry," Aela growled.

"Not a fucking chance. She's pissed at *me*, and I deserve it."

Boothe pulled Maria through the portal, and his face hardened as he released the energy in a whirling fizzle. "What's all this?"

"What do you mean, you deserve it?" Aela snarled. "What did you do?"

"You took that boy off to die," Nadia shouted. She struggled in Charlie's grasp, but he dragged her hands down, pinning them to her hips.

"Nothing," Henry said.

"You took my boy off to die?" Frank turned to Henry. "When was this?"

Boothe rolled his eyes at Frank. "Oh, come on. You know Henry was bringing him to find you."

Maria laughed. "Is that how you remember it? *Moro viejo nunca será buen cristiano.*"

Frank shook his head in confusion. "Is that Spanish?"

Nadia stopped struggling, drilling Henry with a vicious stare. "Not a phone call or message of any kind?"

"Yes, that's how I remember it," Boothe said.

Henry turned back to Aela. "I'm a terrible friend, okay? I'm a terrible *everything*. Just calm the fuck down."

Maria put her hands on her hips. "He was running from *you*, Walden."

Charlie grinned. "Your first name is Walden?"

Henry laughed, "That was *my* reaction."

Aela pulled against Henry's grip, but there was no hope of getting free. She looked up into his eyes, anger curling her lips. "Don't tell me to calm down."

Maria pointed at Boothe's chest. "You were trying to get poor Henry to kill that boy."

Boothe spread his hands. "*Poor Henry?*"

"What?" Nadia cried, her dagger gaze sweeping over to Boothe.

Frank leaned back and crossed his arms. "I knew a demon named Weston, once."

"We've been over this," Boothe said.

"You tried to get Henry to kill Adam?" Nadia said. "Mandyel was right about you."

Boothe turned to her, his brows drawing together. "He was right about me how?"

Aela stomped on Henry's foot, her face turning red. "Let me go, Henry."

"Fuck no."

"Why would you do that?" Nadia demanded.

"I was told to." Boothe turned back to Maria. "I had just gotten you back. I was made an *angel*. How could I lose that? How could I lose *you* again?"

Maria crossed her arms and shook her head. "*Calladita te ves mas bonita.*"

Frank looked at the ceiling. "Or was it Watson?"

Too many people talking and it was building up like some tea kettle's whistle in Henry's mind. He had to shut everyone up and restore civility before someone really got hurt.

Henry tipped his head back and roared.

"Could everyone just shut the *fuck* up?"

Quiet.

All eyes on him.

"We're all on the same side. Everything has been worked out, and whatever misunderstandings there were, who wanted to kill who, that shit's all done now. Now we're all on the same page. We've got a fucking mission to do and no time to stand around bitching."

Aela and Nadia both stood down, relaxing their shoulders.

Henry went to the kitchen, muttering curses to himself, throwing his arms up in frustration and snatched the old plastic pitcher from the counter. He stuck it under the faucet and watched the room recover while he filled the pitcher with cold water.

Maria was the first to speak, "Ladies," she purred. "Let's chat."

Nadia nodded. Aela set her jaw and followed Maria to the kitchenette.

Boothe stood, smoothing his hair. "I'm going out. We need information."

Henry refilled his pitcher, and Charlie looked with a wary glance that slid over Henry to the women sitting around the table. "I think I'll go with you."

Charlie looked at Frank, who was fixing the bottom button on his Hawaiian shirt. "You coming?"

Frank waved him off. "No way." He pointed to the corner behind Henry. "He's got a popcorn machine."

Boothe moved to the front door, and Charlie jogged to catch up. Frank walked by and slapped Henry on the arm. Water sloshed over his face, and Henry bent over to cough up what he'd drawn up his nose.

He slammed the pitcher down and headed to the bedroom. As he closed the door, Maria's voice floated through. "So, Nadia. What did you think of Charlie?"

Henry closed the door behind him and leaned back against it with his eyes aimed at the ceiling. He thought of praying for guidance, but considering this year, he doubted anyone was listening.

Chapter Twenty

HENRY FLOPPED ONTO THE BED, flinging his arm over his eyes. He spun the knob to an empty spot on the dial then fell asleep to silence.

No dreams or dark thoughts to mar his empty bliss.

His own voice woke him. Filtering through the door with the whining Burg City accent he played up on-stage. Laying it on thick for the crowd and the cameras. The special he'd taped before his death. The one that was gonna lead to an extended absence. More writing. Producing. Maybe even some directing. It was the turning point of his career, and he was going to be home so much more.

"So, I'm getting coffee in, let's just say, a *not so safe area*. And ... I don't like to make assumptions about a place or people just because *it's always on the fucking news for murders*, but ... sometimes, well ... you know."

He remembered the awkward grin he gave followed by the audience's groans. Henry also remembered the nervous energy of the mostly liberal crowd thinking he was going to make a racist joke or something. And Henry loved playing with audience expectations.

"So, it's like, barely four in the morning, and I'm not even awake. This black guy comes up to me wearing red from head to toe. Shoes. Tracksuit. Hat. He grins with a mouthful of gold teeth, and he goes, 'Yo, I know you.' And I'm thinking, um … I don't think so, but I don't say that, because, I don't wanna get … well…"

He'd made a finger gesture like a gun shooting and the audience groaned again.

"What? I'm not saying he might have shot me because he's black but because it's fucking Murder City. Did you not hear the part before? Okay, forget it, he was *a white dude* in all red, does that make it better? Jesus."

The audience laughed, but Henry wasn't done yet.

"Anyway, the *very, very, like exceedingly white guy, even whiter than me,* turns all excited and yells to the back. Like, right at the glass wall of coolers with all the energy drinks and liquor. He goes, 'Yo, it's that motherfuckin' clown I was telling you about!' *Really* loud, too. Him calling me a clown, I thought maybe he'd seen my show. Liked my album, you know?"

Henry sat up and crossed his legs underneath him, leaning forward with his elbows on his knees.

"So, I lean out away from all the coffee pots. You've been to Speedway, right? A mountain of twelve pots of coffee with different names, tryin' to be fancy and shit with their descriptions but they all taste exactly the same? Then you've got a pyramid of wrinkled fucking hot dogs that look like dismembered geriatric cocks rolling on a grill since the Johnson administration? Seriously, who the fuck is eating that shit? I'm fat, and not particularly known for my discriminate palette — true story, I once ate a Cinnabon I found on a mall bench — but *I* won't even touch those things. So what *kind of fat fuck* do you have to be to eat those severed old man dicks? I mean, you *really* must hate yourself to be eating those!

"So, anyway, I lean out, and this giant black guy turns toward me, is it okay if *this guy* is black? Because he looks just fucking like Biggie Smalls, and I can't exactly say he's a white dude too, okay? So, Not Biggie lets the cooler shut and comes over. He's wearing a white suit, and he's got a black silk scarf around his neck. I'm not making this up. True story. A white bowler's hat, and a white cane with a gold tip."

Henry nodded. He had told the story exactly as it had happened, only leaving out the six Little Debbies he was going to buy and eat on his way home. He'd hidden the wrappers, too.

"He comes rolling out of the back, driving his cane into the floor like he was making a beat. Like he was about to freestyle, and I actually looked around for cameras, like I had gotten sucked into a music video. Then, one more dude is with him, a short steroid fat dude, you know the kind I'm talking about, used to be on the juice and jacked, but now ... just fat. And he's wearing a puffy coat and gold chains, and a hat at that angle that schlumpy tubs like me can never quite figure out. And I'm like, 'Who the fuck are these people and why do I always run into them?'

"So, Fat Steroids says, in a Russian accent, by the way, and everything *always* sounds so much more sinister in a Russian accent, ya' know? He says, 'Man, what you did to them kids.'

"I fucking freeze. I'm thinking, *what kids? What did I do to them kids?!* Not Biggie reached into his pocket, and I think for sure he's gonna shoot me or something. And *not because he's black!* But he pulls out an iPhone instead, and says, 'Yo, clown, you wanna see the pictures?'

"I taste a little bit of vomit, like, I have no idea what

these pictures are of, but I know I don't want to see them. Nothing good can come from this situation, in Murder City at the ass crack of dawn, with a bunch of shriveled dicks and Not Biggie and his Russian dude and the very, very white dude, and … I just start thinking of all the pedophiles you see on TV and their mugshots, and it's almost always some pasty, balding, fat fucking white dude, just like me. And they must be mistaking me for some piece of shit kiddy diddler, right? So, I just figure I'm dead. I mean, I'm certainly not gonna outrun them. I mean, yeah, he's fucking the size of Biggie, but, look at me, right?

"Anyway, Not Biggie's got his iPhone and starts swiping pictures, and I see a pasty, fat, balding white dude … dressed as a clown. And … the fucker looks just like me. And, … he's in a children's hospital, buncha cancer kids and burn victims and shit. And these three guys are there in the pictures too, with scrubs on and with a bunch of smiling kids. Not Biggie then starts bawling, saying how much my act meant to those kids, and going on about this little girl who was hanging on by a thread and got better after I, or rather the clown, did his show. And he hugs me, right there in the store, in front of the shriveled old man dicks and everything, he's just hugging me. And what am I gonna do? I can't say that's not me. I mean I *should* say that, but … I dunno, I'm kinda enjoying the love! I'm pretty sure *none* of my jokes ever put a smile on *any* kid's face, and I'm standing there trying to figure out what the fuck I'm doing with my life, because here I am kinda pretending to be a clown that visits sick kids and, anyway, long story short, very, very white dude then says, "Yo, your coffee is on us, brotha.' And then we all stood in the parking lot for twenty minutes shooting the shit and I never once corrected them and told them who I really am, and … the worst part is, when one of them asked if I'd come back, what could I say, um, no, you've got the wrong guy? So, I said yeah, I'll come by. And I thought that would be the end of it, but they asked if I could do it next weekend, and … what was I gonna say? So I said yeah."

The audience groaned.

"So, all I can think of is that because I was too chicken shit to tell these guys the truth, somewhere there was a room full of cancer kids and burn victims waiting on a clown that never showed. And whenever they run into the real clown, who is probably like the nicest guy in the world, they're gonna *kick his ass!* And yeah, I'm pretty sure I'm going to hell."

Henry opened the door to laughter and applause in time to see his own incredulous smile as he had waved at the crowd. A surprised look that said he couldn't believe this was happening. "You've been great. Thanks so much," he said from the TV. Henry waved to himself as the credits rolled.

Nadia sat on the end of the couch, leaning over her crystal ashtray with the silver filter held between her teeth. Gray smoke swirled up into her hair.

Frank hugged a bowl to his chest with a few kernels of popcorn rolling around in the bottom. He pointed a remote at the huge panel hanging on the wall, and Henry's special was replaced with a Samsung logo. He looked up at Henry with a grin. "That was some funny shit, man."

Even now, praise made him uncomfortable. Henry gave his standard answer, ducking his head in embarrassment. "Appreciate it."

Nadia smiled at him through her smoke, and Henry sighed in relief.

I guess we're good again.

"You know, I donated half the profits of that show to

Burg City Mercy Children's Hospital. To make up for the whole clown thing."

Frank leaned forward, dropping the empty bowl on the coffee table. "No shit?"

"Yeah, and here's the best part. I handed the check to Pastor Owen right in front of Burg Spires."

The pride on Samantha's face. Smiling at him through her tears. He wondered if that's when the son of a bitch decided to kill him.

"Any word from anybody?"

Nadia pulled the butt from her silver filter and ground it out before answering. "Maria went out. She said she was in the mood to shop. Ramiel's on the roof looking at the stars. No word from Boothe or Charlie."

"What about Aela?"

"She's asleep in the other bedroom."

"This place has another bedroom?"

Nadia smiled. "It has as many as it needs. For a while, it needed two."

"Yeah, well. I think I should apologize. For grabbing her like that."

Nadia waved him away. "I think she understands. Besides, even though she was born in Solitude, she's human. Let her rest, Henry."

Henry nodded. "Then I should apologize to *you.*"

Frank rubbed popcorn butter on the legs of his pants already shiny from napkin service while he watched TV. "Why? What'd you do?"

Henry glared at Frank, but the demon just looked up with a crooked open-mouthed smile. Henry sighed. "I said some shit that I really wish I could take back."

"Who the fuck are you to care about me? You don't fucking know me, lady. You can pretend to be on my side all you want, but just like everybody else, you walk around like you got a secret, and you know

what? Keep it. Because I don't give a fuck about you, either. The only thing I give a fuck about is my daughter!"

"No, Henry. The only person you give a fuck about is you."

Nadia sat back and crossed her legs. He had forgotten how good she looked. Even Frank had a handsome nerd mystique that the ladies probably loved. Surrounded by people *way* better looking than him was how Henry had spent most of his life.

Now I gotta be ugly while I'm dead, too.

"You don't need to apologize, Henry. I've heard the story. That doesn't mean you're off the hook. It just means I understand why you did it."

"That's good enough for me." Henry sighed with an absent nod. "So, I think I'll do some looking around of my own?"

"You should take Frank with you."

"Yeah," Frank said. "You and me. Two guys doing guy stuff. Maybe get a beer or something."

"Because he's annoying the shit out of me."

Henry burst out laughing, and Nadia turned to Frank. "No offense."

"None taken."

"All right. As long as someone will be here if Aela wakes up."

"Don't worry, Henry." She smiled with a knowing lift of her eyebrows. "She'll be fine."

Henry looked away from her smile and walked to the sliding window looking out over the city. Frank padded up next to him while he opened the window and inhaled the heavy air. That feeling of being home nearly knocked him off the window sill.

"So, how we getting down? A fire escape? You gotta car down there?"

Henry shot his hand out and grabbed a handful of

hibiscus, pulling Frank against him with his shirt. "Not exactly."

He dragged Frank into the shadows, wrapping the darkness around them like a sleeping bag. Frank's scream trailed away as they shot through the city, a breath away from the light.

Henry burst out of the dark, pulling Frank into the shadows behind the trees at the edge of the church's property. He turned Frank around and held his coffee can up to his chin under his lips. "Shhh."

Frank nodded with wide eyes. He pumped his fists in a shadow boxing dance, stepping back against Henry and grabbed a fistful of shirt in each hand. "That was awesome!" His grin slipped at the sight of Henry's face.

He followed Henry's eyes, and they looked through the trees together. The Burg Spires Church of Hope was gone.

A pile of blackened rubble. Weeds around the edges. Old yellow tape fluttering in the breeze.

A fire had burned it to the ground.

"That's one Hell of a bingo night," Henry said.

"What is this place?"

Henry blinked his shock away and looked down at Frank. "It's the church."

"What church?"

"The Burg Spires Church of Hope."

Frank's eyebrows shot up, and he took another look. "No way."

A shadow rose from a pile of ash and shook itself like a dog. Henry squinted at the familiar shape. The way it moved. Small gray wings. A grin split Henry's face, and he shouted before he could stop himself. "Ezra!"

The goll froze, turning its glowing eyes toward the sound.

Henry clapped a hand over his mouth, and the pointed ears stood straight up. The goll spun, dove back into the rubble, and scurried out of the light.

"What the Hell did you do that for?" Frank whispered.

"I don't know. I thought I knew him."

"Yeah, but you don't just throw your hands up and yell, *hey guys, I'm over here!*"

"Look, I'm sorry, okay? What's the worst that can happen?"

Frank pointed at the shapes coming out of the darkness. "I guess we can ask *them.*"

Motherfucker!

A woman with traps so big, it looked like she was wearing a jetpack. A neck as thick as her head. Her pink sports bra doing little to disguise her rippling muscles, her hands ending in glittering nails sharpened to wicked points.

Her boyfriend stepped into the light behind her, so hairy that Henry thought it was a bear walking upright. He wore no shirt, steaming in the cool night air, his Order From Chaos tattoo glistening through his chest hair.

The goll bounced at the bear's heels. More green than the familiar gray that Ezra had been, and he moved with more spastic energy than the goll who saved Henry's life.

Henry spread his arms with a nod. "Yeah, that's not Ezra."

Frank gave his eyes a dramatic roll. "No shit, Sherlock."

Sports Bra made wet smooching sounds. "You might as well come on out. We know you're in there." Her voice sounded like a ten-year-old girl's.

Bear tipped his head back, nostrils flaring as he sniffed the air. Silver rings jangled in his cheeks and lips.

Frank put his hand flat on Henry's chest. "I'll handle

this."

Before Henry could argue, Frank stepped out of the trees, his sneakers crunching through gravel at the edge of the parking lot. The goll pressed itself against Bear's calves, leaning out to watch Frank's approach.

"Hey," Frank said. "I'm looking for my pastor. Guy named Owen. You seen him?"

Sports Bra reached up and pulled her blonde ponytail over her shoulder, stroking it with glitter covered fingers. "Maybe," she squeaked. "Who wants to know?" She tossed the ponytail back, and Henry saw the OFC across her throat.

He nodded and crossed his arms, waiting for Frank to *handle it.*

Frank stuffed his hands in his pockets. "I just need to talk to him. He was the one who married me and my wife. We're having some problems, you know?"

"I'm sorry to hear that."

"Yeah," Bear rumbled behind her. "We're real sorry."

"Hey, thanks," Frank said. "So, is he around?"

"Nope. He's uptown with the mayor."

Frank turned at the waist with his hands spread out, looking over his shoulder as if to say, *See?*

Sports Bra stepped forward and launched a kick into Frank's testicles that lifted his Chuck Taylors off the ground almost a foot. He came down on his knees with his hands pressed into his crotch. He wheezed out a whining sigh and fell over on his side.

She drew her foot back again, aiming at Frank's face, and Henry dropped into the night.

He shot across the darkness to rise out of her shadow like the Saturn V rocket. His coffee can hit her chin and her jaw collapsed, splitting apart and popping open like a Diet Coke full of Mentos.

She flew straight up like the rebound of a trampoline, and the rainbow of blood sparkled out in an arcing shower that glittered like rain.

Bear lunged forward with a roar, but Henry dropped to his knees, and the wild slash whistled by without touching him. Henry jumped like he was trying to push the Earth down, slashing up with a roar of his own. Bear's guts spilled out of the hole where his balls had been, and blood shot from his mouth as he landed flat on his back.

Bear's eyes rolled back and forth, fixing on Henry's face as he died. His life energy rose with the steam, and Henry inhaled it. Here was an asshole who truly deserved it, and Henry was only doing his job.

The goll scraped against the ground, watching Henry with wide eyes. He offered his hand as if trying to give a dog his scent. The goll's hand whipped out, and Henry rocked back in shock. Blood gushed from the gash on the back of his knuckles.

The goll jumped from the ground, his claws outstretched. His mouth open in screeching rage. Henry caught him in midair with his hand over the goll's mouth. Like a bird flying into a plate glass window. He drove his hand down, and pie-faced Ezra's evil twin into the asphalt.

Henry jumped back as the goll staggered back to its clawed feet, weaving around in a circle while his wings wilted like flowers in the heat. Henry took a cue from Sports Bra and sent a kick into the goll's back that sent him tumbling through the air, his wail of pain pulsing as he spun into the shadows. A crash as he hit the charred debris in the center of the burned-out church, and Henry turned to help Frank to his feet.

Frank winced as Henry hauled him up. One hand grabbed at Henry's shoulder, the other cradled under his balls. "How'd I do?"

"Oh, you handled it."

"Good."

Henry made sure Frank was steady before turning to look at Sports Bra lying on the ground, staring up into the dark sky, blood coughing and gurgling out of the ragged hole that had once been the bottom of her face.

"Oh fuck," Frank said. "She looks like the Predator's mouth."

Henry squatted down. Her searching hand grabbed his pant leg, and he swatted it away. He leaned over her so she could see his whole face. A bubbling mist of blood burst into the air with every breath.

"I'm not going to tell you what your *cult* did to me. What they did to my family. I don't care if you know or not. I just want to ask you a question."

Her chest heaved, and her squeaking voice blossomed from the spitting blood. Tears poured from the corners of her eyes. Henry rested his hand on her shoulder. "No, no. It's okay. It's okay. One blink for *yes*. Two for *no*. Okay?"

She nodded, her eyes opening to their limits. Her heels dragged back and forth like she was trying to slide away. Just slip to the side and disappear.

"Good," Henry said. "Do you want to die?"

Blink.

Henry didn't wait for the second one. He swiped his claws across the Order tattoo on her throat, and blood splashed, spreading out from her head in a jet that soaked his pants from the knees down.

Another life taken that truly deserved it, and Henry stood with his eyes closed.

"What *are* you?" Frank whispered.

Henry turned and wiped his claws on his shirt. "I'm a comedian."

Chapter Twenty-One

HENRY DUCKED through the window into the living room light.

He got one foot on the floor, and Aela sprang from the couch, running over to give him a hug as he stood to make room for Frank. "You were gone when I woke up." Her eyes were wide and shining. "Where did you go?"

Imagining himself clean was easier every time he tried it. He was starting to understand how the rest of them kept doing it. "Just stomping around the old haunting ground."

Frank squeezed by. "Did you know the pastor's church burned down?"

Boothe stood from leaning on the kitchen counter. The ice in his drink tinkled as he lowered it from his mouth. "Yes. It happened two months ago. On the news, they spoke about the tragedies that have cursed that church, but the mayor has assured the city that he will personally take care of the parish. He's already had two fundraisers, and they've raised more than nine million dollars."

Henry shook his head. "What church needs that much money?"

Ramiel leaned forward from his seat on a kitchen chair made tiny by his massive frame. "So says the Lord, Heaven is My throne, and the earth is My footstool. What is the house that you would build for Me, and what is the place of My rest?"

Aela nodded. "In whom the whole structure, being joined together, grows into a holy temple in the Lord. In Him, you also are being built together into a dwelling place for God by the Spirit."

Frank shrugged. "Yeah, I don't know what that means."

Boothe slid his empty glass toward the sink. "It means one must remain humble if he is to please the Lord. It's just an excuse to keep the good pastor close. As resources or protection, I can't say."

Henry slid from Aela's embrace, crossing the room to the coffee table. "Yeah, me and Frank found a couple of Order stooges patrolling the ashes. They were *not* humble."

"What happened?"

Henry dug into the cargo pouch on the outside of his pant leg and pulled out everything he found on the bodies. "Stuff from the dead guys' pockets."

Charlie leaned forward for a better look, and Henry noticed his hand had been on Nadia's thigh. He glanced over at Maria, and she looked at him over the rim of a coffee cup with a smile in her eyes.

Nobody's safe from her love spells anymore.

"This failed Russian weightlifting experiment and her boyfriend tried to act like tough guys."

Frank spread his arms like he was measuring the fish of his dreams. "This bitch was *huge.*"

"Like a vagina with pecs."

Maria snorted, and coffee bubbled over the edge of her cup.

Frank nodded. "We handled it, though."

"But before we *handled* it, she said the pastor was with the mayor."

Henry swirled his claws through the crap on the coffee table. Two vape pens with massive batteries. One pink. One green. Two giant smartphones, both with cracked screens. A worn wallet made of duct tape. A keyless entry fob to a Mini Cooper, and a yellow prescription bottle of fosfomycin.

One of the phones had a pink slipcase over it. As good a place to start as any. He retracted his claws and collected the phone, turning it over to find any buttons. He felt like an out-of-touch grandpa trying to figure out a terrifying new technology.

The cracked glass flared on, and Henry winced away from the home screen picture. A close-up of Bear's hairy face, the silver rings shining with the flash.

Henry pressed the messaging icon. Sports Bra's last text popped up.

OMG! DID U C? PR ON DL AT GYM. 5 ON EACH SIDE!!! TTYL :)

He shook his head and handed the phone to Boothe. "I'd rather listen to you and Maria argue in Spanish."

Nadia's eyes were intent on the other phone. "Henry. Look at this. It's tomorrow."

"What's tomorrow?"

She held the phone out to him and he took it, raising his eyebrows to get a better look at the tiny words. "What is this, an email?"

Hey Jonnie!

We're sending this message out to let our members know — IT'S BACK!

The Dark Auction has found a new home!

The old Burg City Penitentiary.

As always, refreshments and spectral transport provided by our friends at the Viazo Grand.

Don't forget your mask, and bring Pattie. She'll love it!

-Mark@ofc

P.S. Show them this code at the door.

Henry scrolled down and almost dropped the phone when the Order From Chaos symbol filled the screen. It seemed to crawl as if the pixels were alive. He pressed the buttons on the side of the phone until the evil disappeared. He took a calming breath and met Nadia's eyes.

She sat with her back like a rod, arms crossed under her breasts. She shook her head, and her jaw bunched. "Henry …"

"I know."

Boothe held his hand out. "What is it?"

Henry handed him the phone and looked at Ramiel, his head tipped in appraisal.

Ramiel's eyebrows shot up. "What?"

"You'd look good as a bear." Henry turned back to Nadia. "Does *Mandy's Export Emporium* carry masks for costume parties? Of the animal variety?"

She nodded. "Of course. We have everything for the discerning orgy lover."

Frank held up his hand. "Wait, what?"

Ramiel drove to his feet, and his eyes filled with swirling light. "Am I to understand this is … an event similar to how we met?"

Henry found the angel's blazing gaze and nodded. "I think so, yeah."

Ramiel growled, and the sound set off a primal response deep in Henry's chest. His shoulders heaved, and a growl of his own rose in his throat.

"Wait a minute," Frank said. "What are we talking about?"

Nadia lit a cigarette with shaking hands. "It's an auction where they sell children."

Maria stretched her hand, her eyes wide with horror. "Walden?"

Boothe took her hand and set the phone back on the table. "It ends in sexual sacrifice."

Frank stepped back and lifted his hands as if snatching them from scalding water. "Of the kids?"

"That's why I was locked up," Charlie said.

Nadia drew away with a gasp.

Charlie held his hands up. "Not because of *that*, gimme some fucking credit, okay? No, I ratted out this guy who was smuggling fairy dust over from the UK. Some Order From Chaos bullshit, but I ain't down for that. And I ain't *that* kind of demon."

"Was it Frenchy?" Henry asked. "Frenchy Letters?"

Charlie nodded. "Yeah, and they caught me and chained me up next to that whistling prick at the end of the hall."

"Francesco told me that fairy dust is only used on children. That must be how they keep 'em quiet. They looked like fucking zombies."

Aela clasped her hands in front of her. "If you know where and when it is, you can't let it happen again, can you?"

Boothe pulled Maria to her feet and wrapped his arms around her, pressing her face into his shoulder. "Of course not."

Henry drew a calming breath. "It might be a good way to stick it to the Order while they're busy in Solitude."

"Yeah," Frank agreed. "Split their attention. We just need a plan."

"Don't worry about that. I already have one."

"You do?"

"Yup. Ramiel's gonna dress as Jonnie Bear, then off to the Viazo Grand with a date, ready for action."

"I see," Boothe said. "And the rest of us?"

"We'll meet him at the prison."

Frank shook his head. "No way. That place is on an island. They patrol those waters like it's Vietnam. Between the cops and who knows whatever else they got there, what? We're just gonna walk right in?"

"Maybe. You're a shapeshifter. Why not become someone in the group?"

"I can change my shape, but not my voice to match."

"What about me? Can I change into anyone or just this douche I've been?"

Nadia shook her head. "Frank's the only one who can become anyone."

"Almost anyone. We need to get a good look at them," Frank corrected.

She continued, "But we're kind of limited."

Henry said, "I need to talk to a guy I know."

Frank asked, "Fine, but what about Remmy's date?"

"Oh, I think you can manage."

Frank's jaw fell open. "Me?"

"You *did* get a pretty good look at her when she was kicking your ass."

"The mutant *vagina?*"

"Yeah."

Frank's mouth opened and closed like a fish gasping for water. "Yeah, but …"

"And don't you have some *other* forms you can shift into? Like ones with claws?"

Frank tipped his head to the side and shrugged. "*Yeah*, but …"

"Better decide quick. Tomorrow's only a couple hours away."

Frank's shoulders fell, and he nodded in defeat. "Okay."

"You'll do it?"

"Of *course*, I'll do it. Only because of the children."

"Good enough." Henry turned to Boothe with a smile.

Boothe sighed. "What is it, Henry."

"Nothing, I'm just gonna need your help convincing a guy I know to maybe help us."

"And that guy is?"

"A guy named Mike Stone."

Chapter Twenty-Two

"WHAT ARE WE DOING?" Henry asked.

Boothe reached up and smoothed the jacket on Henry's shoulders. Straightened his tie. "We must look the part."

"Yeah, but if you can just look like whatever you want, why have a closet full of suits?"

"It's the same as traveling. I have to have been there, or I can't teleport to it. Unless I am given the memory, I can't go somewhere if I don't know where it is." He stepped back and straightened his own tie with a smile. "I must have seen myself in this suit in order for *others* to see me in it."

He stepped out of the way, and Henry looked into the mirror at Mike Serafino. It was jarring. Henry almost shifted back to the demon, but he held the image of his alternate form and saw himself nod.

He held up his nubbin, more scarred and twisted in his human form. "Like this shit. If I can make clothes, why can't I make a hand? And if I make clothes and then take 'em off, do they disappear? Did I just take off a piece of *myself*?"

Boothe sighed. "I don't know, Henry. These are things that just *are*."

Henry slid his nubbin into his pocket.

Better keep it there.

"You're saying I should probably get a good long look, so I can do it again when the closet's not around."

"That is exactly what I'm saying, Henry."

"Then I've seen enough." Henry turned away and headed back into the living room.

Aela's were the only eyes watching for his return. She sat on the arm of the couch with her arms crossed. The look he remembered from the attic back in the Forgotten. Careful consideration and mistrust.

Ramiel stood with his arms extended to his sides. He looked at the ceiling with patience while Maria and Nadia flitted around him like moths. Tugging and adjusting, pinning his suit into a perfect fit.

Charlie stood from the table in the kitchenette, pulling a brass phone away from his ear and sliding it into his shirt pocket. He looked at Henry with a nod of approval. "I said what you told me to, and you were right. He said *No*. So, I mentioned our Tracker friend here, and that got his interest back. Not as much as the offer for double time, but either way, he said he'd be here."

Nadia glanced back over his shoulder. "You and Adam *did* destroy his car. He was very angry."

He had turned into the monster with Adam in front of the Burg City Credit Union.

"Francesco's just being a baby," Henry said. "He loves this shit."

Nadia grinned. "He really does. He said the limo business hasn't been the same since Mandyel left."

Boothe placed his hand on Maria's back, and she turned to offer him a kiss. "Good luck, my darling."

Henry turned for a little luck of his own, but Aela still stared with narrow eyes. "I like the other Henry better."

"Well, I can't really walk around outside a police station looking like *Paradise Lost*, can I?"

She shrugged and continued to sit with her arms crossed, like a teenager being forced to join the family party.

Boothe's arm fell across his shoulder.

Henry looked at him from the side of his eye. "Do you need my memory of it, or what?"

"No, thank you. I've actually been near there."

The room compressed to a pinpoint. Henry folded in on himself, and light burst into his eyes. In an instant, they spread through reality to stand across the street from BCPD 6TH Precinct. In the shadow of an awning in front of Desoto's Donuts. The sun burned a line on the horizon as morning raised its head.

Boothe dropped his arm. "What is your next move, dear Henry?"

"I don't know. Charlie said he went from nights to first shift."

Probably to spend more time with Sam. I can't fucking blame him.

"And your plan is to just stand here? Wait for him to notice you, your eyes locking across the distance like fate?"

"I don't know! You get a bunch of monkeys in a room, the one that sounds most confident is almost always the one in charge. This is as far as I thought ahead. It was *your* fault for listening to me."

"It's true. You are the most confident primate I have ever known."

Henry tried to tell Boothe to fuck off, but Stone's

SAWYER BLACK & DAVID W. WRIGHT

brown sedan pulled into the spot right in front of him. Henry's jaw dropped, and he flapped his hand in Boothe's face. He squealed, like a cheerleader freaking out because the quarterback was walking her way. "He just fucking pulled up!"

Boothe shook his head, his face slack with awe. "*Hablando del rey de Roma.*"

"Free will can eat it," Henry said.

Mike Stone stepped out of the driver's side wearing a gray suit. Casual with a black tee underneath. The car rocked as a big square-jawed corn-fed blond man got out on the other side. Stone buttoned his jacket as he shut the door and pointed at the passenger over the roof. He opened his mouth to say something, but Henry interrupted him with a shout.

"Detective Stone!"

Henry had seen enough Hollywood douche nozzles who wielded personality as a weapon. He knew how it put people off their guard. The type of guy that everybody recognized. Loud and full of themselves. Ready to sell.

Stone's head snapped around, but Henry grinned with an artificial joy that reflected the sunlight and stuck his hand out in a Cary Grant shake. Stone's forehead wrinkled, his brain working under the confusion, his feet carrying him up on the sidewalk. His hand rising to return Henry's greeting.

His face lit with recognition, "Serafino, right?" But it was too late. Henry pumped his hand, jerking Stone off balance, and the blond met them at the front of the car with his face clouding in uncertainty.

Boothe touched the blond's upper arm like he was guiding him to his table, and his other hand latched onto Henry's sleeve.

Space and time folded, and the brown sedan twisted

away. The apartment sprang into existence around them, and Henry released Stone's hand as the detective fell to the floor, holding his stomach and retching.

The blond recovered much faster, reaching under his jacket with wide eyes and confused terror.

The point of a black sword scraped the skin under the big man's chin, and he froze. His eyes followed the blade up to the fist, then finally up to Ramiel's face. The angel's eyes swirled with light. The blond dropped his hands and stared.

"Don't you dare spread your wings," Maria shouted. "You'll rip the seams."

Blondie looked at Maria, and his jaw dropped even more.

Stone pushed himself to his knees, and his hand darted for his gun.

The air blurred next to Henry's head, and Charlie Mara streaked by. Stone's jacket blew open from the stiff wind of Charlie's passing, and his hand came out empty. Stone stared at his open fingers, his eyes nearly crossing with the effort to make sense of what was happening.

"This is bullshit!" Frank's voice carried in the sudden silence, and Stone leaned sideways to see past Henry's hip. By the change in his expression from dazed to comically incredulous, Henry knew what he'd see when he turned around.

He cast a look over his shoulder, and Frank stepped into the kitchen. He looked just like her. Down to the smallest detail of Henry's memory. Instead of a pink sports bra, she wore a little black dress stretched tight across her bulging chest and thighs. Black leather boots rising above her swollen calves. Muscles, tattoos, and glittering nails. "I look like one of the Power Puff Girls ate a female Romanian weightlifter."

Frank tossed his head in disgust, and the thick yellow braid looped around his neck like a scarf. He pointed across the room. "Who are those guys?"

Charlie came out of the corner, holding Stone's pistol. He aimed it at Blondie and shrugged in apology. "Can you put your gun on the floor or something? Please?"

Blondie blinked as if coming awake. "Yeah." His hand moved into his jacket as if underwater. "Sure."

He held the gun out, dangling between his thumb and index finger.

Henry looked at Boothe and shrugged. Boothe copied his shrug, and Henry pointed to the gun. Boothe pulled it from the cop's unresisting grasp and set it on the coffee table like it had dirtied his hands.

"Okay." Henry stepped back and swept his arm toward the couch. "You two want to take a seat?"

Stone stood, eyeing Henry like he didn't understand English. Blondie edged away from the sword at his neck, holding his hands up at his shoulders. He crossed between Henry and Stone as Henry eased clear of Ramiel's swing.

Stone lifted his hands and followed Blondie to the couch. They dropped in unison, and Henry jumped with a yelp when a cellphone split the air. A heavy metal song full of drums and screaming. Henry thought it was Blondie's. He looked like he might have been a metal head in his life before being a cop, but Stone pointed to his hip pocket. "You want me to get that?"

"Yeah, just … be cool."

Jesus, Henry. Real fucking smooth.

Stone kept one hand held high while he leaned over and dug into his pocket. He swiped the screen then raised it to his ear with a deep breath. "Yeah, this is Stone."

His eyes darted from face to face. "Nah, I decided to

take Scott down past Bledsoe into the market. Kind of a teachable moment."

Stone rolled his eyes. He was probably taking shit from his boss. That shit was universal.

"Yeah," Stone said with a nod. "No problem."

He pulled the phone from his face with a bitter twist of his lips, then shook his head and slid the phone back into his pocket. "What a cocksucker."

Blondie leaned toward him. "That Murphy?"

Stone nodded. "Of course." He looked at Henry, and he no longer seemed frightened and confused. He raised one eyebrow and pursed his lips. "The fuck do you want, anyway?"

"Hey, don't take your shitty job out on me." Henry pointed to Blondie. "You said you were taking Scott to the market. Is *he* Scott?"

Stone nodded.

"Detective Scott?"

"Sergeant."

"Ah, like a new partner? Showing him the ropes?"

"Yeah, pairing and sharing." Stone leaned forward. "Like I said, what the fuck do you want?"

"Either of you know anybody in Harbor Patrol?"

Stone sat back, the uncertainty returning to his eyes. "Yeah, maybe. So?"

The jacket fell from Henry's shoulders and he reached up to unbutton his shirt. "I'm about to tell you a pretty crazy story." His nubbin bumped his chest, and he looked at Boothe. "I'm not gonna be able ..."

Boothe waved his apology away. "Just get on with it."

"Okay." Henry let Mike Serafino go, and the demon burst out of the suit in his place. Henry remembered to make sure he was wearing the black tee and jeans, and he smiled when he saw the coffee can over his wrist.

And that's how you get to Carnegie Hall.

The detective took it pretty well. The sergeant did not.

His terrified shriek pierced Henry's ears, echoing off the walls. Rebounding from the ceiling. It took him a half hour to stop hyperventilating.

It took Henry what felt like hours to tell his tale.

By the time he got to the second Dark Auction at the Burg City Pen, Stone was leaning forward, his gaze intense and staring. The detective had definitely seen enough to be a believer, but Henry's details about Sam won him over.

Their phones started ringing an hour into the story. An hour later, they were vibrating constantly. Shortly after that, they had to power them down.

Henry leaned back and waved smoke from his face. Nadia had filled the room though only he seemed to notice. Henry jumped up to open a window, and he felt like everyone's eyes were glued to his back. He hadn't tried to make himself look good. In fact, he had probably gone too far in the other direction.

He knew how to tell a story, and even though it was the most important one of his life, he was still waiting for the laughs. Watching their faces and gauging their reactions. Even now, he was performing.

He slid the window open, and a gust of fresh air blew by, sucking the smoke out. It swirled away, and Henry imagined being in an airplane with the clouds flowing by as he ran away to … anywhere. To someplace where he could hide. Where nobody knew him or cared if he lived.

He tore his eyes from the street below and headed for the kitchen. He wasn't thirsty, but he could hide behind the work of filling a pitcher.

"You know, I got suspended because of you," Stone said.

Henry turned with the pitcher in his hand. "Because of *me?*"

"Yeah. The Hooded Angel. I couldn't let it go. I was *obsessed* with finding you."

"What happened?"

"I was on a fast track to Lieutenant before you showed up, and when my son died …" Stone cleared his throat and narrowed his eyes, but true to his name no tears appeared. "My wife was already long gone. Went to her mother's in Kansas. So, I dove into finding you. They passed me over for promotion after promotion. Made me see a bunch of different kinds of therapists. Divorce counselors. Grief counselors. PTSD counselors. Then I met Samantha, you disappeared, and things got better. Kinda returned to normal."

"Yeah, well. I guess I'm sorry." Henry filled the pitcher, lifting it to take a drink.

"I asked her to marry me.

The pitcher fell from his numb fingers, bouncing off the floor and splashing his feet with cold water. He remembered her moving in with him. All of her stuff had fit in the back seat of his Dodge Neon. Even with his TV and shitty laptop, it had still been more than he owned.

They had been in a slow line of cars, waiting to pay the toll so they could cross the South Enon bridge, and he looked down with his stomach dropping out. He didn't have the money to pay. Not a single coin.

He had sat up straight, holding the wheel until he thought his knuckles were going to explode. Sweat burst out in the folds of skin over his gut, and he blurted it out. As unprepared to say it as she must have been to hear it. "Hey, you think we should get married?"

Samantha tilted her head like she needed time to think,

then nodded, her face glowing with a brilliant grin. "Okay."

Henry stared at the pitcher rocking back and forth. Spilling a little water with each change in direction. "So soon?"

"It's been over two years, Henry."

The pitcher blurred as his eyes filled with tears. "What did she say?"

The silence stretched until Henry wanted to scream. Stone sighed, and the couch cushion creaked beneath him as he sat back. "She said 'yes'."

"Congratulations."

The shadow under the dishwasher stretched across the floor. Henry dipped his toe into the darkness, and then he was gone. Screaming through the black that felt emptier the faster he ran.

Chapter Twenty-Three

THERE WAS NOWHERE in the city safe from her memory.

Everywhere Henry went, staring out from the shadows growing smaller with the rise of the sun, he saw Samantha's face.

His vision turned to the hazy red of rage, and people shied from his hiding spot, even though they couldn't see him. A wide berth from a *feeling*, a gut reaction that continuing in his direction meant danger.

His breath steamed, heat rising up to make the shimmering mirage of a distant road in the summer.

She had been his cheat code.

What was he without her?

Nothing.

Without him, she was still Samantha. A beautiful woman. A beautiful *person*.

To share her love with him, so unselfish …

He kept going until he couldn't stand to see the faces of the city anymore. To hear the voices, washing out all the other sounds in a murmuring blur of noise. Pain and sorrow under the joy, like a dark undertow dragging surfers down into the waiting jaws of sharks that circled the freezing depths.

His chest expanded with his heaving breath. Heat shot from his mouth like jets from a grate in winter.

Boothe's apartment was the only place that was clean of her touch. He pressed his fist into his eye. The ridge of the coffee can into the other. He felt the street fold away, turning inside out to become the white living room.

I'll be damned.

He stood leaning in the doorway leading to the bedroom. Everyone else was gone.

"Hey, sailor," Henry said.

Boothe smiled, sympathy and anger. "Hello, Henry."

"The fuck am I supposed to do?"

"I don't know," he said, shaking his head.

"But you know how I feel, don't you?"

Boothe looked down at the floor. "I do."

"Why me?"

"I'm so sorry, Henry. I did what I had to …"

"That's not what I mean."

Boothe looked into Henry's eyes and stood straight. "Then, what *do* you mean?"

"Why am I the one to save fucking *anybody?* I'm just a dead guy too full of hate and selfishness … too blind to …" Tears filled his eyes, and the heat of his anger turned them to steam, sizzling as they rolled down his cheeks. "She was the last of my humanity."

"No."

"Yes! Everybody pushing me to make a fucking decision. *Make a choice, Henry.* Just so's I make the *right* one. But the right one for who? Samantha deserves it. She deserves to live a new life. A *good* life with a *good* man, but I even fucked *that* up!"

"I understand."

The red in Henry's vision deepened. Rage swelled in his chest and brought a dark energy in its wake. His skin was going to burst. He wanted to *fly*.

Boothe's heartbeat pulsed with glowing light. His energy swirling in and out from his center to his fingertips.

Henry was a Paladin. He didn't know what that even meant, but if he unleashed that power into Boothe, he had a sudden certainty that the angel would fall. The realization of his dominion over the being that had been his superior since they'd met brought Henry no pleasure. A quiet sadness dressed like regret.

Henry realized that he had always been better than Boothe.

He had only ever lied to himself.

Henry compressed his rage into a ball, pushing it down to his navel. It spun and twisted, pressing against the confines of his will, and he drew a deep, calming breath. "I believe you, Boothe. At least, I think you *think* you understand. The Order From Chaos has something to do with this Dark Auction nonsense. I'm going to go there, and I won't even ask any questions. I'm going to kill every single fuck that answered that invitation. And then, I'm going to follow Pastor Owen into Hell, and I'm going to save my daughter."

"And then?" Boothe asked.

"I'm going to disappear. Let everybody go on without me, and hopefully, I'll never be asked to make a decision ever again."

Boothe chuckled. A bitter sound without humor. "That's exactly what *I* thought."

Henry growled. "Where is everybody?"

"Waiting in a fishery south of Twyker Island."

"You been there, already?"

Boothe nodded and held out his hand. Henry took it, and the light coming through the living room window was replaced by light pouring through an open overhead door.

Facing the docks, the sun rippled off the waves. Henry squinted into the blaze, and Twyker seemed to float on the waves in the distance. Sprawling rocks and thin grass. The old prison walls capped with shining wire.

"Okay."

Henry turned to the voice. A tall woman dressed in black tactical gear stood in front of a group of men and woman dressed just like her. An AR-15 hung from a sling around her neck. A Burg City Harbor Patrol hat on her head, her dark ponytail poking out of the back. A name badge over her breast pocket under a silver shield. *Hansen.*

"Now I believe you," Hansen said.

Francesco's limo sat in the shadows next to the overhead door. The driver leaned against the front fender. *"There* he is."

Henry grinned. "Hey, Oddjob. It was the double time, wasn't it?"

Francesco grinned, and he tipped his leather driver's hat. "You got that right."

Frank was still shifted. Pattie's muscles rippling as he rocked from foot to foot. Ramiel in his shiny suit, standing with stoic calm.

Aela stood by herself, arms crossed, the black handles of her daggers sticking out from her hips.

Stone's feet scraped on the concrete as he walked up to Henry, ducking his head in apology. "Henry, we gotta talk about your people. They can't be part of this attack."

"Who's in charge, here?"

Stone shrugged and pointed to Hansen.

She stepped forward. "My jurisdiction, so *I'm* in charge."

Henry shook his head. "No, you're not."

"Now, hang on a minute …"

Henry stomped his foot and roared up at the metal rafters. Rage shot hot from his mouth, carrying smoke and embers into the air. He brought his burning gaze down, and Hansen and her men backed up, their eyes wide, weapons rising to the *ready* position.

Henry pointed at Aela and the others. "They go or you and your men will all be dead before you your first casings hit the ground."

Hansen swallowed and stepped forward. "Fuck you. Don't tell me how to run my show."

Henry stepped forward, nodding with respect when she didn't back down. "Is your dick being bigger than mine worth not saving those kids?"

Hansen performed the Holy Sign of the Cross, kissing her knuckles at its close. "Convince me."

One of her men edged up and touched her sleeve. "Jesus Christ, look at 'im, boss. After what they've been saying? *I'm* convinced."

Maria, Nadia, Aela, and Charlie stood in a little cluster off to the side, cigarette smoke swirling around their heads. Charlie crunched into a candy bar. He caught Henry's stare and shrugged with a nervous smile.

Henry shifted his eyes back to Hansen, and she nodded with a single sharp drop of her head. "Fine. What do you propose?"

Henry jerked his thumb at the limo. "Remmy and Frank are gonna ride to the Viazo Grand in style. They'll get transported to the island through a portal, and you'll ferry us there. Remmy will signal us with his holy light once the party starts."

"I don't understand."

"Don't worry, you will. When we hit, I'm gonna get a

running start and kill everything in there. Your job is to shoot anything that's not us, and not Pastor Owen, then get the children to safety."

"Excuse me? We need to *apprehend* these people."

"This isn't your regular assignment. They're not even all human."

"You can't just kill—"

Henry hald up his coffee can, then put it down, and held up his finger on his other hand. "You don't get a say in this. I am going to go in there and kill them all. If you think you can stop me, try. But I'd hate to kill the good guys. All I want is to save the kids and get to Pastor Owen."

He winked at the cops, then turned to Mike. "Can you get my back on this, Stone?"

Mike nodded. "I think we should … yeah, just do what he says."

"How many kids?"

Henry shrugged. "They may have stepped up their game. Thirty? Fifty?"

"What about my men?"

"I don't really care. Nothing matters but those kids. Could you really get up tomorrow and eat breakfast like always, knowing you coulda done something but didn't?"

"Don't fucking lecture me."

"You'd have way bigger problems than the mayor on your hands," Henry said. "Bigger problems than the Order. Maybe you can live with it, but this I can guarantee. Heaven *remembers* the choices you make. Trust me."

Stone asked, "What do you mean? The mayor?"

"Who has the money and resources to cover something like this up?"

"I don't know? Fucking Leonardo DiCaprio?"

"Come on, Mike. You heard my story."

The seconds ticked by in uncomfortable silence. Shuffling feet and loud breathing.

Francesco pushed off the side of the car. "Traffic's gonna make the drive a couple of hours. Better get a move on."

He opened the back door, and Ramiel slid in without a word.

Frank stopped with one foot inside the car. "Henry?" His voice coming from the woman's body. Instead of being hilarious like it should have been, worry wormed into Henry's throat.

Frank swallowed, and the muscles on either side of Pattie's neck flexed and relaxed. "If you see Adam, and I don't get to …"

Henry nodded. "I will."

Frank pressed his lips into a line and ducked into the leather seat. Francesco shut the door and headed to the driver's side with a salute. The rumbling engine echoed off the steel walls, and he pulled away, gravel crunching under the tires.

Henry looked at all the faces staring up at him, then at an imaginary watch, finally calm for the first time all day. "Anybody got any cards?"

THE BOAT ROSE and fell in the troughs of the chop.

Silent on electric motors, the only sounds were of water. The hull's impact against the waves and the spray. Running dark through the night, the lights of the Twyker towers jumped with each surge toward the island.

They were aimed at the utility docks on the east side of the island. Hidden from the city light to a wooden ramp on poles sunk through the muck into the limestone foundation, rock that formed the wall leading up from the water. Hansen knew the patrol schedules. The timing of every boat in the harbor.

She and her men used night-vision to navigate. Henry used his anger to see.

The attendees' glow sparkled through the rock. Single lines of souls collecting to initiate the sacrifice. Gathering in a room in the center of the prison. Surrounded by iron.

The boat swung sideways and drifted against a row of tires hanging over the pier. A jolting impact, then the hands of the Burg City Harbor Patrol tied the boat off before the rebound could send them back into the water. Over the edge in a crouch, and the other boat hit with a squeak of rubber.

Glowing eyes peering out from the dark rock, and the fluttering shape of a goll scampered up the wall.

A lookout? Just one?

Whispered shouts. "The fuck was that?"

"Are we shooting?"

Light bloomed in the distance. Golden shafts bursting into the night. Screams muffled by tons of stone.

"That's it, kids!" Henry bounded over the edge with his feet churning on the pier as Hansen pressed herself against the railing.

"LIGHT 'EM UP!" Hansen screamed, and the night erupted with gunfire.

The goll reached the upper edge of the cliff before catching bullets from every direction. Henry knew they were slippery as fuck and almost as tough, but he wasn't sure a goll could survive that shit.

He ducked as he charged up the ramp, bursting onto the flat plain leading to the stone perimeter — a thick wall topped with chain link and razor wire.

Henry glanced over his shoulder, and his shock nearly broke his rhythm. Aela matched him stride for stride, her hair streaming back, daggers in her hands and teeth bared.

Maria rose from the boat on a shaft of light, glowing, with energy swirling over her heart. Her nude form sparkled, a gold band around her waist and each wrist. She spread her arms, and her hands burst into white fire.

Boothe flew up behind her, his wings churning water into mist. Still a slave to fashion, he wore no armor. A white suit, hanging perfectly, his shoes gleaming. He held a black spear overhead and opened his mouth in a shout that Henry couldn't hear over the wind in his ears.

The Harbor Patrol spread out in a line. Stone and Scott on either end, aiming into the darkness.

Henry faced front and pumped his knees, lowering his head. A step from the wall, he *flared*.

The energy he had held in check, blistering in his gut, spread out with a scream, burning through the air. It hit the mortared stone, and the wall exploded as he stepped into it.

The blur of Charlie Mara's charge sped past his eyes, and they ran through the swelling wave of destruction, carrying themselves into the courtyard, heading for the churning light inside.

Aela's footsteps dug under the patter of falling stones and dust.

White flames burst overhead, splashing against the prison wall. The blocks caved in as if hit by a train. Henry jumped through, pushing into the range as Maria's light filled the air with brilliance, blasting through a haze of dust that moments before was a wall.

Ramiel's voice boomed.

Today is mine to avenge. Your foot has slipped.

He hovered above the floor, his light filling every cell on

the upper tier. Children's terrified faces pressed against the bars. A Hell Hound stood at Ramiel's back, snarling burning pitch into the air. Frank had chosen a pretty good shape to shift into, even though he blistered wherever Ramiel's light touched his skin.

The orgy was in full swing. Naked bodies writhing on the floor. In the center was a stone table, a dirty child held by taut rope, spread out among a circle of flickering candles. A little girl. A man with a dog mask crouching over her, sweat glistening on his back.

Charlie tore through the hole in the wall at Henry's side.

Maria shot over his head like a flaming Spanish arrow with Boothe on her heels. Henry's feet hit the floor, and the naked revelers scattered with screams and wild eyes. Skin bursting as some of their true forms surfaced. Confusion and anger.

Nadia's hot breath heated his shoulder as she landed behind him. She ran forward with her black claws digging through the stone floor, screaming, her raptor's voice ripping through the crowd.

Ramiel raised his black sword overhead.

YOUR DAY OF DISASTER HAS COME!

Time slowed to a fluid crawl, and Henry saw the crowd not as individuals, but as a single entity. Flowing away from the danger at either end of the range, compressing into a swirling mosh pit in the center of the room. The armies of Hell and priests of the Order from Chaos were busy elsewhere. The Dark Auction wasn't ready for this.

It was almost unfair.

Henry found the rhythm of his breath. The growl with every swing. Sucking air with every advancing step.

Flesh parted under his claws. Limbs flew. He darted in

and out, winding his way through the blood and viscera hanging in the air, and he finally knew what it felt like to dance. He reached the table in the center of the room and lifted his hands to free the child, but Aela appeared under his swing, her face covered in scarlet. Her hair slicked back with blood. Her knives parted the ropes before his claws could fall, and he spun to look back the way he had come.

The air was an unholy curtain of red. Glittering as it hung in the slow motion of his vision. He sighed, slamming back into normal time as shock dropped onto his shoulders.

Blood fell to the floor like rain.

Screams and moans. Nadia's shriek as she tore a woman in a lobster mask in half. Frank's Hell Hound growl as he jerked his head side to side, the body in his mouth tearing apart from the force.

Charlie flashed by and drove his shoulder into a woman backpedaling into the wall. The impact split her in half and caved the stone in behind her. She fell into a splattering heap on either side of him, and Charlie stepped back, whipping blood from his hands in an arc that painted the floor at his heels.

Henry turned, and a grim satisfaction rose to compete with his roiling bile.

What have I become?

A whimpering at his knees drew Henry's eyes to the man in the dog mask, the one that had been straddling the kid. He knelt at Henry's feet, hands clasped in front of him and shaking with his sobs. "Please," he whispered.

Aela scooped the child into her arms. The kid squeezed her like she was the only thing in the world, a fierce gesture of relief. She walked away, stepping gingerly through the carnage smeared across the floor.

Dog Man's eyes filled with a terrified light behind the mask. Maria glided over Henry's shoulder. He stepped back, and Maria looked down at Dog Man. Her beauty stung his eyes. Her black hair rippled in the rise of her power. She held her hands out, palms swimming with white fire, and Dog Man reached up and slid the mask from his head.

His face full of awe. Rapturous joy. He took her flaming hands, and the fire shot up his arms, swirling around his head and falling to swallow his body as she pulled him to his feet.

He screamed, and his voice rose to fill the silence with agony far beyond what a normal human could suffer.

Henry turned, swallowing his vomit. The scream rose further, her flames growling and roaring.

But that scream …

He jogged to the steps leading up to the row of cells overlooking the range. He hit the top and leaned out to see the blackened husk of Maria's victim fall to the floor, trailing smoke as it toppled. Charlie Mara rose out of the stairwell, his eyes wide with haunted shock.

Henry spun to the first cell. The child inside backed away, looking at him in terror. That look split his heart. The fear told him that he was indeed a monster. He would never be anything other than the demon he'd become. He swung in anger, and his claws passed through the heavy iron lock as if it were cardboard.

Charlie turned the corner, back in human form. Jolly smiles and outspread arms. He gestured for the child to come out. *He* wasn't a monster, and the child listened. Henry walked down the range, slicing through every lock without looking back.

They hustled the kids through the hole in the wall, herding them like sheep.

Ramiel disappeared under a mound of children, trotting along with them hanging on with both hands. Henry thought he even saw a smile or two. Adam's grin popped into his mind, and he wished he could feel those little arms around his leg.

Pastor Owen wasn't here. So, his work was far from done.

He looked around at the bodies, what felt like hundreds, and he could feel their souls feeding him, fueling him further, making him want more blood to shed.

He saw Aela looking at him and he stopped, knowing that she was looking right into the core of what he'd become, maybe always had been.

He'd never feel Amélie's hug again. Even if they got out of this whole thing alive, she was lost to him. How could she see past what he had become?

Through the perimeter, they ran among the rocks and sparse grass.

Red and blue lights in the harbor. Distant sirens.

They handed the kids off to the waiting arms of the Harbor Patrol, and Stone rushed up. "They were fucking everywhere!"

"What was?" Henry squinted into the darkness, and golls lay scattered around the top of the ramp.

"They just kept coming. Took a whole magazine, and they wouldn't go down. Halfway through, they just took off."

"Where'd they go?"

"You tell me. We got kinda banged up, but Scott took a hit to his side. Got blood all over him."

"Is he okay?"

"No way. He's dying, but he wouldn't let us take him out. Said to wait for the kids. We weren't sure if you were even coming back."

Henry broke into a run, but before he could get there, Aela lowered to her knees. She held the child out, and somebody took her. Henry thought it was Hansen, but he couldn't be sure. His eyes were glued to Aela.

She leaned over Scott's body and pressed her hands to his side. He gasped in pain, and Henry stopped when light sprang from Aela's body. Glowing like she had the night he rejected her in Solitude, the light traced wings behind her back.

Feathers of light rose and fell, like a butterfly on a flower, and the light pulsed down her arms to enter Scott through the wound in his side. He growled, gritting his teeth, and the light flashed before dying, dropping to a single point over her heart. Scott stared at her face with sobbing awe. "You're an angel."

Aela reeled to her feet, catching her breath and shaking her head. "No, I'm *not*."

She stomped up to Henry, not looking him in the eyes, then crossed her arms and stared at his feet. "Take me back home."

Boothe stepped up with Maria back at his side. In her dress. Clean and neat. He looked at Aela with careful consideration and dropped his hand on Henry's shoulder. "She's right. We should go. The police have it under control."

Boothe stepped back, and Henry nodded. He took Aela into his arms. She pressed her face into his chest but didn't return his embrace. He looked at Scott getting to his feet as he thought of Boothe's apartment, and the island disappeared.

The living room unfolded around them. Aela forced herself away, turning and running into the bedroom. She slammed the door, and the apartment filled with the sound of celebration.

Henry was sure they'd done a good thing. The right thing. But looking at all the smiles made him wonder what they would have to pay later.

Chapter Twenty-Four

FRANK WANTED to know if it was on TV. He sat on the edge of the couch with a wild grin, the remote dangling from his fingers.

It was on every channel.

Satanic cult sex traffickers, broken up by Burg City's finest. They didn't get an interview with Stone or Hansen, but they caught Mayor Lucius on the front porch of his mansion, and Commissioner Voight standing behind him in the shadows. The mayor looked like his brother. Slick gray hair, but without the goatee.

"Tonight," the mayor said as if he wasn't complicit in the evil, "working in concert with the Burg City Harbor Patrol, the 6th Precinct of the Burg City Police Department has won a victory for the children of this great city. Heroes, every one."

He looked at the camera, and Henry felt like the man could see him through the TV. "But rest assured, evil shall not win."

Henry wanted to be there whenever this man was brought down.

They left the apartment in small groups. Boothe and Maria first. Nadia and Charlie with Frank tagging along like a small yapping dog, running at their heels for attention.

Ramiel said he was going to look at the stars and pray. He stood and looked at Henry before leaving.

"What?" Henry said. "You don't feel good about what we did?"

"I feel good about the result."

"Just not the methods?"

Ramiel lowered his head. "I wonder if it was truly God's vengeance …"

"Or if it was your own?"

"Yes."

Henry looked at the closed bedroom door. He had hoped that Aela would come out, but seeing her face after she healed Scott, he wasn't sure she'd ever come back out. "Look, I gotta say goodbye to someone. Why don't you go up there and ask Him?"

Ramiel nodded then left by the front door, his head hanging down in thought.

Henry pulled Mike Serafino over his shoulders like he had pulled on the hoodie for so many months, and instead of dropping into the shadows, he thought of his house on La Paz. The front porch with the *Gnome Sweet Gnome* welcome mat, the little cartoon face smiling out from the upper corner.

He had a sudden certainty that his power had grown tonight, perhaps fueled by the carnage. Maybe he could do Boothe's trick and teleport back to his old place.

Might as well try.

The apartment compressed into a dot that resolved into his old front door. It swung open into a foyer full of shadows.

It worked! Fuck yeah!

He looked around, but the neighborhood was dark. A few porch lights. Streetlamps on the corners. He took a hesitant step inside, drawing a breath to shout Samantha's name.

A dark trail on the floor. A faint glimmer of reflected light. Glistening red. His breath left him as he charged inside. Henry's memory put Amélie at the top of the stairs, screaming for him to save her. Samantha standing with horror in her eyes.

Henry dismissed it as he slipped in blood turning into the living room. It bloomed out into a pentagram scrawled on the floor. The furniture had been pushed back to accommodate the artist, and there was so much fucking blood.

If that's her blood, she's dead.

Please be someone else's blood.

Nobody.

His eyes adjusted to the dark, and he searched in every corner. Feeling along the shelves of the entertainment center. Under the cushions. On the coffee table, he found a note taped to the remote control. The remote was a big color touchscreen that some local installer had programmed for him. It could handle the whole house, but he had only ever used it for music, and to flip between Comedy Central and the History Channel.

He snatched the note and held it to his eyes. Words in marker. He could still smell the ink.

Watch the movie.

He tapped the remote and the screen lit in his hands. He closed his eyes, trying to remember the sequence that turned everything on and started the DVD player. He looked down, and the icons swam together. The TV came on with a pop of power. He pointed the remote at the

DVD player, even though he knew it wasn't line-of-sight. He could have pressed play from the bathroom.

The hum of the player as the disc spun up to speed, then the TV brightened on a scene from Henry's nightmares.

Samantha sat at the head of a table. A white gag in her mouth tangled in her black hair. Another strip of white tied over her eyes. Her hands were under the table, but she struggled to prove she was tied. He tossed the remote on the couch behind him and walked to the center of the room as the speakers filled with her whimpering cries.

"Henry."

Pastor Owen's voice. Calm and sympathetic. Soft yet passionate. A voice that had helped him through some of his darkest times. A voice that led Samantha back into the light after Henry's death. It sounded like betrayal and pain. The biggest lie he'd ever been told.

"There was a time when I thought I might try to recruit you. When your lust for killing had so overwhelmed any voice of reason that there was a possibility you might listen to *mine*. As we both know, that never happened. Probably because, and I know you would never admit it, you are a good man. And this woman is the reason. My biggest mistake was not killing her, too. You see, Henry, *you* were at the heart of a prophecy. Well, maybe not the *heart*, for that honor was Adam's, but you were still there. It took me far too long to see that, but when I discovered it, I thought she would be the key to controlling you, and in a way, she was.

"Let no one deceive you by any means, for that day will not come unless the falling away comes first. The man of sin will be revealed, the son of perdition, who opposes and exalts himself above all that is called God or that is worshiped, so that he sits as God in His temple, showing himself that he *is* God.

"Where is Adam now, Henry? In his temple in Solitude. With his congregation, who worship him above Jehovah. Is that not the destiny of the Antichrist?"

Henry remembered Adam's prayer in the forest. Praying not to God, but to himself, like he was reassuring himself of his own power. Henry shook his head, ready to deny the pastor in spite of his own memories, but Pastor Owen continued.

"And I saw one of his heads as if it had been mortally wounded, and his deadly wound was healed. And all the world marveled and followed the beast."

Adam had healed himself after the Lost had attacked, but so what?

I heal all the time.

But then again, I'm a demon.

"Who is a liar but he who denies that Jesus is Christ? Not me, Henry. I have believed my entire life. Devoted my every waking moment to His word. And what does His word tell us, Henry? Every spirit who confesses Jesus Christ has come in the flesh is from God. That's *me*. For the mystery of lawlessness is already at work, but only until the one who now restrains it is removed."

Pastor Owen stepped into view. Wearing the red robe of an Order From Chaos priest, he stood behind Samantha and put his hands on her shoulders. She jumped and cried out. The pastor smiled.

"And that's *you*. The false prophet. But we will not allow the boy to ascend to Heaven, where he will be destroyed. Nor will we let him descend into Hell. Even if the result is that the devil is thrown into the lake of fire and sulfur, where the beast and the false prophet drown, we will not let him be tormented day and night forever.

"Adam's day will not come until the rebellion comes first, and it has already begun. And in that rebellion, the

Lord will not be able to smite him with His breath as is foretold in the bible. Because *we* will have secured Adam's reign. I have prepared for his coming for over forty years, laying his kingdom bare for him, and you have strengthened his resolve. You, his false prophet, and me, his general. His Paladin."

Pastor Owen reached inside his robes and pulled free a knife. Curved with a golden handle, jewels glittered on the hilt. He laid the blade against Samantha's arm. "You will come to me, Henry. In two days, I will summon you. I apologize for making you wait, but my attention is divided at the moment. When you receive my message, I urge you to follow its instructions. I see now that you are the key to my victory, for the boy loves you. He will do whatever you ask. *Whatever* you ask, Henry.

"We will do great things together. And lest you think you will not do as I tell you, if you don't, I will kill Samantha. But first, every Ravager under my control will rape her. Over and over, devouring her soul one bloody bite at a time."

Henry's legs folded, and his knees hit the floor in the center of the pentagram. Even now, she suffered for him.

Pastor Owen turned the knife so the edge was against her arm. "Tell me, Henry. Have you started killing again?"

He swiped the knife in a savage slash that split her arm open below her shoulder. Blood pulsed out to splash on the table, flooding over the pastor's hand. Samantha's scream was severed by the video's death.

Henry tipped his head back and howled. The pentagram burst into flame, fire exploding in a shower of sparks. He drew a breath full of heat and smoke then howled again. His voice cracked and split. But still, he howled. His steaming breath plumed with the smoke.

The flames grew like a beast that swelled as it ate,

growing into an inferno, feasting on every room. His home had betrayed him. Betrayed his family. He fed the flames with his rage, and by the time the fire department arrived, it was a swirling tornado.

He sat in the center of a previous life, and he watched the firefighters prepare their hoses. Scurrying to battle.

Henry pulled the heat into his heart, and the flames died in a rush. Swirling smoke. Frantic shouts. In the sudden darkness, Henry made his escape, roaring into the shadows.

He only had to keep living for another two days.

Chapter Twenty-Five

IN AN ALLEY BEHIND A LIQUOR STORE. *Cane Street Beverage.* Squinting into the bright lights bleeding across the sidewalk.

Numb fingers.

Henry felt the fear and tension from inside. Even through his stumbling rage, it called him.

Two tries for him to pull the Serafino suit on. Hauling it from his fragmenting memories. Samantha's face, smiling at him from across the table. Morning sun shining through the steam rising from her coffee. The thumping steps of Amélie in the hallway upstairs. His daughter's exuberant shout, and he was pretty sure that she'd slid down the banister.

Sam's eyes had risen over his shoulders, and her smile became a grin. Amélie stood in the doorway, her face flush and eyes wide. "Waffles!"

Their last morning as a family.

Samantha looking over his shoulder at the top of the stairs. The gun digging into the back of his head.

The blood flowing down her arm.

Henry dried his cheeks on his jacket sleeve and emerged from the shadows. An empty sidewalk and a single car rolling by, bass shaking the storefront windows. A bell jangled overhead as he opened the door. The reek of disinfectant. The tang of panic in the air.

"*As-salaam-alaikum.*" The voice was pinched, as if speaking caused him pain.

Henry turned to the man behind the counter. His jaw was set in a forced smile, standing with his hands behind his back. His face was ravaged with deep acne scarring, and his scrappy beard stuck out like a pine tree. His eyes shifted to the side and back.

Henry followed the line of the man's eyes, and two men stepped out from behind a Red Bull cooler at the end of the aisle. White men with cruel faces that looked like Pastor Owen's. Another man walked out of a door behind the counter. A third white man, taller than the other two. Owen Number Three. He sidled up to the clerk, and Henry tasted more fear as the cashier inhaled deep and closed his eyes.

Henry waved. "*Alaikum-salaam.*"

"What are you doin' in here, man?" Owen One said.

Henry pointed to the store's interior. "Well, see, I wanna get super drunk, and this place happens to have the exact thing I need to make that happen, so …"

"Man, shut the fuck up."

"You asked! I'm just trying to have a conversation."

Owen Two pulled a gun. "Have a conversation with *this*, bitch."

"Oh, I get it. This is a robbery."

"That's right." Owen Two shifted his pistol toward the clerk. "We're robbing this motherfucker right here."

Owen One slid a gun from the back of his waistband. "You might as well give us all *your* money, too."

Henry didn't care what Owen Three was doing. He pinched the bridge of his nose and closed his eyes. "You know what? I'm not really in the mood for this shit tonight, guys. I'm just gonna kill you. How's that?"

He opened his eyes. The Owens stared at him as if were a talking bug. Before they could gather whatever brains they had for a comeback, Henry stepped out of Mike Serafino, and the demon spread his hands. "Ta-da, motherfuckers!"

Owen One opened fire, his tripping feet carrying him back. Screaming.

Henry walked forward with a smile, steam jetting from his nostrils. Bullets ripped into him, struck his chest, his neck. Black blood splattered out.

Over the screams and thunder, Henry's own laughter sounded cruel in his ears.

Owen One fell on his ass as Owen Two dove into the aisle. Henry swung, and his claws tore the gun away, along with the hand holding it. Owen One screamed and looked at the flowing stump with horror. His blood spurted up to mix with Henry's as it dripped down his arm. Henry kicked the fucker in the shoulder, laying him out flat. He dropped a knee on the center of Owen One's chest, and he wrapped his hand around the asshole's throat.

He bent to stare into the terror in the guy's eyes as he squeezed. His fingertips met through his fleshy neck. Blood sprayed into his face and into his open mouth. The life-force rose up and Henry breathed him in. It wasn't enough.

He jumped up and launched himself down the aisle.

Owen Two scrambled back. A frantic crabwalk, the gun clacking and sliding along the tile floor.

Henry jumped, spreading out and falling, then he dropped his fist onto the guy's face like a red hammer.

His head exploded like a ketchup packet under a boot heel. Spreading to either side, splashing up on the pork rinds and corn nuts. Covering Henry from forehead to belly button. The guy's life-force joined the other.

Henry still wasn't satisfied.

He stood and turned to face the clerk and Owen Three. They stood pressed against each other, their horror bridging the gap between race and religion. The clerk whispered. *"A'oodhu bi kalimat-illah il-tammati min ghadabihi wa 'iqabihi."*

Henry broke into a run, and the clerk's whisper became a shout. *"Wa min sharri 'ibadihi wa min hamazat al-shayateeni wa an yahduroon!"*

Henry leaped over the counter.

Owen Three stepped around the clerk, a silent scream stretching his lips, and the knife he'd been holding to the clerk's back rose up. His head split apart under Henry's claws, and the knife went into Henry's chest to the hilt.

His weight crushed Owen Three against the wall of cigarettes behind the counter. The knife twisted from his death grip, and Henry spun away, doubling over the blade that hung between his ribs.

It pressed against his lungs, scraping blood into his breath. He left it there as he pulled in the swirling energy that had once made a man and limped out from behind the counter. His feet slid in the blood, and he threw his arms out for balance. The clerk whimpered behind him, and he didn't bother to tell the guy that it was all okay.

Because it wasn't.

Behind the loose bottles of whiskey, he found it by the case. A bottled-in-bond rye. He stood with the box under his arm and walked toward the back of the store. Into the shadows through a dark doorway.

He spread through Burg City, stretching from the dark

of a back doorstep to the shadow under a dumpster to the gap between a pair of abandoned warehouses. Faster than thought, Henry shot up his building and landed on the roof. He emerged from a corner hidden from the stars by a corrugated overhang, then slid down to sit with his back against the wall.

He propped his elbow on the booze and dug his claws through the box looking for a bottle.

"You talk to God, yet?"

Ramiel sat with crossed legs, looking up at the sky. "I did."

Henry stuck the bottle between the vice of his thighs and spun off the cap. "What did He say?"

"He set my heart at ease. There are often no answers to the most difficult questions during strange days."

"Uh-huh." Henry brought the bottle to his lips, wincing as the blade ground against bone in his chest. Blood welled from his right eye, dripping onto his hand as he took a deep drink.

Must have got shot in the face, too.

He sighed in pleasure and tipped his head back. "Well, I got a question for you. What do you say?"

Ramiel lowered his gaze, eyes widening at the sight of Henry's blood. The knife sticking out, bobbing with his breath. "What is your question?"

"Can you heal me?"

The angel shook his head. "I cannot."

"But you can end my suffering, right?"

"Yes."

"Because it wasn't you that healed me in Solitude, was it? It was *Aela.*"

Ramiel nodded, lowering his eyes. "She asked me not to tell."

"Oh, man. Now you're a *liar*, too. I guess I'm a bad influence."

Henry drained the bottle and tossed it to the side. It didn't break, rolling in a crooked spiral to rest on the roof's edge. "It doesn't matter. I don't have much time left."

"What does that mean?"

Henry opened another bottle. "It means, ol' Remmy ol' pal, that I'm going to get as drunk as I can while I wait for Pastor Owen to *summon* me. This shit'll probably heal itself, anyway. Right?"

"What has happened, Henry?"

Henry lowered the bottle, tears mixing with the blood that poured from his eye. "I am the false prophet. The Antichrist's general has kidnapped my wife, and he's going to kill her if I … I don't know … build the church of the beast."

"When was this?"

"Just now. He's gonna call me in two days. If I don't do what he wants, he'll throw her into the asylum with ten thousand maniacs. Fooling myself, really. Thinking she was safe."

Henry grabbed the knife handle and gave it a twist as he pulled it out. Black blood filled his lap. Clogged his throat. He took the energy from the lives he had ended at the liquor store and thought of a better Henry.

"Would you look at that?" He emptied the second bottle and threw it away. It clinked against the first one. He reached in for another, with a hand clean of the blood. And he whispered, "Good as new."

"What would you have me do?"

"I'm not your fucking boss, man. *You* figure it out."

"You are wrong, Henry. I have sworn my life to you. I am your vassal. Sworn to obey you, though you have yet commanded me anything."

Henry ran the tip of the bottle in the shape of a cross through the air. Ramiel's flat stare, hard at the edges. Sad underneath. Whiskey splashed Henry's feet. "I doth command you to fuck off. Fly hence and find the pastor, that I may smite him." The bottle cracked against his fangs as he tried to take another drink. He giggled, choking and sputtering on the burning liquid. He caught his breath and tried again. This time the booze made it down his throat. Another empty bottle.

Ramiel stood, the light growing over his heart to stab Henry's eyes.

Henry squinted and giggled again. "Smite him … with my *dick!*" The light continued to swell, blinding Henry with shimmering waves of gold. He heard Ramiel's wings. Felt the air drying his tears, blowing the dust into swirling eddies.

He couldn't get a deep breath. Couldn't lift his arms. Henry slid sideways down the wall as Ramiel rose into the sky. His light shrank with distance, and Henry's cheek scraped against the cool roof.

I was only kidding.

Drool spread out in a sticky puddle, and Henry passed out.

Chapter Twenty-Six

Yellow light pounded against Henry's eyelids. Heat spreading across his face. Henry cracked his eyes open, and the sun hung directly overhead in the center of his field of view.

The cracks in his lips stung as he worked up enough spit to swallow. He sat up, and his head pounded with the change in elevation. Henry groaned, shielding his eyes with his nubbin and holding his stomach. His claws tangled in his shirt, tearing holes as he stood. Swaying, he pushed off the wall behind him.

The sun beat on the top of his head, but the only shadow was the small blob under his feet. Henry thought about the apartment below, but when space began to fold around him, vomit flooded his mouth. He slapped his hand over his lips and bent over, banishing the image of the apartment from his mind.

I guess I'll take the stairs.

The stairwell was cool and dark. Henry took each step while hanging onto the rail like Abraham and his cane.

Lights in the short white hallway stabbed with beaming

shards. He squeezed his eyes shut and felt along the wall for his front door. The apartment was blessedly dark. The blinds drawn. Quiet.

He shuffled to the refrigerator and reeled back from the light.

The fuck am I doing?

The pitcher was on the counter. He needed some water. He swung the door shut, and black blood glistened on the floor. He snatched the door back open, letting it swing all the way out, and the blood led to his feet. Footprints.

He spread his fingers over his chest. Down his arms. He blinked the grit from his eyes and shook his head. The footprints ended a few feet inside the front door. The edge of a pool. So much blood. He rushed to the entry and snapped on the foyer light. The puddle spread from under the chair facing the couch in the living room. A slumped figure. Wings torn and bloody. Blackened and charred.

Ramiel!

Henry rushed away from the open fridge. His feet hit the puddle of blood, and they came out from under him. He smashed onto the floor with a shuddering crash, floundering over to his hands and knees. He lunged around the chair, and drew back in shock.

Ramiel's ribs protruded through a burned hole in his chest. The mangled fingers of his left hand rested in his lap. Gashes crisscrossed his legs, some showing bone. His swollen face, burned and bloody, hung forward. The entire chair shimmered with black blood.

"Help!" Henry shouted. "Somebody!"

He raised his hand, but drew it back, unsure of where to touch. Henry turned his face up to the ceiling. "BOOTHE!"

Ramiel's eyelids fluttered, and the right one rose to

reveal a battered black eye, filling with blood. "I found your pastor."

Henry leaned forward and dropped his nubbin on Ramiel's shoulder. He put his hand against the angel's cheek, and Ramiel rested his head in Henry's palm.

"Ah, fuck, Remmy. I didn't mean for you to get yourself *killed*. I was … just what the fuck did you think you were doing?"

"He is with the mayor." Ramiel's voice sounded thick and wet. He gasped in a bubbling breath. "In his mansion. By a park with a stream. Lovely …"

Henry turned to shout over his shoulder. "Is anybody still fucking here? I need some *Goddamn* HELP!"

He stood, and dizziness hit him like a rocking subway. He fell back to his knees, using the arm of the chair for support and closing his eyes.

"Jesus, fuck."

He fought to calm his gagging throat. His thoughts ran to Ramiel's words.

"The taxes paid for that golf course … right next to the estate. The fees are fucking astronomical. It's got a …" Henry swallowed and caught his breath. Panic was spiking with every beat of his heart. "Nature reserve …"

The bedroom door clicked open, and Aela peeked through the gap. Her eyes widened. She threw the door open and ran to Henry's side. "What happened?" Her eyelids and cheeks were red and raw. Puffy from crying.

"I don't know. I told him to find Pastor Owen, and he just took off."

Ramiel nodded. "I fought many. My net was very full."

"Why did you ask him to do that?"

Henry pulled away and faced her. "I didn't ask him to do *this*. I was drunk. Pastor Owen has Samantha, and he's gonna kill her."

"Your wife?" Aela looked down at the floor.

"Yes, my fucking wife. Ramiel said it was *you* who healed me in Solitude."

She sat back on her heels, and her shoulders fell.

Henry stabbed a finger at the bleeding angel. "Heal *him*. Please."

"It hurts," she whispered.

"Please."

Ramiel smiled.

Blood dribbled from the corner of his mouth. "Do not fret, child. Do not blame yourself, for He chose us in Him before the creation of the world to be holy and blameless in His sight." The angel reached out and patted the air, his hand seeking her touch.

He can't fucking see!

Henry took Ramiel's hand, and the angel's smile became a grin, his teeth soaked with black and lips cracking. "Do not mourn for me. *No* man can lay a foundation that has *already* been laid by our Father. Instead, rejoice and be glad, for my reward in Heaven will be great."

"Okay." Tears streamed from Aela's eyes. She rose on her knees and put her hands on the Tracker's forearm. "I'll do it."

Ramiel shooed her hand away, looking for her face like a man staring out of the dark. "Nay, save it for another. I will live on in His memory, even though I die in your hearts." He took a small gasping breath. "Henry, my friend. I will now do as you asked …" Another gasp, his head falling back down, the smile still spreading. "I … I will fuck off."

Ramiel sagged forward in the chair. A spot of light formed over his heart. Swirling and growing, it spread to fill his body from toe to wingtip. A glow grew on the ceiling to match the light below. It spun, swelling into a cone that stretched into the infinite ether above.

The angel of light that settled over the angel of flesh rose into the air, and the flesh crumbled to dust.

Ramiel paused before rising into the tunnel of light. He looked down at Aela and Henry still kneeling on the floor, and he spread his arms.

Even you, a demon created through careless sin and design, and you, an angel shrouded in flightless wings of pain and doubt. Your citizenship is of Heaven. Paladin and Healer. There is no greater proof of His design than in your union.

You are everything good for doing His will.

He raised his face, pointing the light of his gaze into the light of his ascent, and then he was gone with a flash and a clap of thunder.

Henry leaned into Aela's shoulder. "Jesus, I barely *knew* that bastard."

Aela nodded into his chest. "Why does it hurt so much, then?"

"I don't know. I can't fucking think. How am I supposed to make sense of that shit?"

The compression of air at his back, and Maria's gasp foretold Boothe's arrival.

About time, although I don't know what he could've done.

"What is this?"

Henry told them about his trip to his house. The video. The liquor store.

Aela told them about Ramiel.

Maria sat on the edge of the couch, smoothing her skirt. "And what will you do now, Henry?"

Henry dropped to his ass and leaned back against the chair still soaked with an angel's blood. The pain in his head spiked with every move, and his heart refused to quit galloping. "I'm gonna burn that place down and kill everyone inside."

Maria smiled, leaning back in satisfaction. "Good."

Aela stood and pointed to the empty chair. "Henry, look."

Henry struggled to his feet, catching his breath once upright, swaying as though pushed by a breeze. He looked at the chair, and the handle of Ramiel's black sword poked above the back cushions. The blade that had killed Mandyel's golem.

Struck down dragons.

Saved his life.

"Take it," Aela said.

Bitterness flooded Henry's mouth, and he shook his head. The thought of holding it disgusted him. *Offended* him. "Fuck no. *I'm* not touching that thing."

"It is an angel's blade," Boothe said.

Aela looked back and forth between the demon and the angel, her eyes settling on the latter. "Then, *you* take it."

Boothe shook his head. "I am not that angel. But he left it for a reason, don't you think? You should take it."

She threw her hands up in defeat, and her face crumpled in anger.

"Everybody knows what I should do. Keep telling me what's best for me. *Fine.* My grandmother was an angel. I guess so am I? Fine."

She shook her head and snatched the sword from the chair. It swirled with creeping black energy, and wings of light erupted from her back, charged with fire. Her eyes widened, staring into a space Henry couldn't see. Her head tipped, listening to a voice Henry couldn't hear. Jealousy twisted in his gut, and he looked away.

The tip of the sword dug into the floor at her feet, and

when he looked back, she was just Aela. Tired and scared. Leaning on the hilt of a black sword with tears in her eyes.

The front door exploded open, and Frank strolled in with an armful of junk food. Bright packaging, crinkling with every step. He slurped from a straw stuffed into the biggest slushie Henry had ever seen. A *bucket* of frozen sugar. He crossed to the large sliding window between the living room and bedroom, juggling snacks to get a free hand for the blinds.

Light flooded the apartment. He dug out a red rope of licorice out and flipped the end into his mouth. He turned and froze, the licorice hanging from blue-stained lips.

"Hey guys," he said. "What's going on?"

Chapter Twenty-Seven

THE CITY'S sorrow continued to batter Henry's senses. He saw fire and smoke wherever he looked, and his head split with throbbing pain. It was hard to concentrate on anything but the lure of so many souls in need of punishment. Despite his resistance, he had to *feed* soon.

Henry sat next to Frank on the couch, gobbling popcorn and Twizzlers, watching coverage of the Siege of Twyker.

Sounds like a fucking Lord of the Rings book.

They'd been at it for hours. The sun was setting, turning the walls and floor purple as it sank. "It's like we're watching the OJ coverage."

Frank nodded, pulling on the straw digging into the bottom of his slushie. He was nearing the end, and the straw glugged in between slurps. He released it with a loud smack of his lips, his wide eyes still fixed on the TV. "I had a thing for Marcia Clark back in the day. I think it was the perm. I always thought she'd be dirty behind closed doors, you know?"

"I guess."

Frank tipped his giant cup at the TV, pointing with the straw. "Uh-oh, we got a *breaking news* update."

It was about Mike Stone. His Burg City ID picture hanging over the shoulder of a serious blonde with a tight sweater fitted for ratings. His smiling face replaced with that of his younger version, stern and unforgiving in a military dress uniform. Metals gleaming on his chest.

A third picture of a bearded Stone under a mountain of military gear and a campaign hat. Sand from a middle eastern desert.

"Holy shit," Henry said. "No wonder Samantha fell for this guy. He's a fucking badass."

Frank worked a final echoing slurp from the bottom of his cup then abandoned it on the coffee table. "I know. I think *I'm* about to have sex with him."

Henry focused on the blonde's mouth, her perfect teeth flashing the impossible white of modern dentistry.

"... in stable condition at Riverside South, he has been identified as one of the Heroes of Twyker Island, saving over twenty-five children from a satanic cult practicing their religion in the abandoned Twyker Penitentiary.

"He was wounded during an attack on the mayoral estate early this morning that left several dead and parts of the estate damaged before the fire was put under control. Police aren't releasing details about whether or not this attack involved the cult, where the mayor is now, or if the mayor is among the injured or dead, saying an investigation is under way and more details will be released later."

The camera angle changed, and she turned to match it. A new picture over her shoulder. This one of Henry in a stained hoodie, bending into the shadows. "You may remember Detective Stone from his public investigation of the so-called 'Hooded Angel,' a Burg City vigilante that saved victims with bloody justice."

Another picture of Henry. This one his professional black and white head shot. Vague surprise, like he couldn't figure out why his picture was being taken.

I kinda liked that one.

"Detective Stone has *also* been flirting with Hollywood, often seen with the widow of Henry Black, beloved comedian murdered in his home in the El Matanso suburb."

Henry's face was replaced with the graphic of a house fire.

"The very same home that burned to the ground last night. There were no victims recovered from the fire, and foul play *is* suspected. Attempts to find Samantha Black have been unsuccessful. The Black's daughter was also murdered in the home invasion that claimed her father's life. Connections are currently under investigation."

That's it?

"They couldn't even use *her* picture? They just stuck my face up there and instead of being her own fucking person, she's the *wife* of some dead guy. Amélie is the *daughter* of some dead guy? Fucking assholes. They're worth more than just being *lucky* enough to be associated with *me*."

I was the lucky one.

Henry jumped up, kicking the coffee table. Candy wrappers scattered. Tortilla chips flew. Rage filled his chest, and his headache blustered away like brittle leaves.

"Boothe!"

Frank stood, watching Henry pace with staring eyes. "What are you doing?"

"Getting ready."

Boothe emerged from a blink in space, standing with his hands behind his back. "I can't just drop everything and come whenever you call, Henry. I have things to do."

"Like what."

He tipped his head with a shrug. "At the moment, nothing."

"Then why are you bitching?"

Boothe clenched his jaw, his eyes narrowing. "What do you want, Henry?"

"I'm not gonna wait for Pastor Owen."

"Then what are you going to do?"

"You know where the mayor's estate is?"

"Yes."

"Can you open a portal there?"

"Knowing where it is and having been there are two different things."

"You've never been there?"

"Not exactly."

"The fuck does that mean?"

"It means I've played golf there."

"Golf?"

"Yes, Henry. Golf. As a man of culture and refinement, I often find myself in situations—"

"Sure, sure. Whatever." Henry flapped his hand for silence. "I've played it, too. As a man *pretending* to be cultured and refined, I've shaken a lot of dirty hands. Anyway, the ninth hole is practically in his back yard. Can you open a portal right on the tees?"

"Yes, I can. Now, why do you want me to do that?"

"You ever been to the hospital?"

Boothe reached up and covered his eyes. "Which one, Henry?"

"Riverside South."

"No, I have not. Have you?"

Looking at Samantha through the window. Tubes in her nose. Her hand strapped to the rails after she tried to kill herself. Pain caused by the Order. By Henry himself.

My fault.

"Yeah, I've been there." He spun around and entered the bedroom.

"What are you going to do?"

Henry paused with his hand on the doorknob. "I'm gonna get everybody I can find with a little hate in their hearts, and we're gonna tear that mansion to the ground."

Boothe nodded. "That will actually please Maria very much."

"Then go get her. I'll be back in a couple of hours."

Boothe disappeared in a bending twist of light as Henry turned and entered the bedroom.

Aela sat on the bed with Ramiel's sword on her knees. Looking down at her hands, her eyes still red.

Henry resisted the urge to sigh and roll his eyes. "You been in here crying this whole time?"

"Yes."

"You done?"

"Yes."

"Good. Get your shit and let's go, but leave the fucking sword. I don't think the hospital will like that."

She looked up in confusion, and Henry pulled Mike Serafino out of the dark, dressed in the good old hoodie and jeans.

Aela pulled back with a sneer, turning to put the sword onto the bed. "Where are we going?"

"I told you, to the hospital. Hurry up."

Henry returned to the living room, pacing behind the couch, staring out the window at the darkening night.

Frank came around the couch to stand in Henry's path. "It's really happening, isn't it?" He slid his hands into his pockets. "We're finally getting to the end, aren't we?"

Henry nodded. "I think so."

"What do you want me to do?"

"You know where Nadia and Charlie Mara are?"

Frank shook his head. "No, but I can find them."

"Then go find 'em."

Frank nodded and reached into his shirt pocket. He pulled out his sunglasses and dropped them on his nose. Opened his mouth as if he was going to say something, but then snapped it shut and spun on his heel.

He stepped into the hall at the same time Aela exited the bedroom, and the doors shut in unison.

Henry almost told her to leave the daggers, but he shrugged and offered his hand. "You ready?"

She took it, shaking her head. "I don't think I'll ever be ready for anything ever again."

"Good."

Henry dropped into the shadows, dragging her with him as she clung to his shoulders and moaned into his neck. They spiraled through the darkness, through the lightless corners and alleys. Up the concrete block wall of the hospital. The ledge outside the windows where Samantha had slept. Where Henry had been haunted by his daughter, waiting for his wife to wake up.

Aela caught her breath and looked over Henry's shoulder. She gasped and pressed her face into his chest, clutching and digging with her fingers. He looked over the side with a chuckle. Lots of air before hitting the pavement, but he knew it wouldn't work. He leaned against the wall and peered into the window. An old woman, her face furrowed with pain, her fear pecking at the window like a bird.

Nope.

Henry dropped in and out of the shadows to the next window.

Aela caught her breath but made no more noise, clinging to him with trembling terror.

He worried they would have to figure out how to navigate the brightly lit corridors, then he finally found him. Lying in bed, surrounded by cops, Mike Stone stared out the window with hooded eyes, his pale face slack and gray.

"Well," Henry said. "Let's do this."

He pulled Aela into the dark and swam up into the shadows in the corner of Stone's room. The corner next to the curtain and the beeping IV machine.

Everyone froze at the sudden appearance of a stranger with a blonde woman hanging from his shoulders, but Sergeant Scott jumped up and rushed toward Aela. Henry pushed her off his feet, and she drew back with a hiss as Scott wrapped her in a hug.

She held her arms away from him as he murmured in her ear, but as the moments passed, and he wasn't letting go, her arms fell to hug him back.

Hansen stood on the other side of the bed. She looked even rougher out of uniform, her hair in a messy ponytail, her hands covered in bruises and cuts.

Henry recognized a few of the other faces, but he was fixed on the pair men at the foot of the bed. Dressed in nearly identical ensembles — jeans, tight tees and curled baseball caps. They were bearded, thick, and quietly menacing.

Hansen's eyes left Aela and Scott's embrace, then settled on Henry in confusion. He pointed to himself and shrugged. "This is how I look when I'm trying to fit in. I'm still Henry."

She narrowed her eyes and said nothing, leaning back and crossing her arms.

Scott pulled out of Aela's arms, turning to the room with teary eyes. "This is the angel that saved my life."

Aela hugged herself, rubbing her arms. "I'm not an angel."

"She healed me."

Henry stepped out of the corner. "What's wrong with him?"

Scott looked at Henry as if he were transparent, like he couldn't focus his eyes. "Shot and burned, mostly. A bunch of broken ribs. Bullet in his right lung. They had to re-inflate it twice, and now there's a tube in his chest, sucking the blood out. Stabbed through the thigh, through the femoral artery. They say he'll probably lose the leg. Burns on his other leg up to his hip. Once he's more stable, they're gonna prep him for grafts. Probably take the skin from his back."

"What happened?"

Scott looked at the floor. "We followed you."

"How the fuck did you do that?"

"Well, we didn't really *follow* you. Mike remembered following you last year to your apartment over in Martins-burg. He was sure that's where you lived, but after that night, you never came back. We didn't find you *this* time, either, but we saw light on the roof and the angel fly away." He turned to Aela. "Was it *you*?"

She shook her head. "I'm not an angel."

Henry was sick of her denial. "You followed him to the mayor's mansion?"

"That's right, But I don't know what happened. He made me wait in the car while he checked it out, but then the fucking place just about exploded. I'm talking every color you could think of, like fireworks. I jumped out and it was *Saving Private Ryan*. So much screaming. And the angel shot straight into the air like a rocket. Stone came stag-gering out of the shadows, smoking and bleeding. I brought him here, but the mayor's security detail was already at the doors. Not the city ones, but his private assholes, and they were throwing their weight around. They took off with the mayor before we could stop him."

Henry was going to ask why they didn't just go arrest the man following the rescue of the children, but he knew the answer. They couldn't just arrest the man on his word that he was part of this big conspiracy. They needed to actually do an investigation. Still, they should've at least had *someone* watching the mayor and the fucking pastor. Maybe Sam would be safe now.

Hansen dropped her arms and leaned on the bedside rail. "That's when Scott called me, and we made it clear that he was the Hero of Twyker Island like they keep saying in the papers and on TV. Rolled heavy with my boys from the harbor and half the 6th. Locked the whole floor down."

Scott nodded. "Yeah, there's something not right about this shit. Not fucking right."

Stone muttered something behind his oxygen mask, writhing in pain, his face twisting. Condensation on the inside of the plastic cup covering his mouth and nose was tinged with red.

The two bearded men both reached down, placing a hand on each of Mike Stone's feet, and the detective settled back into the pillow.

Scott looked at Aela bending at the knees to lower himself into her gaze. "Are you here to heal him?"

She looked at Henry, her eyes full of panic, but he stared back and said nothing. She swallowed and nodded. "Yes, I guess I am."

Chapter Twenty-Eight

AELA FLICKED her hands at the floor as if she were throwing something away. Scott stepped out of her way and she walked to Stone's side. His hand reached out for her, and she took it. Then she raised his fist to her lips, kissed it, pressed it back into the cushion beside him, and placed her other hand on the seeping bandage over the tube dangling from his chest.

Her fingertips pulsed with light. Tears tracked down her cheeks, glistening as her hand blossomed into white fire.

Stone stretched under her touch. The muscles bulged in his neck.

Aela grabbed the tube, pulling the tape from his skin like releasing Velcro. He hissed in pain, his heart monitor ringing out in alarm. The light grew to a blinding flame that spread through Stone's torso.

The tube came free with a wet popping sound.

Stone screamed.

Two burly bearded men who were in the room, and not in uniform, started toward Stone. "What the hell?"

Henry wasn't sure if they were cops or worked at the hospital, but he wasn't going to let them interrupt. He threw Serafino into the dark and stepped in to intercept them with a growl, his claws ready.

Stone's scream died with a gasping moan.

The bearded men halted with unbelieving eyes tracking up the length of Henry's body.

Aela's healing light grew even brighter, and Henry's skin tightened across the back of his neck. The light reflected in every eye. Monitors shrieked. Her wings spread, feathers of burning light, and Stone bucked under her hand.

Bones mended.

Burns cooled.

A final groan through the detective's gritted teeth, and the light died.

Aela collapsed to the floor, and Henry spun, catching her before her head made contact.

He pulled her to the chair under the window, setting her in his lap and bending over, pressing his lips to her forehead. Her breath fluttered into his face. She looked into his eyes and smiled.

He shook with a joy that teased laughter.

Scott squatted next to his legs and looked at her face. "Is she okay?"

Henry grinned and shook his head. "Oh, yes. She's fine."

Stone threw the sheet aside and bounced out of bed as if his mattress was on fire.

The room's door popped open and slammed into the wall. One of the Harbor Patrol officers from the Siege on Twyker rushed in. "Fucking nurses are coming like it's the Boston Marathon."

Stone turned while he pulled sticky pads from the hair

in his chest. Snatching the IV from his arm. "Keep 'em outta here!" He bent down and jerked a gray plug from the wall. Monitors trailed off, screens flickering to black.

"What?" The man stared at Stone with a hanging jaw.

Hansen turned and knifed her hand at the hallway. "You heard him! Keep 'em busy."

"You got it, boss." He whipped around, slamming the door shut behind him. Hansen leaned against the handle.

Stone tore the hospital bracelet off with an annoyed grimace, then dropped to his knees next to Scott and looked at Aela. "He was right. I don't give a shit what you say or think or *feel*. You're an angel. You healed me. I saw you shining out in the sky like a bird made of fire. A beautiful bird ..." Tears found his eyes. "A bird with sad eyes. Always flying away."

Aela reached for him, and just like *she* had, he brought her hand to his lips for a kiss. "Detective Stone?"

"Yes?"

"Put your pants on."

He dropped her hand and looked down with an embarrassed flush. Then back at her with a grin. "Right."

Shouts from the hallway as he jumped up. Knocking on the door followed by pounding. Hansen held the handle firm. Shouts receded.

Aela pushed from Henry's lap and stood. "It always hurt before. It felt *good* to heal him this time. I don't understand."

"I know when I do shit, it's like finding that thing you were made for, and doing it. Contentment?"

She nodded with an empty expression. He stood, lifting her to her feet, then stayed behind her with his hand on her shoulder.

"Henry," Stone said, sliding the other leg into his pants and tipping his head to the two bearded men handing him clothes from a duffel. He pointed to the one with sandy blond hair, then the black streaked with gray. "This is Howser and Weego. Friends from Afghanistan."

Henry waved. "They look like southern Ohio to me."

Stone barked laughter and pulled a T-shirt over his head. "Don't let that fool you. Howser's an electrical engineer, and Weego's a neuroscientist. They helped a guy start a private security firm for a bio-research company. Called it Dark Water before they turned independent and moved out to Seattle."

"Kinda far from home, huh?"

"They were here for me, doing a fundraiser for the Burg City VA. Traumatic brain injury research." He spoke like an announcer at the end of a commercial. Cramming as many words in as possible.

"Mike!" Henry shouted.

Stone looked up from tying his shoe. "Yeah?"

"They got Samantha."

"What?"

"They took her, and they burned down my house. If I don't show when he calls, he'll kill her."

"Who, Pastor Owen?"

"Yeah."

"He's the reason my son died."

"I know."

"Your daughter."

"I know that, too."

Stone threw his hands out in frustrated disgust. "I *liked* that house."

You and me both, and only one of us paid for it.

"I need your help."

Stone smiled, his lips pressing into a hard line. "You have it."

Henry sighed, relief loosening his knees. He held onto Aela to stay upright. "Thank you."

"What are we gonna do?"

"We're gonna play a round of golf."

Stone grinned with a knowing nod. "I like that. What clubs are we gonna use?"

"We need a full set?"

"I don't think so. Just the big ones. The drivers."

Henry grinned with him. "Then, how about we meet at the clubhouse for drinks? Say midnight?"

"You got it." Stone turned to Howser and Weego. "Did you bring the wagons?"

His two bearded friends traded a glance then nodded in unison. The blond, Howser, turned back and smiled. "You know it."

"Good. There's a fire station about three blocks down. The chief's an old salty bastard named Williams, but he knows me." He spun to Henry, his eyes fevered with excitement. "Me and a couple of guys'll hump it up to the clubhouse, and after we talk, I'll call the rest of 'em in."

Henry raised his hand. "How hard do you want to do this, Mike?"

"How hard do I need to be?"

"You know when people say they had to go through Hell and back, and that shit's just a metaphor?"

Stone nodded with a confused shrug.

Henry spread his hands, and turned so everyone in the room could see him. "This is not a metaphor."

He wrapped his arms around Aela and thought about the apartment. He hoped it worked, otherwise he'd end up standing in Stone's hospital room looking like he was trying to fart.

Time folded and scattered behind them, pulling space with it.

They stood in Boothe's living room. Aela's knees buckled, but Henry held her up, scooping her into his arms and carrying her into the bedroom. He laid her down and pushed the hair from her forehead. He turned to leave, but her hand caught his sleeve. "Don't go."

"Okay." She scooted over, and he sat on the edge of the bed.

"My grandmother was an angel."

"Not your mother?"

"No, my mother was a prostitute in the Forgotten."

"That seems … *difficult*."

"I guess."

Henry scrubbed his eyes with his fist. Weariness settled across his shoulders. He spun the dial to static and blocked out the city. Aela kicked her shoes to the floor. Henry sighed and stretched his neck. "What about your father?"

"Just a man. In Solitude somewhere."

"Oh. Well, we all gotta be somewhere."

"I never knew him, and I had my grandfather."

Henry knew there was more to that old man than even Aela knew. "He was good to me. And Adam. The look on his face when Adam gave him his bible."

Aela laughed. A single chuckle of air. "He has maybe a thousand. In a thousand different languages, but that one was special."

"So's that boy."

She flopped on to her side. "What's it like being a demon?"

He looked at her to see if she was joking. Her face was serious under the fall of her hair. "Shit. I don't know. A lot like *not* being a demon, I guess. Maybe I'd have a better answer if I knew what it was *supposed* to be like."

"You have powers, though."

"*You* have powers."

"It's not the same."

"How would *I* know? I don't think Boothe had a plan for me beyond getting Maria back. What's it like to heal people?"

"Terrifying. At first, I felt exposed, like God could see me. Like he was judging me for using this… accidental gift. Like I wasn't supposed to. Like I was taking advantage of Him."

"But not anymore?"

"No, it was still terrifying, but this time … I don't know. It felt like the right thing. I could tell he was a good man when I touched him."

"I know. It pisses me off."

"Why?"

"It makes it harder to hate him. In fact, it gets harder to hate *anything* every day."

"That's what makes *you* a good man, too."

Henry growled and shook his head. He pushed off the bed to stand, but dropped back down. Nervous energy flooded his thoughts. He didn't deserve anyone's admiration. "That's what Pastor Owen said. That whether I admitted it or not, I was a good man."

"But, you *are.*"

"I'm not!"

"You're going through an awful lot to save your daughter. I don't think a bad man would do that. The way you fought for Adam. I don't think a bad man would do that, either."

"You don't understand."

"And now you're fighting for your wife."

"Not really. She's my widow."

"But do you still love her?"

He looked down into his lap and closed his eyes. "Yes."

"And *that's* why you're a good man. A pretty girl in your

bed, a girl that already tried to have sex with you, and you told the *truth.*"

"Maybe I'm just dumb."

She laughed. A true moment of humor, and Henry realized he was a prostitute, too. Only, he trafficked in jokes.

Anything for a laugh.

She put her hand flat on his back, teasing with her nails through his T-shirt. "Sometimes, you *are* dumb. You see so many details, but then you're surprised by the big picture."

"Yeah." He leaned into her touch and looked up at the ceiling. "That's me."

"Henry, I want you."

"Okay."

"Close the door."

He rose and walked across the room, afraid to turn around and see her laughing at him. The nervous energy still burned in his brain, but his feet felt heavy. He closed and latched the door, locking Aela in with the monster. He switched off the light before turning around.

And still Aela glowed as she had under Solitude. Faint. Right at the edge of vision. He walked to her and sat back on the bed. He loosened the laces at her waist, clumsy with only one hand. She lifted her hands overhead and let him do it on his own. He worked the leather free from her skin and slid her pants down, one side at a time.

He stood and leaned over the foot of the bed, pulling her pants free with the sound of silk. He climbed over the footboard, and she spread her legs so he could plant his knees inside of hers.

When she grabbed his horns and pushed his head down, he let her.

Chapter Twenty-Nine

THE NEIGHBORHOOD WAS SILENT. The golf course dark. Only the spritzing rhythm of the lawn sprinklers' breath. And distant traffic.

They stood in a clump of trees next to the concrete path that wound through every hole. A big roundabout at the rear of the clubhouse lit with landscape spotlights. Electric golf carts charging in a neat line.

Henry spread his senses. He couldn't figure out how he was doing *anything*, but if he asked hard enough, his mind usually offered the answer on instinct. He felt the souls crying for help. Voices raised in prayer and desperation. The shuttered homes in the mayor's exclusive community were full of muttering dreams, but his estate seemed empty of will. Like it didn't even exist, even though Henry was looking right at its shadow.

The place was covered in police tape. The front entrance was charred, with boards over the front windows and where the door had been.

Charlie Mara leaned forward, staring into the dark with narrowed eyes. "There is a glamour on this place."

The mansion was lit like the clubhouse. All the windows dark, but with spot and path lights aimed to highlight every detail. The sprinkler sprang back at the bottom of the iron fence surrounding the yard, and the sheet of water from its nozzle splattered off the air like a sheet of glass. Henry squinted into the spray, and water trickled down from a point above the ground. A straight line of moisture puddling on the lawn.

"What, like what you did under the Viazo?" Henry pointed at the water running down the windowpane of reality. "Because it looks like there's a wall there."

"No, it's more like an enchantment *hidden* by a glamour. The entire mansion is shrouded in energy. Grounded in another plane. We're seeing an illusion that's supposed to mask whatever spell is just under the glamour's surface."

"Are they trying to disguise the mansion as something else?"

"By making it look like it *always* does?"

"I don't know," Henry said, his voice gaining volume with his frustration.

Boothe dropped a hand on Henry's shoulder and whispered, "Calm down, Henry. Charlie can't answer, because the glamour is so thin. Like a soap bubble on top of another bubble. It is the underneath that has him worried, because he can't see it. Whatever it is, it's focused outward instead of in on itself."

"Well, then, let's toss Frank at it and see what happens."

"Hey!" Frank hissed in an offended stage whisper. "That's not funny."

Boothe looked up, his eyes tracing an arc over the mansion roof. "It *feels* like a portal. A very large gateway placed over the property. As if somebody were expecting an intruder, only they didn't know from what side of the building they might approach."

Charlie nodded. "I think you got it."

Henry pointed at the sprinkler. "But what about that shit? If the water can't make it through, what's to say *we* won't just splash against it and run down the side."

"I think it's just bad work," Charlie said. "Such a large glamour probably isn't easy to maintain."

"I agree," Boothe said. "There could be any number of things making it more difficult, as well. Spacial dilation. Time transposition. Maintaining transmission frequencies."

Henry watched Charlie nod at Boothe in knowing agreement. Two guys talking shop. His mouth twisted with bitterness. "Woulda been nice to have a mentor willing to teach me some shit so that I could follow along with whatever the fuck you're talking about. All I got was sleep and water."

Boothe turned to face Henry, hands behind his back and black suit gathering reflections from the path's low light. "You know, there is an actual science to magic."

"No, I *didn't* know. Do tell."

"I tried to discuss the vibratory transmutation of invisibility, but your eyes glazed over."

"That was at my fucking funeral. They were burying my daughter, and I was kinda preoccupied."

"You were impatient."

Henry snarled. "You wanted to keep me dumb."

"So, you admit you started out that way?"

Henry raised a clawed finger to point at Boothe's smug smile. Frank stepped between them, peering through the glamour. "Hey, can anybody on the other side of that thing see us?"

Charlie shrugged. "Maybe, if they knew where to look."

Henry dropped his hand and looked down. His emotions were swirling. Colliding. A logjam at the crest of a waterfall. Plunging over the edge, only to be replaced by another. The heat of Aela's hand on his back, and his heartbeat slowed. He drew a deep breath, and looked back into Boothe's face. The angel gave him a sheepish shrug, and Henry grunted to keep his laughter at bay.

"You people are too fucking loud." Stone's voice startled Henry into a crouch a second before the detective stepped into their group, melting into existence as if he were one with the shadows, traveling like a demon. The rippling darkness behind him resolved into the body of Stone's buddy, Howser. Both wore black clothes and matching gear. Same for their body armor, and the grease on their faces.

They each held a rifle pointed at the ground in front of their feet.

Henry seemed to be the only one surprised by his sudden appearance. Maria and Nadia gave Stone and Howser a fleeting look, then went back to chatting in breathy whispers with their heads nearly touching. Frank and Charlie kept staring at the glamour. Boothe kept his eyes on Henry, and Aela stepped around with her arms crossed. Henry's back felt cold without her behind him.

Stone shook his head. "We could have dropped a grenade right in the middle of your bickering, and only the flash would have told you we were here."

Boothe turned to Stone, his hands sliding into his pockets. "I felt you coming before you finished the Lord's Prayer in the parking lot of the fire station. Smelled you before you even entered the trees."

Henry realized *he* could smell them, too. Metal and oil.

Excitement and fear. The energy of their souls pressing against the meat vehicles around him. The two men's thoughts bursting across the surface of their minds. He looked at Stone. "You're thinking about Samantha. About the day you proposed to her in Lake County, California over a bottle of Merlot. Sweating because it had cost you a hundred and seventeen dollars. She was beautiful with the sun shining through her hair as the dry wind pulled it away from her face."

Stone's mouth dropped open, and he lowered his weapon further, the tip pointing at his toes. Henry turned to Howser. "And *you're* wondering if your Brianna could see you, if she would be proud of you. You always thought she was when she was alive, but without her around to ask, you can't be sure. A small blonde in a rocking chair. Kicking her feet and watching the ducks in the river."

Howser stood like a rock, his expression bored. Like a man who hadn't heard a word Henry had said. Another thought flitted across his mind.

Henry nodded. "I expect you're right. If Hell doesn't claim you when you die, you can ask her then."

Howser tipped his head, and Henry tore his eyes from the man's gaze. His internal suffering tasted too good, and Henry felt dirty for sitting in his thoughts for so long.

"So, what do we do now?" Henry asked.

Stone swallowed and glanced at the mansion. "There's been zero activity from that place for hours. No shadows across the windows. No calls in or out. No cars. It's like … I don't know."

Howser released his rifle, letting it hang from a sling around his neck. "It's like a static video feed. Or a *picture* of the place hanging over it. Like the way we used to hide from air surveillance with netting in the desert."

Charlie nodded, crossing his arms over his chest. "I

think your guess is actually right. I think there is a glamour cast over the property. Like a dome of smoke, and the mansion is projected onto the inside surface to hide what else might be there."

"What else might be there?" Stone asked.

"I think it's a portal," Boothe said. "A nodal transport portal that will most likely take us into an ambush."

"To where?"

"The place that makes the most sense? Nowhere."

Stone shook his head in confusion.

But Henry smiled in realization. "Of course. Wherever that Lincoln Log bullshit fort was past the trees." His heart pounded in anticipation. "They had generators and shit, so if they have guns, they probably work. If he has anybody to spare from whatever's going on at Solitude, we might be fucked. *But*, if all he has at the front door are a bunch of those Ravager assholes?"

"This all sounds like you guys are guessing," Stone said. "And, I don't even know what any of that shit meant. Is Samantha in there? You think they would've actually come back here?"

Henry nodded. "I wasn't sure, but now, yes, I do think they came back here. I think, despite the police investigating this place, they feel safest here right now."

Stone sighed. He pointed at the mansion behind its glamour. "What if we just walk in there?"

Henry shrugged.

Charlie held up his hand. "Unlike the water in the sprinklers, we'll go right through to wherever the portal takes us. It looks like it's set on a trigger. After the portal sends us to wherever, the glamour blows away and the mansion returns to normal. Whatever that means."

Aela growled. Frustration and impatience. "Can we just get on with it, please?"

Stone spread his hands. "Okay, okay. Weego and Hansen are sitting in the wagons as we speak."

"What the Hell *are* the wagons?" Henry said.

Howser pulled his rifle up to the ready again. "Prototypes of the TDVs we built for Dark Water."

"Oh."

"Tactical Defense Vehicles. Urban armored response transport."

"Got it."

"Do you?"

Henry shook his head. "Not really."

Howser grinned, a chuckle escaping through his teeth. "How about we call 'em in, and you can see for yourself?"

"So, are we just gonna walk through?"

"I wish we had more time to plan this shit." Stone pointed to Henry's horns. "But I don't really know *what* to plan for."

"Fuck it," Henry said. "Call 'em in, and we'll break on through to the other side."

Engines rumbled in front of the clubhouse. Howser dropped his hand from a black band around his neck — one of those fancy throat mics.

"I already did," he said with a smile.

Howser waved for them to follow and spun to jog out of the trees. Henry broke into motion to join him, freezing at the sight of two vehicles growling under the golf course entrance lighting. "Okay, I *didn't* see those coming."

Charlie and Frank both crashed into Henry's back. He looked at them over his shoulder, and they shared the same look of astonished wonder. That expression that men shared at car shows and breweries.

The *wagons* were two giant SUV's. Flat black with wide stances and billowing exhaust. They looked mean, their dark grills like grim smiles. They seemed to pull the light into themselves, and Henry felt their purpose like a mugger's intentions. The doors opened, and there were no interior lights.

"It's like what the Devil would drive," Henry said.

"Damn straight," said Stone as he walked by.

Henry looked around him with his senses stretched as far as he could reach. Still the sleepers blanketed in their dreams. The firemen off in the distance and their quiet laughter at Stone's manic secrecy. Silence from the mansion behind him. Henry drew his thoughts back into himself, and turned to survey his friends standing in a semi-circle at the edge of the trees.

Helping him save his wife. His daughter. A miracle of a boy. Henry realized for the first time in his life, he didn't have a joke. "Fuck it." He turned back to the TDVs. "Now what?"

Weego shrugged his body armor higher onto his shoulders and rocked his head side to side, stretching his neck. He pulled away from his quiet conversation with Howser and Stone and smiled. It looked to Henry like an expression he only invited to his darkest times. "I say we send the wagons through, and you and your ... *squad* here can come through on our bumpers. We'll pop the guns and see what's up."

Henry had no better answer.

Is this really where I am?

Everybody looking at me?

Without turning to the faces behind him, Henry nodded. Defeat was at war with excitement. Hanging heavy over every head.

He took a deep breath that tasted like diesel exhaust. "Let's do it."

. . .

THE ENGINES REVVED, and the fat tires dug through the perfect grass of the ninth hole tee. Henry kept pace across the lawn, inhaling smoke from the armored vehicle's tailpipe. Exhaling with the heat of his rising anger.

Why me?

The gun still hadn't left the back of his head, even after taking his life.

The TDVs hit the edge of the glamour just before the iron fence. The nose of the lead vehicle disappeared, and the illusion shrouding the mayor's mansion rippled. Green sparkles of light traced away from the breach like fleeing insects.

The TDV was swallowed. The glamour closed over it like the shrinking iris of a film student transition. The second vehicle hit one lane over, vanishing to the front tire before Henry hit the sizzling power with his horns.

Daddy's coming.

The gut-wrenching twist of moving through space and time preceded the forest's wet scent at the edge of the Forgotten.

Broken asphalt under his claws was slick with oil. A darkness different than the night above the golf course. Thick and pressing, like a canopy directly overhead.

The SUVs slid to a stop, each veering to the outside to face away from each other, forming a *V*. Henry slid to his own stop at the lead vehicle's left-front fender, and his knees locked. Shock swamped his heart, and he grabbed the darkness around him. Shadows under the vehicles rumbling beside him. The black under his own feet.

He dragged it in like pulling a soaking sail from the ocean, and he spun with it unfurling behind his head. He saw Aela's wide eyes. The grim set of Boothe's jaw.

Charlie's speed had left him, and he stood at Nadia's

side, staring. Maria slowed with her hands spread out, white fire dying in her palms.

Frank met his eyes, horror pulling his chin to his chest.

The strain pulled something loose in Henry's gut. Lancing pain shot up into his head, spreading to his temples as the energy to gather mountains of darkness burned through him. His shroud settled over them, and he cinched it tight, spreading it to bury them in shadows. His claws scratched through the road as he spun to take in the enemy.

Red fire arced through the air from the front of a block building set into the center of the road. A ball, spinning and roaring, trailing yellow light. It fell from the sky, angling toward the two vehicles. Coming at Henry as he cowered under his cloak of shadow with the rest of his friends gathered around him.

Under the falling boulder of fire, was a writhing mass of Ravagers standing in ragged ranks at the base of the building.

The windows on the top floor were lit from inside. Creatures made of fire reflected off the ground floor's wall of dark windows. Demons and golls took to the air, screaming as weapons were readied. So many, and Henry couldn't see any space between them.

The ground shook with their pounding feet as they charged. The air ripped with their combined voice. Henry looked over his shoulder, and the golf course was gone. Charlie and Boothe had been right, and he sent them through, anyway.

Why the fuck would anybody listen to me?

Henry knew the darkness wouldn't protect them, but maybe it would hide them long enough for somebody *else* to make a decision.

The ball of fire pounded the ground right in the notch

of the *V.* Flames exploded into the steel. A crash that drowned the screaming voices and pounding feet. The TDVs lifted up and rocked from the impact, but there was no shattering glass or crumple of metal. The fire broke apart, like water splashing against a break wall.

The TDVs bounced, the springs in their suspension creaking, and a hatch in the center of each roof popped open. Howser rose out of one and Weego from the other. The thick metal of a mini-gun barrel led each man into the open.

Henry's jaw dropped further, and in his shock, he lost his grip on the shadows.

Howser and Weego opened fire, and the concussion of their guns drove Henry back into Boothe's arms.

Ravagers exploded as the bullets tore into their ranks. Driving through the men and women in the front, bullets blowing craters into the concrete wall behind them, spreading the blood in streaks of crimson and black.

Maria shot into the air, shedding her clothes in favor of a robe made from the white fire of her undiluted power. Her scream rose above the thundering guns, and her hands met in front of her, a shaft of energy sweeping out from her fingers and knocking winged creatures into the path of the destruction on the ground.

Boothe leapt up on white wings, and a spear left his hand to stab the side of a demon flying in a slow arc with a black sword overhead. She dropped in a screeching spiral, the mini-guns shredding her wings and tearing chunks of flesh away in an explosion of blood.

The guns spun into silence, and both men ducked back inside.

Henry felt slow. His thoughts slogging through mud. He shook his head, but the haze over his eyes clung to him like gauze over his face.

Are they reloading?

Are they done?

Swirling balls of energy like the ones coming down the hill in front of the Viazo Grand roared at the vehicles. Probably the same magic that had killed Ezra as Henry ran for his life with Adam in his arms.

The hatches slammed shut just before the direct impact of energy, and Henry caught flame and heat against his chest, but the vehicles fared as well as last time. The asphalt cracked. Black chunks and dark dust rising into the impact's wake. The hatches popped back open, and Howser and Weego opened fire again.

Nadia pushed Henry around the outside of the vehicle and dragged him into a stumbling run.

He couldn't think past the noise.

Grit in his eyes.

Lights flashing through his eyelids.

Panicked thoughts of the Ravagers as they died.

His senses were overloaded. Motivation frozen by his inability to decide on a course of action.

Nadia's claws dug into his arm, and her raptor's cry tore through his ear. Henry ducked away from her voice.

A Ravager with bandoleers crossed over his chest ran at them from the edge of the trees, skirting the guns' reach. He held a pistol in each hand like Billy the Kid, and he grinned with brown teeth, his eyes showing white all around. Henry felt hands at his shoulders. Fingers tangling in his shirt, pulling him out of the Ravager's path.

Henry's feet collided and his knees gave out. He tipped over, his arms held out straight in front of him. His palms scraped the road, and the impact jarred his jaw shut with a clopping bite that caught his bottom lip between his teeth. Black blood glistened like syrup as it stretched through a line of drool that traced the ground like a snail trail.

He looked up from under his brows, and the lights burst over his head like flashing neon in a darkened casino. Black lights sparkling from all the white T-shirts as the kids danced to the pulsing beat. Lasers beaming through the crowd.

He looked into the Ravagers fevered eyes and saw his vision reflected in the man's maniacal gaze.

The hands still pulled. Under his armpits, digging into his ribs.

"Henry, what is wrong with you?"

He couldn't tell who was talking.

He felt eyes on his back. Staring and hateful.

Guns belched fire as the Ravager pulled the triggers over and over.

Henry looked away from his attacker, snaking his head through the thick air. Windows on the second floor were blazing.

A dark figure stood in the center of a square of glass. Robed with his hands behind his back. Outlined by light. Even across the distance of the battlefield, their eyes locked.

Henry stared into Pastor Owen's gaze, and his muscles turned to pudding.

The noise around him grew to the screaming rush of his own blood in his ears.

His vision dulled to a dirty gray.

The Ravager hit him with every bullet he fired.

Chapter Thirty

HE FELT THE IMPACT, but no pain. Somebody screaming through the pounding in his head.

A cruel hand on his ankle. The ground dragging against his back.

Henry opened his eyes, and colors streaked by. Swirling clouds above that. Faint light at the reaches of his vision.

Deep vibrations through his bones.

The colors wheeled and danced, forming shapes in his imagination, like gazing at clouds on a hill.

That one's a giraffe.

Trees slid by on his left, so close they intruded on his view of a charred sky.

Blurring shapes whipped by on his right.

Henry pushed his chin into his chest, rolling his eyes down his body. Seeping holes spreading black blood through his shirt. One leg rising from the ground to end in the grip of the Ravager with the Old West rig.

Henry dropped his head and drew a breath that tasted like salt and mud.

The sluice of wet earth beneath him changed to flat

and the symphony of battle stayed behind him. The block wall loomed ahead, its second story window still blazing with light and power. Pastor Owen with his face against the glass, watching Henry disappear into the front door.

The interior was dark. Grease and gasoline. Dust and ashes.

Henry's head bounced against the stairs on their way up, and his sinuses filled with blood.

A tight squeeze through a doorway at the top, and the ceiling turned from concrete to steel. Old signs hung from rusty trusses. Vintage gas and oil. Automobilia. The kind of crap the American Pickers always found in a New England barn.

The light at the end of the room brightened as they neared. From blue to orange. Dancing and cheery, like a log cabin's fireplace. Heat swept across the floor, drying his lips and the blood crusting around his nostrils.

The Ravager let go of his ankle, and Henry's boot slapped on the floor, the echoes louder than the dying sounds of the conflict outside.

Footsteps scraping away. The squeal of metal chair legs, and the grunt of someone sitting after a long time on their feet.

"Please join us, Henry."

The pastor's voice washed over him like the rolling waves of the ocean. Holding Henry in place, then lifting him up. Crashing against him.

Henry rolled to his side and pushed off the floor without meaning or wanting to. He stood and steadied himself on the back of a metal chair in front of an iron table set for six. Sparkling white plates and silver cutlery. Crystal glasses. Servers and bowls. All empty. A woman sat at the end of the table. Blindfolded and gagged. A bloody bandage on her arm.

Samantha.

Henry smiled at the sight of her. A tightness around his chest, being so close, yet unsure how he was going to save her.

He pulled the chair out and slid to his seat, leaning forward on his elbows to stare at his wife.

"Thank you, Henry."

Henry turned, and Pastor Owen left the window. He walked to stand behind Samantha, opened his robe, and let it fall to the floor behind him.

He crossed behind her and stood in front of an iron frame full of Hell. The burning light glistened off the sweat on his chest, his tattoo shining as if glowing bugs tracked the ink under the surface of his skin.

The Ravager tipped his chair back and slung his boots onto the table. The place setting jangled from the impact. He popped the wheels on his guns, and the brass cartridges scattered the light as they tinkled to the floor. Fingers black with mud and blood fished fresh rounds from the belts across his chest.

The pastor moved up to Samantha's back. He slid the blindfold from her eyes, dragging hair across her face. He leaned in and whispered, "As promised. Here is what your Henry has become."

Her eyes widened, and she rocked back into the chair, tears streaming down her cheeks. Henry could tell she could see the monster, and the last of Henry's will poured into the floor. He hung his head over his shining plate and stared into the eyes of his reflection.

Hate and anger roiled under the surface. Screaming and wailing defiance ready to burst into rage, but he could only shrug and nod. He looked up from under his brow, directly into her shaking horror.

"Hey, babe."

Pastor Owen smiled. Proud that his patient had come so far. Samantha shuddered under his hands as he rubbed her shoulders. Rocking from her sobs.

Something inside Henry begged him to look away. He tore his gaze from her face, but nothing else could satisfy his eyes. He focused on Pastor Owen's mouth and tried to ignore her gagging cries.

The pastor dropped his hands from Samantha's shoulders then leaned back, still smiling. "We have come so far. Right to the finish of things, I think. I have made a few recent deals that have changed the terms of our victory, but it will be a victory nonetheless. Thank you, Henry."

Henry shrugged again. "Don't mention it."

The pastor nodded. "I have bound you to me. To our quest. With the one thing you loved above everything else. Your dear wife. Samantha's blood. Hidden under the glamour you walked through on your way to revenge. I will admit, the weapons you have brought to bear against me … were unexpected. But I *did* expect you. A spell to bend you to my will as you entered my domain, and the bullets to drive my control into your soul, coated with the life you loved so very much."

The pastor lifted his arm to indicate the Ravager sitting with his arms crossed, his bored expression at odds with the fever of battle he'd shown in the trees. Henry shook his head and thought back to that moment.

Was someone else there?

The pastor snapped and Henry left his memory, sitting up straight like a schoolboy caught in a daydream.

"His name is Blane. Son of Botis. Part of the agreement I've made with my new dealings with Hell. I knew him from when I started my quest. He aided me when I needed my church destroyed. Once, to kill the spirit of its people. A massacre that killed many children. And once, to kill its body with fire. It was all for you, Henry."

Owen lifted his hands, the palms glowing with red fire. The flames behind him rippled, and a hot wash blew across the table. He balled his hands into fists, and Henry hissed in pain.

Searing heat from the entry wounds in his chest and belly spiked and spread out, blending into a mass of agony over his heart. His muscles locked him in position. His teeth ground together. Tears squeezed from the corners of his eyes.

Pastor Owen smiled. "I have been given dominion over you, Henry. You are the demon that will lead my charge. This portal into Hell remains open so you can see what you have lost, but it also shows what you yet have to gain."

The flames in the frame parted, and a figure of shadow stepped forward. Opalescent skin. Hairless with jet black eyes. Satan wore a crisp suit and tie, and a small figure stood before him, matching his steps as he neared the portal's border.

Amélie.

The heat over Henry's heart blossomed into an inferno of rage. He pushed against Owen's control as if they were chains. Struggling, his voice whining in a labored rumble of agony, Henry looked into Lucifer's eyes and was suddenly free.

He sagged back into the chair as the eyes claimed control, removing his will to fight back.

The devil smiled.

"Resist me," Pastor Owen said, "and Samantha dies. If you try to go to Hell without me, Samantha dies. If you do anything other than the work set out before you … Samantha dies. The perfect bonds for someone like you, Henry. The only thing that will truly keep you at my side."

The black in Satan's eyes swirled beyond his eyelids, spreading out from his face to cover his head like a cowl.

"And here are my generals," Pastor Owen continued.

Big Ben stepped out from the shadows in the corner. Dressed all in black, a shining steel pauldron over his left shoulder. Heavy plates down the arm. Demon Piercer hanging from his back.

Petrov Obisev followed. Looking better here in Nowhere than the last time Henry had seen him. Dressed identically to Big Ben, a sword at his hip and a shotgun in his hands.

They took their places at the table. Henry stared at Satan from the last supper he would ever have.

With the devil's hands on her shoulders, Amélie stood strong. Chest high and hands at her sides. Chin up and out. As the black from Satan's eyes poured down to cover her face, filling the portal to Hell, Amélie winked.

Listen to the pastor's words, young son.

Lucifer's hissing voice rose into Henry's thoughts, rolling and cracking through his mind. Whispering echoes pulsing in and out of the shadows.

He has made a deal with me, but my dealing is not yet done.

Pastor Owen spread his hands, the power pushing through his fingers leaving trails in the air as they moved. "And when the sky is blackened by the smoke of the bottomless pit, and the locusts and scorpions have had their fill, we shall leave this place with a new army that is on the move even now. You will be my commander in the sacking of Solitude, and the boy will fall victim to your claws."

He stepped from Samantha's side, blocking Henry's view of the swirling oil coating the passage to the underworld. "Or Samantha will die, and if you think her reunion with your sweet Amélie will be joyous in Hell, I can assure you, you are mistaken."

A voice like the crawling of centipedes through moist earth. *A front divided is a front controlled.*

"They will both be tortured for an infinity of time. New degradations that have not even been imagined."

I do not want the pastor to rule on earth in my stead, young son.

The inky flow of black rolled to the portal's edges. Satan's gaze blocked the light of Hell, and Pastor Owen's voice boomed with his passion. "Order will be torn apart as Chaos spreads to cover humanity. We will cleanse the *love* of the Oppressor from the earth, and a *new* Order shall emerge. A new balance with me at the head and you at my side, your wife and daughter an eternal reward for your service. The prophecy will fulfill, and a new age will dawn. Henry, can't you *see* it?"

He could see Samantha's eyes, weeping and wide with horror. Sweat rolling down the pastor's forehead. Henry saw every bad decision he had ever made. Every selfish move. Every pain he had unintentionally caused. Henry closed his eyes, and for the first time in his life, he prayed.

But the voice he heard in his mind was not God's.

Young son. Come treat with me.

Time rolled into a moment of thought. Henry rose from his body to hover over the slowing tableau, rising and falling back as the pastor's word made slow progress into the air. Through the wall to hang in the stairwell. Stone barely moved in his headlong rush up the stairs. Bloody and frantic, he led the way to Henry's rescue. Teeth gleaming out of the blood. Aela at his back, covered in shining splashes of black and red.

The frozen light of Maria's power pushing against the shadows, Boothe hanging from her shoulder. Nadia's raptor form snaking onto the lower landing. Frank's Hell Hound slinging lava from its tongue. Charlie Mara's blur as he overtook them all, and the humans, Howser and Weego staggering in the rear, facing back with weapons drawn, staring into the Ravagers coming at them from the field.

Every eye dark and hollow with terror and exhaustion. Every wound and injury pulling them down, nearly frozen as Henry flew out into the mist. It was the final charge of friends he hardly knew. Another column of names he had betrayed to add to his list.

As he slid over the trees, the pastor's building receded in the distance, the wooden fort taking its place to fall away as well. Swallowed by fog and darkness. The trees ended at the cemetery. The cemetery ended at the Forgotten.

The noise a drone of slow passage. A single note as the clocks ground over to the next second in time.

Through the mists leading to Solitude and the armies of Hell battling the armies of Heaven yawning beneath him. Blinking lights twinkling through the battle that churned the mud and blood into a red haze that hung above the city's walls. The fight tumbled through the halls, and Henry looked away.

The light turned to a dirty gray as he left the Forgotten and parted the mists as he descended into Nowhere. The Tree's beauty ached in his chest. Its sadness and fear radiating like the aroma of dying flowers.

At its base was a table big enough for a hundred, but only four places were set at the end. Shining dishes and gleaming cutlery. A full chessboard in the center.

Samantha's wispy soul occupied one of the chairs. Still bound and gagged, her eyes watched him fall, the edges of her form flowing away from an unseen wind. Amélie sat across from her. The ghost of a beautiful girl, the table showing through her glowing body.

Henry eased into the chair next to his daughter, and when he reached for her, his hands passed right through her light. Like Samantha, he was barely there.

Satan sat forward in his chair across from Henry, his glossy skin shining like polished stone.

He sat on the white side of the board, and when he steepled his fingers together, the pawn in front of his king slid forward.

"Let us begin, young son."

Chapter Thirty-One

"CHESS IS A GAME OF POSSIBILITIES," Satan said. "One could even say that it is an exercise in *choices.*"

Henry remembered chess from school. Drunken parties. Under the spring shade in the park. His dismissal of a pursuit that he tried to convince himself was an unnecessary mental exercise. Really, he just didn't understand it.

He focused on the board. Black pieces awaiting his command. The pawn in front of his king slid forward.

"Ah, yes. A standard response, but a solid one. An opening for the church and an agreement to deal. Shall I make an offer?"

Satan's knight rose from the board. From the king's side of the line, it dropped in front of the bishop's pawn.

"I put in front of you, entrance into Hell."

Henry's eyes slid up, but he couldn't meet the abyss of Satan's gaze. His eyes bounced to the side, and he pushed his fist into his belly to catch his breath. He looked back down to the board, and the pawn in front of his king's bishop slid forward one space.

"A timid move. Offensively useless, but it pulls your ears to my words. You are willing to negotiate. Very well."

The white knight rose again, wrapping the white pawn to take Henry's man from his opening move. The black pawn turned to dust and blew to nothing.

"Again, I will offer you entrance, but I will not release the souls in my possession out of hand."

Henry was no better off. He could get into Hell, but he would still have to fight for his daughter. For Adam's mother. Unacceptable.

With Satan's knight unprotected, the black bishop's pawn slid diagonally to clear the white knight from the board.

"An assertive move, but a ploy that only opens you up for attack. It *does* illustrate your position, however …"

The white queen came out, sliding through the gap left by the king's pawn. To the edge of the board, she lined up with Henry's king, and Henry groaned.

Satan folded his hands together. "You are not in a position of strength, young son. I am still willing to keep my original offer extended, even as you are in check."

Henry scanned the board, his eyes roving frantically. "I don't know what to do."

"Do not express such weakness, young son. Your panic strengthens my strategy."

"Shut up." Words bitten through gritted teeth.

"Your friends are nearing the top of the stairs, young son. Time is inexorable."

"Shut the *fuck* up, old man!"

His king hopped forward, and he looked up into the swirling depths of Satan's gaze, holding his terrifying eyes until Henry's guts quivered with an arctic dread.

Satan grinned, and his teeth ran with blood. "*Now* it is a game. Truly."

The white queen slid sideways, again lining up with Henry's king.

"In check again, you have nowhere to run, young son. I will allow you into my home, but what is mine remains mine. Can you take it from me?"

Henry's king jumped in front of his bishop. Now in a pawn's square, he stood in the front ranks of the battle. Exposed.

"Still denying my terms. Very well. If not what I ask, then what do you offer?"

The white bishop came forward, sliding through the gap in the king's defense to sit diagonally from Henry's king. Another Check.

"I am still holding out for agreement, as you have not yet shown me a willingness to fight for what you want. Earn your leverage, young son."

The black queen's pawn slid forward to block the white bishop.

"Time to think. Time to plan. You buy yourself only time."

The white bishop took the pawn.

"My offer is strengthened, and I now may be in a position to demand further concessions. What say you?"

Henry's king moved diagonally to sit in front of his knight's pawn. Leading the charge, and his bishop and queen with no defense, Henry swallowed the vomit that frothed into his throat.

Satan leaned back, the corner of his lips rising in a sardonic smile.

"A bold denial, to which I agree."

The white pawn in front of the king's rook stepped forward two squares.

"And I will expose my battlements. To my gain? My detriment?"

Henry slid the opposing pawn forward, mirroring Satan's move.

"Precarious, yet I see the need. Now, I will sow the seeds of false agreement. Be wary, young son."

The white bishop in the center of the field ranged across the board to take the pawn in front of the black queen's knight.

"And with the break in your line, I will offer one soul for you to take. The daughter or the mother. Your blood or Adam's?"

The black bishop took the white bishop, and Henry's line was restored, but the gap around his queen widened.

"It seems you have chosen the daughter. *Very* selfish, young son, and as you have experienced, selfishness requires punishment."

The white queen slid over one square. In line with Henry's exposed bishop. A single diagonal square from his king.

"In check, you see the error of your ways. Of your *decisions*. What do you now offer?"

Henry's king ran from the danger, moving over one space to the edge. Blocking his rook. A pawn in front. His king had nowhere to go.

"So it is both souls or *neither*, then."

The white queen's pawn rocked forward, dragging two spaces to sit next to the opening white pawn's position.

"I will take time to consider your offer, young son. Can you sweeten your plea?"

The black pawn in front of the king's knight came forward. Slow and reluctant. It seemed to strengthen the king's position, with a pair of pawns in front of him, but Henry saw the empty space behind and covered his fear with a fierce glare.

Satan nodded. "A strong rebuttal. Still willing to negotiate, even as your king suffers. I will counter, then."

The white queen attacked, rushing forward to sit in front of the black bishop. She was poised to move on Henry's king, and he saw no defense. Only his own queen sitting behind the lines.

"There is a way out for you, but you are only a few moves from checkmate, young son. If you kill the pastor, voiding his control over my intent, I will grant you entrance into Hell, and I will release the trapped souls of your daughter and Adam's mother to you. Everything you have asked for."

His bottomless eyes rolled to the side, and the devil turned his head to stare at Samantha. "Of course, *she* will die, but you will be free of the pastor's control. My offer stands, and there will be no further negotiations."

Henry couldn't hear her, but Samantha's form rocked with her sobs. Her eyes roving with fear and helplessness. Her mouth wide in a wail of grief and rage. Her eyes locked onto his, then swung to Amélie's. His daughter held her hands out, but there was no contact. Or comfort.

He could finally save his daughter, but the cost was his wife. More dear than his soul, how could he agree? He looked back at the board, and suddenly realized he wasn't the king. He was one of the pawns.

Was Owen his bishop? And Amélie his rook?

Henry's breath came in hitching gasps. *This* was the choice that Mandyel had warned him about. The one he had felt coming since his death. The hardest choice. To save the world from prophecy made worse by a false profit. The price too dear.

But Pastor Owen had named *Henry* the false profit.

Henry was a Paladin. The *pastor* was the false profit.

Henry looked into the torment of Samantha's eyes.

And you are my queen. Dear God. No!

Her eyes widened further, and she looked at the board. Satan leaned forward, his eyes intent on her face.

Henry swept his arm across the board, but his fingers passed through the pieces like brick colored smoke.

NO!

Satan pointed at the table. "Unless the queen was sacrificed. Coming out in the defense of the black."

Amélie's voice joining his screams, bouncing through the vast echoes of Satan's dark words, twining around them like the vines in a tattoo.

The black queen quivered in her square, and Satan reached out to put his finger on the white king's crown. Like Randall under the Tree before, Satan tipped the king on its side. "The white king concedes, and you are free to meet *your* end of our bargain, young son."

The smoke of Samantha's hands crawled up the table.

Henry couldn't look away from her face. The beauty and the love etched in the lines around her mouth. Unconditional acceptance of his every fault. He had found her. Somehow, she had been his.

Samantha's hands solidified as they neared the silver knife next to the plate in front of her. Her fingers closed around the handle, and she lifted it to her neck.

Henry's breath left in a rush, and the crushing pain of her sacrifice lodged in his throat. He couldn't breathe.

She smiled as she slashed the knife across her throat.

Blood washed across the table, sweeping pieces off the board.

The air denied him finally filled Henry's lungs, and he threw his head back and screamed. The spell that had held him shattered in the face of his agony, and he rose from the chair, hurtling back toward his body, the devil's laughter like thunder in his wake.

He sailed into the mist, the light surrounding the Tree dimming to ash. The battle in Solitude swinging out of his sight as he soared through broken buildings of the Forgotten. The trees whipping by as he broke from the fog to fly over the cracked asphalt leading to the broken fort before the open field through the glamour.

The TDVs, crumpled and charred. A glittering pool of expended brass scattered in a shining arc through the sticky, bloody mud. Dead and dying Ravagers. Demons piled from an onslaught greater than preparation.

Samantha was gone.

Henry reached down as he rocketed across the battlefield, and he scooped up the life energy of his enemies. Adam's enemies. His wife's torturers. His daughter's murderers.

The energy filled him, and he stuffed it down to make more room.

More and more energy joined the rush hanging behind him as he slipped through the block walls.

Screaming Ravagers at the base of the stairs, their insanity lit by the gunfire as Henry's friends tore up the stairwell and into the twisted dining room. Stone bursting through the door with his weapon raised. The others crowded in behind him, their faces stretched with the same horror that split the detective's mouth in a panicked snarl.

The blood pouring out from Samantha's throat to wash across the table in a slow-motion fan. Pastor Owen's face naked with shock, staring at her sacrifice.

Big Ben spinning with his hand on the hilt of his black sword.

Petrov Obisev diving under the table.

Blane, son of Botis, pulling leather with a manic grin.

Henry slammed into his body, rocking forward. Driving his chest into the table, he sent dishes and silverware hither and yon. His scream hit like the shattering of a sonic boom. The energy he dragged behind him roared like a gas explosion, and his eyes found hers. As soulfire raged into his body, the light left her eyes. Her smile died as she fell from the chair at Pastor Owen's feet.

She was gone. Not free.

But Marisol was free. *Amélie* was free.

Henry was free.

Finally.

Henry lifted his hands over his head. He drove his fist and his coffee can hand down with a roar that tore blood from his throat to mix with the sparks that shot from his mouth. The table split in half, warping like molten steel. He *flared*, sending every molecule of energy he had captured from his center in an exploding wave of rolling white fire.

It hit Big Ben first, and the heat ripped the skin from his body, driving him back in a splatter of blood and bone. Blane, son of Botis disappeared in a mist of flayed skin and muscle.

Pastor Owen threw his hands up, crossing his forearms in front of his chest, and the energy drove him back, splitting out from his defense.

Henry launched from his seat with his claws overhead, the heat from his roar rippling his vision in a gnarled haze.

The power passed through Henry's friends, his family in arms. It rolled into the Ravagers crowding into the stairwell, and they split apart from the force, showering the concrete walls with gore. The power slowed as it left the building. He felt it die as he reached the apex of his attack, and gravity brought him down on the pastor.

His claws hit Owen at the base of his throat.

He may have defended against Henry's *flare*, but his flesh was no defense against the blow fueled by a demon's rage. Henry's claws passed through the pastor's body, pulling his rib cage away, breaking through the bones in his arms.

The cascade of blood and intestines splattered out to paint Henry's arms and face, showering his chest with bits of bone.

Quivering meat following his slash to paint the floor at the pastor's feet with his own life, and the empty body slid down in a boneless heap.

"NO!"

Stone's anguish tore into Henry's ears, and he turned to watch the detective slip through the blood, fetching up against his fiancée's chair, reaching for her still form.

Trumpets in the distance.

Henry looked up, his head cocked.

Empty of thought and emotion, he stood while Pastor Owen's life force swirled at his feet.

The flowing black curtain in the portal's frame distended, and Satan stepped through, his goat's foot dripping sizzling lava on the concrete floor. A black twist of horns poked through, and Henry turned away.

Aela rushed to Stone's side. She cast a haunted look up at Henry's face. Dark hollows under her eyes turning blue like somebody diving through freezing water.

Shadows darkening his periphery as the rest of them neared, but Henry's eyes were on Aela as she took Samantha's head into her lap.

The trumpets grew louder, and Satan's hand reached over Henry's shoulder. He grabbed the pastor's sinking soul as his hind foot popped free of the portal's grasp. He pulled it to his snuffling nose and inhaled.

His demonic form swelled, inky smoke spinning around his horns and pulsing wings.

A deep sigh of pleasure sounded like a rock slide.

Henry's shoulders fell, and he collapsed into the alabaster man in a silk business suit. Neat and dapper. All black. Satan smiled at Henry, and a sparkling light reflected in his ebony eyes.

Henry turned, and Aela's healing glow flowed from her fingers into Samantha's face. Spreading out in glistening wings. She bent forward, her hair hanging over Samantha's eyes. One woman had saved him while he was alive. The other was saving him now. His knees buckled, and he fell into the sticky pool that had been an enemy to Hell itself.

Samantha opened her eyes. She looked around, but she didn't seek Henry with her gaze. Her eyes locked on Stone, and Henry grinned with a nod.

Fucking payment in full.

Satan's hand fell on his shoulder. Bitter cold that shot through his bones. Seized his muscles and clamped his teeth like a Taser shock.

The hissing voice in his ears. "Not the sacrifice as I had expected, but effective. Well played, young son."

The portal erupted in an explosion of black liquid.

It struck Henry in the back, driving him to the floor as it spread over him, washing across Samantha's body as she rolled into Stone's arms.

It crushed into Aela, and she disappeared in its flow.

The roar of dark power filled Henry's ears. He tumbled into its depths and sank to the bottom.

There was no more light, and when he opened his mouth in a panicked bid for air, the burning oil flowed into his mouth, choking his will as it filled his lungs and coated his mouth with the bitter suffering of a million lost souls.

Chapter Thirty-Two

HENRY OPENED HIS EYES.

He pushed himself to all fours and looked at a red carpet threaded with gold. The black smear of oil from his face under his eyes. Grunts and groans behind him.

Draped in dripping pitch that barely covered the blood, they all made it to their feet, leaning into each other and holding on, trying to recover from the entry into Hell.

The large room was exotic wood. Dressed panels on the walls and ceiling. Contrasting grains and species, the expanse on each wall broken only by a single door. Three were hand-carved, with intricate vines surrounding the sculpted faces of suffering. The fourth opening was filled with the twin panels of an elevator. Wrought iron decoration, a vintage arrow pointing to the floor. Vines entwining a zero of black metal.

Henry stood and scanned for Samantha, but she wasn't there. Wide eyes stared back at him from filthy faces, but none were hers. He didn't see Stone or his war buddies, either.

What the fuck?

The elevator *dinged* behind him. Henry spun around, slinging bits of sticky black from his hair and fingers. The arrow stopped on '1', and the doors slid aside. Satan stepped into the tasteful lighting and approached Henry with his hands behind his back.

He stepped forward with his fist raised. "Where's Samantha?"

Satan stopped with his heels pressed together and smiled. "This is hardly the place for humans, young son. They have *many* years left in which to make the mistakes that will send them here."

"And where the fuck is *here*?"

Satan's smile widened. The seeping oil glistened at the corners of his mouth. "This is my Edifice. Below us is Hell. Above us is your escape."

"What escape? We had a *deal.*"

Satan's mouth split in a dripping grin. "And so we do, young son, and as a gift to you, I have made it so that your precious Samantha is back in her life with no memory of her time with the pastor."

Henry's fist fell to his side, and he sagged with relief. "She's back?"

"Oh, yes. And she has spread her arms for her returning hero. A life lived together because of you."

Henry reached up to wipe at his tears, but his sticky black fingers soured his mouth in disgust. "Where is Amélie? Where's Adam's mother?"

"They are ready to be freed."

"The fuck does *ready* mean?" Henry growled.

Satan closed his eyes in pleasure, as if Henry's anger satisfied a craving. "I must have something in return, young son."

"And what is that, fucker?"

Satan laughed, his hands coming from behind his back

to clap in front of his chest. "I have decided that only *one* of you must make it out. *Then* I will free the souls you so desperately seek."

Henry opened his mouth, but Satan lifted a finger to forestall his protest. The mirth left his face, and Henry rocked back from the rotting devil's breath. "No, young son. Negotiation is over. Escape the Edifice, and the souls are released. However, if they, or Adam, ever venture from Solitude …"

Satan rushed forward, and Henry drew back, but the devil had his hands on Henry's face before he could draw breath. His hissing voice filled Henry's ears and mind. It echoed from the wood panels, multiplying to compress the space with his words.

"Our contract will be at an end, and I will fill that place with every despicable torture I can muster to my command for *all of you*. There will be no place safe from my gaze, and the souls I have given up to you will be drawn back to *pay*."

Henry blinked his stench away, and Satan stood with that soft smile, his hands behind him. "And I promise you, young son. You *will all* pay."

He turned on his toes, and walked back to the elevator. The doors swept open at his approach, and Satan turned as he nestled into its depths. "Mind yourself, young son. Your power may be your downfall."

The doors closed on his smile with another *ding*, and the arrow slid to the bottom of the scale as the elevator descended to Hell.

Henry turned, and they all stared at him still. He held his hand out to Aela, and his throat closed with the fear that she would leave it hanging there. She took an unsteady step and held her arms open. Relief choked him, a sigh of pleasure fighting his constricting fear. She pressed into his chest. He could smell her even through all the filth, and his anger and fear fell away.

He rubbed his hand through the grime in her hair and caught Boothe's eye. "So, now what?"

Maria pushed herself away from her husband's embrace. "We go up."

"That's it?"

Her eyes looked through him, haunted and wide. "No, Henry. That's *not* it."

The three doors opened with a shocking clang, then demons boiled through the openings in a frantic throng. They poured into the room, rolling and tumbling over each other in their attempt to be the first inside.

Maria's fire sparked into life. Aela pushed Henry away, her unfurling wings glowing as she turned, drawing Ramiel's massive sword from her back.

"To the elevator!" Boothe shouted.

Henry spun without thought. He dug his claws into the carpet and sprinted toward Satan's exit. As he darted across the room, the arrow above the elevator twitched to life, ascending from Hell. Only a few steps away, the doors split, and Henry hurled himself through the widening gap.

He slammed into the back of the car, denting the enameled metal with his shoulder. He twisted to throw his hands out to catch the doors, but they were already closing. As they slid shut, Henry saw the demon horde close around Maria's light, Boothe rising on tattered wings with his spear overhead.

"NO!" Henry's voice folded back into his ears when the doors pressed together. He flung himself forward, digging his claws into the gap, and the lights died with a flicker. His stomach fell as the elevator rose, and he smelled dry ocean air.

The doors were no longer under his hand. Waves

crashed in the distance. Laughter. Moans of pleasure. Cries of ecstasy.

A sultry groan at his feet, and the darkness shrank back from a brightening sun.

A beach covered with nude women stretched before him. Toasting to their health. Teeth flashing in smiles of celebration. Shouts of pleasured release. Hands groping his thighs.

Henry looked down. At his feet were two naked women. One a blonde with full breasts, her lips parted in pleasure. Another beauty so dark, her skin shone with blue highlights. The blonde pressed herself against his hips, while the other pulled the button on his waistband loose.

Henry's erection sprang out fully engorged as she lowered his zipper. She took his cock into her mouth as the blonde rose and breathed into his face. He smelled wine and weed. He bent to kiss her, his hips bucking. The women pulled away, and the smell of their sex filled his nostrils, driving away the other scents of the beach. Replacing his rational thought with desire.

Hands on his shoulders. On his back. Moans that sent fresh blood to his throbbing cock. The blonde turned with her finger between her teeth, and she bent over, pressing her ass against his thighs.

Henry grabbed her hips, and looked over his shoulder. In the space between a redhead's arm and her right breast as she raised her hand to sweep her thick hair aside, Henry saw the elevator doors closing.

Shock dropped over his mind like ice. He raised his hands to push the women away, and a blistering hand grabbed his erection, pulling him back around. The blonde had him in an iron grip. She stepped to the side to line him up, and an image of Aela smiling underneath him weakened his knees.

The closing doors fell to the back of Henry's mind, and he let the blonde guide him closer to entering her.

Her forked tongue flickered out from between her fangs, and Henry jerked his hips back. His claws sunk into the flesh over the rise of her ass, and black blood welled out as she hissed in delight. His memory of Aela swept away. He blinked and shook his head.

The doors are still closing.

Henry shoved the blonde and turned, driving his legs to reach the elevator. He pushed a plastic cup of beer aside. Knocked a joint from an offering hand. Swatted a hand from his dick. His heart pounded.

The sand in front of him was laden with the kind of ass he had only been able to dream about during puberty. Spread legs. Hungry fingers probing down the sides of his pants. Breasts lifted for his examination. They clogged his path — hands fondling his balls, hands groping at every inch of exposed skin. He swung his claws, and blood splattered the nipples of a brunette with her eyes rolled back in pleasure.

His claws dug through the skin of another blonde, and the scaled demon beneath her rose from the slits. She gasped in pleasure, pulling his claws up to her lips.

Bodies so thick in front of him, Henry couldn't get his feet under him. He stumbled under their lust. Pawing and clawing. Lips and teeth. Pants stripped to his knees.

Panic blinded him. They blotted the sun, plunging Henry into shadow. He swung his claws in every direction. Black blood spattered his face. Dripped into his mouth. Strong hands spreading his ass cheeks apart. Nails splitting the skin over his dick. Digging into his back.

Henry screamed. A pathetic and helpless sound, swallowed by the rising moans. The manic pleas for release. He *flared*, and the tiny amount of fuel in his tank pushed them back. The doors were almost touching.

The women tumbled back in a desperate recoil. He swung and they fell around him, blood coating his arm and showering his shoulders. A woman grabbed his horns and dug her pubic hair into his face, screaming in ecstasy, rubbing and grinding. His nose crunched against her pelvis, and his blood filled his mouth.

Weight on his back, pushing him into the sand. Hands under his body, spinning him to face the sun, pulling his pants to his ankles. Scratching and fighting to be the first one to ride him, they tore his pants to shreds with their claws. Spiked wings bursting from their backs, splitting the skin in a torrent of gore that rained on his chest.

Moans becoming wails. Tentacles and tails. Cruel grins full of curved fangs.

Henry skittered back, thrashing his head, roaring in wordless terror. His coffee can hand clanged off the edge of the door, and his claws skidded on the elevator's metal floor. The doors sprang back open, and Henry hurled himself into the car, his back flattening against the rear wall.

He stared out into the silence of the beach. The sun dimmed, and the demons burst into their true forms. They leaned forward, their breasts swinging in front of them, their legs spread wide. They screamed in unison, and in their blended breath was the scent of passion so strong, his bruised and bleeding penis throbbed toward a fresh erection. Henry bent forward, driving his hand against the floor to push to his knees.

Beautiful in their horror, they called to him, and his body responded, fighting to join the orgy promised by their cries. Lust Beach was a helluva place for a party.

SAWYER BLACK & DAVID W. WRIGHT

The doors clanged shut, and Henry fell back with a gasp.

What the fucking fuck?

His stomach flopped as the elevator rose to the next level, and as before, the light flickered before plunging him into darkness.

308

Chapter Thirty-Three

THE LIGHT STUNG Henry's eyes, and he looked down, squinting against the glare.

He stood in a thick fluid that shimmered and glowed from reflected light, and a shining luminescence from underneath. There appeared to be no bottom, but the fluid only reached to his ankles. He lifted his right foot, and the sticky goo clung to his skin like rubber cement.

It smelled like cloves and sugar. A sharp pain lanced up his obliques, and he dropped his foot with a wince. Pink scratches and gashes weeping black blood covered his legs. Crisscrossed over his penis, and down the shaft itself. Bruises darkened his skin from hips to shins.

He took a deep breath and stretched up to relieve his fatigue, then froze with his hands over his head. The elevator stood in the center of an endless lake of the sticky sweet fluid, its doors split wide, waiting for him.

It was only ten or so yards away.

His heart bolted in his chest, and Henry heaved his foot out of the muck to take the first step toward his escape. It clung to his ankle like it was trying to keep him in place. He slung his foot forward, dropping it to splat in front of him. It pressed the surface before breaking through with a gurgling bubble, and he dragged his other foot out of the sugar glue for another step.

This ain't nothing.

He took a deep breath and pulled his back foot out for another two feet of progress. The glow under the ripples flickered like the elevator lights. Two points rose from the turbid liquid, and a pair of hands slid through. They fell toward him, and he tried to backpedal, but the syrup held him firm. Hands grabbed him around his ankles, and he sank further into the surface, air bubbling up around his skin as he lowered into its depths.

Henry thrashed but barely moved. He kicked but the hands held firm. Thick liquid splashed into his face, clinging to the hair hanging across his forehead. He tipped forward, and his chest smacked the surface. Another hand rose like a melting arm in reverse, and it grabbed his nubbin at the wrist. His coffee can stuck to the molasses lake, and his nubbin jerked out and dropped below the surface.

The liquid closed over Henry's hips as he threw his body into panicked convulsions. Bits splashed into his mouth, coating his tongue with cloying sweetness. The fluid weight pressed against his ribs, murdering his air, and he forced in a deep breath. Henry roared as his face neared the amber lake, and the heat of his breath melted the goo to flow away like water. He dropped below the surface, but when he kicked, the liquid poured around his flailing arms, and he rose above the surface for another stolen breath. He roared again, sparks and embers landing against the splashing waves, and he made progress toward the elevator.

Hands rose from every side. Dragging at his shirt.

Digging into his exposed skin. He rolled through the thinning liquid around him and slashed his claws. Severed fingers flew in guttering spouts of blood, but new hands shot out of the depth to replace those he defeated.

Sugary sweetness spilled down his throat, and a burst of power energized his mind. He drank more, until his belly swelled and his progress slowed. He roared again, and swam through the melting slog with his claws parting flesh with every swing, then his questing nubbin fell against the threshold of the elevator.

Henry scissored his legs in a frog kick, sliding his arms on the elevator floor until he was inside. He spun on his back, struggling to sit up as the doors slid closed. Seeking hands plunged back below the surface, and he leaned back to catch his breath as he licked his claws clean of blood and syrup, every swallow returning life to his body.

Lights flickered as his guts lurched, and Henry hung his head in defeat.

GOLD GLITTERED BENEATH HIS LEGS. Reflected twinkles of light sparkling in his eyes. he shifted his weight and pulled his hand into his lap. The sticky bullshit from the Lake of Gluttony clung to his skin like tar. Coins and jewels embedded in the webs and strings stretched from his fingers to the floor around him.

The shining gems glittered out of the shadows, rising into piles of silver and gold. The wealth gathered in the center, and Henry's eyes climbed the thick mountain up and up to the elevator. He was going to have to climb.

Henry shook his head. *Big deal.*

A hundred dollar bill was pasted to his knuckles. He slung his hand to the side, but the paper hung tight. He wiped against the coins near his leg, and his hand came up heavier with coins and stones cemented to his skin with drying sugar.

I'm already rich, though. What do I give a fuck about money?

"That's *mine*, motherfucker!"

Henry lifted his head toward the angry voice, but his vision clouded when a meaty fist smashed into his temple. He flew away from the blow, landing on his back, staring up at the dancing light bouncing off the dark ceiling. A weight landed on his chest, and his air choked off as fingers squeezed against his throat. A fat face bloomed into view, with eyes glaring red from the effort to kill him.

Henry swung his hand from his hip, a shining arc of money flying from his arm as his claws drove into the soft skin on the side of the fucker's teeth. Through muscle and bone, molars and gums flying, blood splashed into Henry's eyes. The pressure left his throat, and he took a whooping breath, following his attacker as the gurgling lump fell to the side. Another slash to the throat, and blood jetted out onto Henry's thighs, mixing with the sugar and turning plasma into jam.

The fat fuck's life force rose into him, and Henry sat up straight as the power filled his reserves. *I would've given a million dollars for that shit.*

The thought made him freeze. *It's not money that's the root of all evil.*

Shadows from the corners, stepping around the pile of money and jewels and coins. Henry shoved the dead fuck off his legs. He stood with a carapace of metal and stone sticking into the syrup that crunched into brittle flakes as he straightened to his full height.

It's the fucking LOVE of money. The eyes on him glittered with greed, reflected and amplified by the sliding piles of coins at their feet. Henry dug his claws into the fabric of his T-shirt, tearing it away from his body with a roar.

Let me tell you something, brother!

Women in yoga pants and hoodies. Dresses. Pantsuits. Men with flapping ties. Jeans and boots. All of them focused on the intruder coming to threaten their riches. At an unheard signal, they opened their mouths to return his roar. Then they charged, slipping and digging through the unsure footing.

He ran to meet them, and his first swing took the reaching hand of a thin woman in a white sweater stretched tight across her tits. She reeled back with a snarl, her stump spraying blood in a fanning arc. She reached with her other hand, but was knocked aside by a redneck with a rebel flag cap on his greasy mullet and a wallet chain swinging at his waste.

Henry dug in, swinging and biting as the greedy tide crashed against him. Black fingers in his mouth, and he snapped them off with his fangs, spitting them into the surprised face of a fat chick swinging her purse at his head. Blood splashing his chest from a swing that opened him from nipple to navel. He tripped over his own intestines, and Henry drank him in when he died.

Attacks against his back, and Henry heard his own ribs creak under an impact below his armpit. He curled in and hitched in a breath, swinging out and eating another one.

That's another dollar.

A polished nail digging into his eye and blood burst down his cheek.

Henry shook his head away from her fingers and snapped his teeth over her wrist with a wet crunch. He fell to his knees, dragging her down with him. A howling man in a policeman's uniform fell across him with his arms wide in a bear hug that nobody wanted, and Henry severed the cop's spine with a swipe to the back of his neck.

He dug the claws of his right foot into the face of the

woman who tried to pierce his brain through the eye, then rose up the pile as two more of his victims filled him with their dying energy. He looked back, surprised to see he had made progress up Mount Greed, but the frenzied crowd still stared, clawing and digging, pulling the ground from under his feet.

He slid back down, and a hand clamped onto his ankle. He kicked as more of the coins came out from under his hands. Losing ground, he spun, twisting his foot out of the grasp. Swinging blindly, he growled his frustration and scrambled up the hill. "Here! Take it back, fuckers!"

He *flared*, sending all the captured energy back to their upturned faces. Except for the shit stuck to the film of drying syrup on his limbs, it was his only currency.

Power flowed down the mountain of money, and they paused as it washed over them. They breathed in as if smelling a breeze full of the aroma of a summer cookout. Henry fell on his ass, and the base of the elevator's opening dug into his lower back. Sweating and breathless, he pulled himself inside.

The doors closed with a hiss.

He flicked a few coins from his nubbin, and the lights went out.

His stomach lurched as he rose to the next level.

HENRY SAT in a drizzling rain in the middle of the street in the Forgotten.

Faces pressed into the windows above him pulled back into the shadows as he looked up. Water softened the gummy residue, and the money fell into the mud. He scrubbed himself as clean as he could, and stood with a groan.

He dug his nubbin into his back as he straightened,

and the grunt rushed from his lungs in a long deflating sigh. His eyes widened, and he reached up to wipe the rain from his face.

Aela ran around the corner into the street, her face white with stark terror. She held a squirming bundle in her right arm pressed against her chest. Her left arm trailed behind her, gripping the hand of a man staggering along behind her, clutching the front of his shirt, blood gushing out between his fingers.

She ran past without seeing him, as if he wasn't there. The demon's heat sizzled the water from Henry's skin and steamed the rain right out of the air.

It slid in the muck, its claws churning up the puddles. The demon's tail whipped into an arc as it straightened, righting itself as it passed through Henry as if he were smoke.

The demon roared in pursuit of Aela as the baby's wail rose in the spaces between broken buildings.

Chapter Thirty-Four

THE STENCH of wet fur and burning shit washed over Henry as the demon passed. Henry pushed off into labored jog, pulling energy out of his asshole to get his speed to a run, but still the demon disappeared into the distance.

The baby's cries, pitiful and squealing, echoed from every angle, and Henry couldn't tell where Aela had gone. How far she was ahead.

At the mouth of an alley, he heard the snort of the demon as it jammed its snout into the mortar joints in a brick wall. The baby's wail rose in a crescendo of piercing sound that lifted the demon's matted fur.

Steaming breath plumed out in twin jets, and it leaned back before driving its horned forehead into the wall. The impact shuddered through the ground and killed the baby's cries. The silence seemed to stoke the flames in its lungs. Beastly eyes glowed with flaring light as it leaned back and charged the wall. Over and over, the demon bashed its skull against the brick, and the hollow thud deepened as the joints loosened and the bricks caved an inch at a time.

The demon would be inside soon. And then it would devour Aela's soul.

He pressed his hand to the wall as the demon readied itself for another run. Henry's fingers sank into the greasy bricks, and he pushed, passing through the wall like sinking into a lake made of heavy syrup. Into the dark of the interior, and he stood in the center of a Way Home.

Aela curled over the baby, crying and shushing. The baby fussed, its tiny voice rising and falling as she traced a frantic hand over its face. Rocking it in her lap.

She turned to the man who had followed, and her rocking slowed. The baby shrieked and the wall shook with a *BOOM!*

Aela jumped, a scream squeaking past her lips, and she rubbed the man's thigh.

"Gerald?" her voice broke, and she cleared her throat.

Gerald's hand fell to his lap. Blood filled his palm. Soaked the front of his shirt. Glistened in his lap.

"Gerald? Darling, no. No!"

Henry's heart skipped into sympathy. His stomach heaved. He swallowed all of the acid and sugar back down. He ached to reach out to her, but in this torturous memory, he had no form. No power.

Gerald slumped, and his body fell over, his head smacking the stone floor with a dull crack. She reached for him, her fingers clawing through his shirt, but the fabric slipped through her grasp.

The building shook with the demon's impact, and the baby screamed in Aela's arms. Shelves along the wall collapsed, scattering the good work of the Sisters of Solitude across the floor. Cans and bundles spilled atop Gerald's body. The baby squealed, its anger splitting Henry's ears, and the demon outside roared in response.

Aela bent forward, her eyes dazed, rocking and bouncing.

"Shhh, little one. My sweet baby, shhh."

Oh, fucking Christ.

Her hand, coated with her lover's blood, patted the baby's chest. The baby's forehead. Fluttering over the baby's face, it settled over its little mouth, and the cries fell to a muffled whine. Aela curled over it, bearing down to keep the baby quiet, and the wall crumbled in, filling the air with brick dust and rotten heat.

The demon bellowed in triumph. Aela didn't flinch, and her eyes stayed fixed on the darkness. She rocked the baby in her lap, and Henry noticed it was no longer crying.

The demon raised its head to get her scent. Then it froze, head cocked to the side.

A golden glow grew from the alley, and the demon's fur smoked and sizzled. A Tracker's song swelled as a counterpoint to the quiet rain, and the demon turned to offer its face to the angel as it slowly descended from the sky. Its eyes boiled away as it stared, and still it stood, waiting in a wash of holy light.

Begone from here, vile creature.

The booming command pressed into Henry. He almost turned and ran.

An end to your pain will end the torment you cause.

Suffer no more.

The glittering web descended, and the demon sagged under its weight. Its hideous face split into a burning smile, and the Tracker lifted the net, slinging its evil burden over his shoulder. It turned to rise back into the sky, and Aela jumped to her feet.

"Wait" The Tracker lowered his net and turned back. Aela held the baby out with shaking hands. "Please."

I am sorry, little sister, but he is lost to me.

Without a change in expression, the angel re-shouldered his net and rose on a beat of his wings that sent a tornado of wet grit into the air to swirl around Aela's head.

She squeezed her eyes shut and turned her head. Henry closed his eyes to her pain.

Aela groaned, her voice rising into a keening moan that opened wide into a wail of grief. A ragged breath and a scream. Fury into the retreating light of an angel that hadn't even tried.

Henry opened his eyes, and Aela collapsed to her knees. Her dead child rolled from her arms, and she sat back, chest heaving as she inhaled and exhaled with painful, shuddering sobs. She lifted her right hand and dug her nails through her cheeks. Blood poured from the wounds and spattered into her lap.

Her other hand lit with white fire, and she passed it over her face, healing her own damage with her angelic birthright. Aela dug her claws in then healed herself again. Digging and healing, until her lap was soaked with her own blood. And still she reached for her face, her hand frozen in a bloody claw.

Henry felt the trick of it all. He was supposed to be angry. Furious at a woman who would kill her son while he was going through Hell to save his daughter. Even if it *had* been a mistake. A desperate act that could never be taken back. Or punished enough. He couldn't do it. The sound of her nails scraping through her own skin made him want to vomit.

He squatted behind her as she passed the light over her face again, and before she reached back up to cut herself, Henry whispered, "I know I don't have the right, but I forgive you."

Aela's hands fell to her lap, and she sighed, slumping forward with her head down.

The elevator *dinged* behind him, and Henry pushed against his knees, grimacing in pain as he stood.

Exhaustion settled across his shoulders, and he turned with a sigh of his own.

He stepped into the elevator, and the doors slid closed.

HENRY'S STOMACH pitched as the elevator shot up another level.

This time the lights didn't flicker. The car came to a stop and the doors opened. He stepped out into the tasteful lighting of the first level of the Edifice. *Back where I fucking started.*

But he wasn't.

Like before, they groaned in a pile on the floor, coated with the oil that lubricated their passage through Hell's portal. Aela rising to her feet with a groan. Boothe pulling Maria up, her hands on his shoulder for support. Nadia and Charlie Mara, their arms entwined as they stood.

Henry looked across the room at the elevator that he started on, and the arrow was all the way to the top. *Hot damn.*

He broke into a shuffling run, his breath sending stabbing pain through his ribs. Naked and bleeding, still wet from the rain of the Forgotten, he stumbled up to Aela and swept her into his arms. He pressed his mouth to her ear. "I love you," he said, his voice breaking from the emotion he'd held inside for too long. "It wasn't your fault."

She stiffened against him, but he wouldn't let go. "Your son. Your baby. It wasn't your fault."

Aela struggled in his embrace, twisting in his arms, and he crushed her to him, afraid to let her go. "No, no. Please. From someone who has hated himself all his fucking miserable life, please. I *love* you. Someone loved me when I never thought it was possible, and now *I* love you. Yes, I believe our souls can be saved."

He rocked her as she had her baby, and she sagged into his chest, pressing her face against the twisted pucker of his scar. He stroked the black slick from her hair and leaned against her, moving his feet, pushing her into a walk toward the elevator. "We gotta move," he said over his shoulder.

Aela stepped away, pushing off to walk by his side. She wiped at her tears, smearing the greasy black into a raccoon mask. "How did you find out?"

"Oh, I've been through some shit, lady."

They made it to the elevator, and when he turned back to them, they looked at him with confusion. Wanting direction.

I'm not a leader, dammit.

He took a breath to start his story, and the three doors opened. Like before, the demons tumbled out.

Fire belched from the opening to accompany their arrival, and they screamed in ravenous hunger as their numbers swelled. They gathered amid an inferno, and their churning mass settled. They calmed as they looked at Henry across the carpeted distance, and before he could shout a warning, they charged.

Frank jumped into a spin, shifting into the massive shape of the Hell Hound. The demons didn't slow.

Maria shed the form of the seductress and swept fire across the demons' path to join the flames that Frank belched out of his terrible maw.

Henry spun to the elevator as the threat drew nearer, but the doors didn't slide open. He beat against the metal and send a booming echo into the car.

Boothe stepped beside him, laid his hand flat against

the door, then turned back, shaking his head. "There is a great enchantment on this door."

"So fucking *break* it."

"It is beyond me, Henry. I'm sorry."

Fucking sorry doesn't cut it, you piece of shit.

The demons broke through Maria's flames, and Nadia burst into her raptor form, jaws wide to receive an enemy between her teeth. Charlie blurred into action, and Frank stomped into their midst, burning and biting.

Henry shoved Boothe aside and raised his claws, and as he passed, he saw the demon's face.

Boothe stared at Maria with a love so radiant that Henry was struck dumb by his beauty. The angel's eyes flicked to meet Henry's gaze, and they shone with unshed tears. Henry stumbled, falling to one knee, and Boothe smiled.

Henry couldn't hear what the angel said, but his lips formed a single word. And before Henry fell to the floor, he saw it.

Redemption.

Henry struggled to his knees, and a blade of fire sheared through his upper arm. He punched his nubbin into the slavering mouth of the demon that stabbed him, and jerked his claws up into its balls. The demon squealed around Henry's stump and fell forward, trapping Henry under his dead weight.

Henry rolled his head up, and he heard Maria scream. Her goddess voice echoing like the voice of a Tracker.

My love!

Boothe grabbed Aela by the arm that held Ramiel's sword, and spun her around as he pressed his back to the elevator doors. He curled forward, grabbing her resisting wrist in both hands. Henry remembered trying to break that grip during his funeral, and his voice joined Maria's. Crying out for his friend.

Boothe jerked Aela's hand forward, and the black sword punched through his chest, sliding out his back and into the gap between the doors. His life force exploded in a thunderous rush, bursting from his filthy suit in a wave as strong as Henry's flare.

Everyone was swept from their feet, pressed into the floor by angel's energy, flames guttered out in a hollow whoosh.

The elevator doors *dinged* as they opened.

Charlie blurred from the floor, catching Boothe as his lifeless body fell forward. Charlie eased him to the carpet and thrust out his hand to hold the doors. They bounced open, and Charlie entered the car, leaning against the doors to keep them wide.

Maria ran to her husband's body. Her wail as she lifted his head into her lap cut through Henry.

Shuffling and grunts. Demons rising to their feet. Growls and howls.

Henry struggled out from under the body that had trapped him, sliding the blade from his arm with teeth gritted against the pain. Now just rusty steel without the life force of the demon behind it, the sword clattered to the carpet with a vibrating ring. Henry staggered up and found Aela there to catch him. He leaned on her as they staggered to the elevator as one. Nadia joined Charlie at the door, twirling the silver ring on her finger. Frank stumbled into the car, his Hawaiian shirt in bloody tatters. He held his hand to a flowing wound on his forehead.

They crowded into the elevator, pressing against each other as they turned to face front. Maria looked up from Boothe's face, her eyes blazing with white fire. "He was a *good* husband."

She stood, and the fire burst from her hands to spread along the curves of her body. The gold hoop around her waist glowed like the heart of a volcano. She turned to face the demons, roiling with anticipation. She lifted her hands, fire swelling into swirling globes.

GO!

The demons charged, and Charlie stepped inside, squeezing into a gap between Nadia and Frank. As the doors slid closed, a sickening explosion filled the elevator with pressure. An explosion they probably heard all the way in the basement. The doors hissed closed, severing the song of terror and agony.

A hum underfoot as the elevator rose.

"Where is it going?" Nadia asked.

Charlie pulled her into his side. "Who gives a shit?"

Henry smiled. *Dammit. That's my line.*

Chapter Thirty-Five

THE ELEVATOR OPENED onto the gas lights of Solitude.

The swaying branches of the Dreaming Tree hanging heavy with pods as nuns climbed the spiral to harvest.

Charlie stepped out, pulling Nadia behind him, stopping to hold the door for the rest of them. Henry pushed off the wall, still leaning on Aela, and walked into the thick scent of white flowers. A deep breath made his head swim.

"Henry!" Like a little white bullet, Adam shot across the room. The nuns halted their procession to watch, and Henry pulled Aela down with him as he opened his arms to catch the little angel in a hug that he didn't know he'd been waiting for.

The little boy's hair smelled like the Dreaming Tree. Fresh and clean ... and *right*.

Henry squeezed the child and looked up through his tears. A radiant beauty with strawberry blonde hair and sharp features stood over Adam's shoulder. Her lip twitched with a smile, her eyes shining with tears. She looked up from Henry's gaze, and the tears fell. She lifted her arms, and Frank stumbled out, crushing himself against her in an embrace that turned Henry's face even redder with its passion.

Frank had been starving for the sight of her and found his plate filled with so much more. Adam turned and his mouth opened in a joyous cry. He untangled himself from Henry and flung himself at Frank's leg. The demon rocked into the angel.

"Daddy!" His small voice was muffled against Frank's dirty pants.

His father scooped Adam onto his hip, and the family spun in a small circle while staring into each other's eyes.

Henry looked behind him. The elevator was gone. He chuckled, shaking his head, and pushed on Aela's shoulder as he stood. He looked around. Behind every black robe. In every corner. Up in the swaying limbs.

Where is she?

"Is she here?" he whispered. "Is she in Heaven?"

He swallowed his bitterness, and hissed in pain as Aela bore down on his arm, fingers digging into the skin under his wound. He saw her frozen face, staring past his shoulder, and the shit he was about to give her died on his lips.

Henry followed her gaze as Abraham stepped around the trunk of the Dreaming Tree carrying a beautiful girl on his shoulders.

My little angel. My baby girl. My Amélie.

Henry pulled Aela into his side, leaning on her to stay standing. His daughter had already seen the monster he'd become, but still he wanted to hide his face. He took a shuffling step forward, and Aela followed. The next step was easier.

After the third step, Amélie looked up from her conversation with the old man.

Her gaze hit his face with a wallop. He caught his

breath and eased to a stop. Tears rolled down his cheeks and dripped onto his chest.

"Daddy?"

He heard her choked whisper from many yards away.

He felt hands pressing into the skin of his abdomen, and he looked down to find sister Gladys holding a rough blanket around his waist. He threw his head back and laughed. Great bellows that came back to him in the dancing branches overhead.

Aela slipped out from under his arm, joining Sister Gladys to tie the blanket around him with a heavy knot at the base of his spine. Henry laughed.

"Daddy!"

Henry caught his breath and put his hands on his hips, shaking his head. Abraham slid the little girl over his head, her feet kicking the air in excitement. He planted her on the ground and then she was running. Henry dropped to his knees, and her squeal of delight was a favorite song on the trumpets of Heaven.

She jumped into his arms. He pressed her into his skin as she sobbed. His hand stroking her hair. His tears mingling with hers.

She leaned back and looked up into his eyes. "I've been waiting here for *weeks*, Daddy."

"I'm so sorry, baby girl. I got hung up, you know?"

Her eyes narrowed, and her mouth twitched into a smile. "Oh, yeah? Doing what?"

"Planting flowers, mostly. And watching cartoons."

Amélie giggled, and it was the best laugh of any of his lives. "That's not funny, Daddy."

"Then why are you laughing?"

He pulled her back into his chest, and when Aela dropped her hand on his head, Henry finally felt like everything was going to be okay. For the first time since his death, things were *good*.

HENRY OPENED his eyes in the room full of clocks, grinning as he stretched. He threw the sheet aside and slid over, dropping his feet to the floor. Aela's side of the bed was still warm, so she must not have been gone for too long.

He imagined himself all clean and shiny, dressed in a black tee and the canvas jeans he'd learned to love. He stood, wiggling his toes inside his boots, and leaned over for the pitcher of water that someone had left for him on the nightstand.

With his belly sloshing, Henry stepped into Solitude, and not a single person looked at him like a stranger.

He took the route he remembered weaving through the stone halls with confidence, until he stood at the base of the stairs that would take him to the city's highest point. He ascended the steps two at a time, and hit the top one with no labor in his breath.

He walked up to the rail, and inspected Adam's work. No swirling mist. Just clear air. Only puffy clouds flowing by under the bright glow of a summer sun. Shimmering blue skies and birds wheeling overhead, their faint cries reminding Henry of falcons.

Straight building along the curving streets of the Forgotten. Bright parks with green grass. People, no longer lost, walking on the cobblestones. Lovers holding hands on the sidewalks instead of cowering in the dark behind filthy glass.

It looks like the fucking Shire.

Rolling hills, swaying plants, leaves spreading out to catch the light. Even the tops of the trees at the edge of the cemetery looked bright and happy, despite their shadows.

Mind, body, and soul, this place had been healed. As the boy grew up, so would everything around him, and one day, he might even desire to become *more*. But for now, he was a beautiful boy who could heal the whole world.

He smelled his sweet Amélie before he heard her footsteps echoing on the stairs. She ran up to him, and he swept her up with his right arm, swinging her out and sitting her on the railing. Her giggles worked into his heart, and he was sure that the universe didn't have a single better sound.

She kicked her feet as she looked out over the Forgotten and reached her breast pocket. She snatched a flower up like a magic trick and said, "I brought you a flower."

"For *me?*" Henry took it from her fingers and brought it to his nose. "You know, I think this is one of the flowers I planted while you were gone."

"No, it's not, Daddy."

"No, really. I put a bunch of 'em by the road coming into Solitude. You know why they smell so good?"

"Why?"

"Because fairies pee on 'em." He took a dramatic sniff, and Amélie giggled again, losing her breath and doubling over. "Ewww!"

"Hey," Henry said, sticking the flower behind his ear. "I'm going to the Tree. You wanna be a thorn in my side?"

"Okay."

She held her arms out, and he put her on his hip. He thought of the tree, and time and space twisted away, and they stood at the roots, looking up into branches crackling with green leaves. Stretching into the sky higher than even a giant could climb.

Next to the Tree was a table big enough for a hundred, where only two people sat. Randall in a white robe. Charlie Mara in a black mechanic's shirt. The demon turned as Henry appeared, and his face lit with a grin. "Hey, my man. I gotta new job."

Henry laughed. "I hear the pay sucks."

"Yeah, but you can't beat the benefits."

Randall looked up from the chessboard, his brow furrowed in concentration. "Hello, Henry. Amélie."

She waved as Henry put her feet on the ground. "Hi, Randall. Hi, Charlie."

Charlie shook his head. "You're right, Henry. She's *very* plain."

"I am not!"

"Yeah," Henry said. "Let's just hope she's smart, right?"

"Daddy!" She swatted his leg, and he pretended to buckle from the pain.

"All right, all right. You look *okay.*"

"That's better."

Henry laughed as he led his daughter past the table. Around the back of the Tree to the headstone that glittered in the sun. Polished granite sparkled as they neared. Nestled among the roots it was the perfect spot. Henry came here often, and though he asked many questions, he was always on his own for the answers.

Just like when we first met.

There was no inscription in the stone. Just two names. *Boothe* and *Maria.* A golden ring encircled them. The hoop around the waist of a goddess. The halo over an angel's head.

Henry pulled Amélie's flower from behind his ear and squatted down to set it atop the stone. The surface so shiny, it was like two flowers in an embrace.

"Is Mom happy?"

The question surprised him. Amélie had hardly spoken about Samantha since his return. With time moving so much slower in Nowhere, Henry didn't know if she was happy or not. He'd made a deal with the devil, and he was damn sure going to keep his word on this one.

"Of course she is, baby girl."

"Can I see her ever again?"

"I don't think so, honey. We have to stay here in Nowhere."

"For how long?"

"I guess forever. Is that so bad?"

She shrugged then reached out and touched one of his horns with her index finger. Pushing on it as if making sure it was real. He couldn't bring himself to take any other form, and he walked around as a demon all the time, now.

She nodded and drew her hand back. "No, that's not so bad."

"Even if I look like a monster forever?"

"That doesn't matter." His baby girl leaned over and rested her head on his shoulder. "Because you're not a monster on the *inside.*"

THE END

A Special Request

Thank you for reading *Monstrous Book Three*.

If you enjoyed this book please consider writing a review of it on your favorite bookselling site so other readers can enjoy it too. Just a couple of sentences would mean a lot to me.

Thank you!

SB & DWW

About the Authors

Sawyer Black writes dark and violent fiction for people who secretly love puppies and rainbows. In addition to being a U.S. Army veteran, he's also a beardsman. In fact, that's where all his ideas come from. The beard. Speculative stories about struggle and triumph and brutal emotion, written mostly for his ideal reader, his wife of nearly twenty-five years. He's an independent woman who likes cigars and margaritas, and he holds the deep belief that the earth is round.

～

David W. Wright is the co-author of edge-of-your-seat thrillers including the best-selling post-apocalyptic series *Yesterday's Gone,* the paranoid sci-fi *WhiteSpace* series, and the vigilante series, *No Justice,* as well as standalone thrillers *12,* and *Crash* which was recently optioned for a movie.

David is an accomplished, though intermittent, cartoonist who lives in [LOCATION REDACTED] with his wife and son [NAMES REDACTED.]

He is not at all paranoid.

He is "the grumpy one" on *The Story Studio Podcast* with fellow Sterling and Stone founders, Sean Platt and Johnny B. Truant.

You can email him at david@sterlingandstone.net

We swear, he almost never bites. Unless you feed him after midnight.

~

For any questions about Sterling & Stone books or products, or help with anything at all, please send an email to help@sterlingandstone.net. Thank you for reading.

Also By Sawyer Black

The Monstrous Series

Soulless

Monstrous Book One

Monstrous Book Two

Monstrous Book Three

Stand Alone Novels

Zoomers vs Boomers

Analog Heart

Born To Die

Also By David W. Wright

Cold Vengeance

Cold Vengeance

Cold Reckoning

Hidden Justice

Hidden Justice

Hidden Honor

Hidden Shame

Hidden Virtue

No Justice

No Justice

No Escape

No Hope

No Return

No Stopping

No Fear

Karma Police

Jumper

Karma Police

The Collectors

Deviant

The Fall

Homecoming

Yesterday's Gone

October's Gone

Yesterday's Gone Season One

Yesterday's Gone Season Two

Yesterday's Gone Season Three

Yesterday's Gone Season Four

Yesterday's Gone Season Five

Yesterday's Gone Season Six

Tomorrow's Gone

Tomorrow's Gone Season One

Tomorrow's Gone Season Two

Tomorrow's Gone Season Three

Available Darkness

Darkness Itself

Available Darkness Book One

Available Darkness Book Two

Available Darkness Book Three

WhiteSpace

WhiteSpace Season One

WhiteSpace Season Two

WhiteSpace Season Three

Stand Alone Novels

12

Crash

Emily's List

Threshold

The Secret Within

www.ingramcontent.com/pod-product-compliance
Lightning Source LLC
Chambersburg PA
CBHW010527100726
47903CB00011B/2923